STATE SECRET

Tim McClure

Rated M for Mature Audiences.

This book by Tim McClure is published by the author.

ISBN: 979-8-9898687-0-4

Other novels by Tim McClure will soon be available on Amazon.com

Printed in the USA by Amazon

Cover design by Alison McClure Blair. Cover illustration by Bryan Peterson.

STATE SECRET

Every State has its share of secrets.
But Texas has the biggest secret of all!

Tim McClure
Author, *Don't Mess With Texas!*

Contents

Map of the Five Proposed States of Texas

Prologue

The President of the United States glared across the desk at the President of Texas.

"By God, Houston, you are one ornery sonofabitch!"

"I've been called worse."

Weathered boots propped up on his weathered oaken desk, smoldering cigar tucked into his right cheek, the first and third President of the Republic of Texas was clearly in a negotiating mood. On his terms, of course

Houston's predecessor, Mirabeau B. Lamar, had terminated efforts to join the Union with the Martin Van Buren administration in 1838. But now, six years later, Texas was an attractive prize to U.S. President John Tyler. Having ratified the Webster-Ashburton Treaty, Taylor was ready to make Texas his top priority.

Indeed, in September 1843, Tyler had opened secret talks to negotiate annexation of Texas by treaty, the only annexation of its kind. But the one thing he hadn't counted on was the gentleman indecorously sprawled across the desk in front of him.

"Here's the deal, Tyler. And it is non-negotiable. Agree to my three demands, and the Lone Star State will sign your treaty to join the Union.

"And just what might those demands be, Houston?"

"First, you will agree that Texas reserves the right, in perpetuity, to fly our Lone Star flag at the same height as the Stars and Stripes."

"Never happen."

"Next, Texas will have permission, in perpetuity, to withdraw from the Union should we ever so choose."

"Agree to secession? Preposterous!"

"Lastly, Texas reserves the right, in perpetuity, to divide our great state into as many as five states."

"Now you have clearly lost your mind, Houston!"

In a blur, Houston retracted his boots from his wooden desk, slid open a concealed drawer, withdrew an enormous knife, and violently stabbed it into his battle-scarred desktop.

"No, President Tyler, you have just lost Texas!"

"Are you threatening me, President Houston?"

"Of course not, Mr. President. I don't make threats. I make promises! That knife belonged to Jim Bowie, the namesake knife he so bravely wielded at the Battle of the Alamo. I retrieved it from General Santa Anna when I attacked his army during their afternoon siesta at the Battle of San Jacinto. The battle only lasted eighteen minutes. But I damned near lost my foot to a stray bullet."

"Let me get this straight, Houston. You're willing to forego Texas joining the Union over a few ridiculous demands?"

"Get *this* straight, Tyler! Either you agree to my three demands, or the Republic of Texas will go it on our own from here on out!"

"And if I decide to wait until the next President of the Republic takes office, Houston?"

"Anson Jones is more afraid of Bowie's blade than you are, Tyler. So you see, it cuts both ways."

"We'll have to keep this all a secret between us Presidents, Houston."

"Why certainly, Mr. President. As long as my three demands are properly recorded in the official Treaty of Annexation Agreement. In the fine print, if you insist."

"I insist!"

"Then assuming you can get Texas President-elect Jones to go along, I predict that you have just added your 28th State."

Glancing again at the Bowie knife still quivering in the desktop, Tyler abruptly made his way toward the door. His exasperated parting whisper was nonetheless overheard by Houston.

"Damn you, Houston!" Tyler cursed under his breath.

"And may God bless Texas!" Sam Houston solemnly swore.

Part I:

Project Pentagram

1

Governor Beauregard Swaggart strode into his new office in the Texas State Capitol and chuckled. "Your house is now *my* house, Texas!"

Beauregard much preferred his nickname "Bo" and would kick anybody's ass who called him Beauregard. Bo was a distant relative of a disgraced televangelist whose telecasts were once transmitted to over 3,000 stations and cable systems every week. Unlike his infamous uncle, Bo knew how to keep it in his pants. And while shocked congregants defrocked his uncle for sexual scandals with prostitutes, Bo had quietly and efficiently been building a political constituency among the Texas alt-right.

When the previous Texas governor decided not to run for re-election for health reasons, Bo was quick to measure the disgruntled Texas electorate, both Republicans and Democrats, and won the Governor's seat with his fiery secessionist rhetoric while blatantly plagiarizing the State's popular anti-litter battle cry, *Don't mess with Texas!*

Bo dared Texans not to vote for him.

"Before Texas was a State, it was a Nation!" he repeatedly reminded voters. "It's high time we are a Nation again, my fellow Texans!"

True, Texas is big, the second largest state in the Union behind Alaska. "But if you melt all that ice," Bo reminded voters, "Texas would be bigger than Seward's Folly!" Bo was known to put a little hair on his stories, but Texans seemed to admire his bravado.

The biggest state in the continental United States might only be a midsize nation in terms of land area, the world's 40th largest, to be exact, but it is an economic powerhouse. It is the 10th largest economy in the world, bigger than South Korea or Mexico, and roughly the equivalent of two Netherlands.

Texas has lots of oil to fuel these boasts, producing about 2 million barrels a day. Houston, the state's largest city, calls itself the Energy Capital of the World, and with good reason. Oil giant ConocoPhillips is based there, as well as many other energy firms. ExxonMobil, arguably the largest company in the world by revenue, is headquartered outside Dallas.

For the time being, Texas was one big state. Texans had elected Governor Bo Swaggart believing he would deliver on his promise to secede from the Union, making Texas a sovereign nation of some 30 million people.

Bo had no such intention. He had a state secret up his sleeve that would change the course of Texas and United States history.

Bo's plan was on a wrinkled map scribbled on a Cloak Room cocktail napkin. The funky little dive a few steps from the Capitol was frequented by members of the Legislature when they were in session and old-school pols on a far more regular basis.

Bo's hand-drawn map divided Texas into five states: North, East, Central, South, and West. In each of these five states, Bo had penciled in a state capital: Dallas, Houston, Austin, Laredo, and El Paso. He called his plan Project Pentagram.

Each state would need a governor. Bo had already created a list of suspects in his own mind, but he was far too shrewd to share that list with anyone. In his mind, there would be two Anglo governors, two Hispanic governors, and one Hispanic governors. Asians would just have to wait their turn.

When he took office, Bo's trusted chief of staff had discovered President Sam Houston's old oaken desk in off-site storage. It still bore the stab wounds from Jim Bowie's original knife. Bo promptly replaced the traditional desk in his office with Houston's antique.

He had only been in office for a few months when he discovered a secret cabinet in Houston's desk. Inside was Jim Bowie's prodigious blade, sheathed in worn leather and wrapped in purple velvet.

2

The Texas Capitol is taller than the United States Capitol.

At the time of its construction, the Texas capitol building was billed as "The Seventh Largest Building in the World." Surveyors measured Austin's domed pink-granite building at 302.64 feet, almost 15 feet taller than the 288-foot-high U.S. Capitol.

"Them's braggin' rights!" Governor Swaggart boasted loudly and often.

From his office on the second floor, Governor Swaggart surveyed the line of people passing through security at the front steps of the Capitol. State troopers with M4 carbines had been posted at each door to the building, a change made shortly after the November 2015 terrorist attacks in Paris that left 130 dead and dozens injured. A few weeks later, 14 people were shot dead and another 21 injured in an attack on a government building in San Bernardino, California. This was what pundits were now calling "the new normal."

Governor Swaggart hated that guests were screened on the doorstep of Every Texan's Second Home, but he begrudgingly admitted that the world had become a dangerous place. Glancing down from his office, he noticed some interesting characters on his doorstep – a Native American in full buckskin regalia topped with an impressive war bonnet. Several uniformed soldiers in full camo, probably from the local Camp Mabry military installation, home of the Texas Army National Guard. And a dozen women dressed in those prim and proper red robes and white bonnets made popular by a popular television series.

"Takes all kinds," the governor mused to himself. After all, these were the very Texans, some of them at least, who had recently elected him.

There was a soft knock at the door, and Marina Alvarez, Bo's personal chambermaid, entered quietly, bowing as she always did to the Governor of Texas.

"*Buenos dias*, Marina," the Governor drawled.

"*Buenos dias, Señor Gobernador*, Marina whispered, and quietly went about her business, dusting the highly polished surfaces of his office while avoiding his massive oaken desk.

"My desk, actually President Sam Houston's desk, is strictly off-limits, Marina," the Governor had told her when he took office. "Everything else in here is fair game." *If only that old desk could talk*, he thought to himself. He was pretty sure Sam Houston haunted the relic.

A second knock at the door startled the Governor out of his brief reverie. Entering his office, computer tablet in hand, was Julie Truman, the Governor's chief of staff. Julie had been with him since the old days, back when he was a young firebrand politician trying to get someone's attention on the political scene in Texas.

It was Julie who first suggested he trot out his first secessionist speech, carefully watered down to test the waters. It was Julie who had suggested the fiery rhetoric, "Before Texas was a State, we were a Nation!" Crowds, small at first but then rapidly growing in numbers and loyalty, ate it up. Less than a dozen years later, Bo Swaggart would assume the highest office in the Lone Star State.

"Jules, I need to meet privately, *very* privately, with these four people ASAP," Governor Swaggart said. He handed her a folded sheet from his yellow pad.

"All together, or one at a time, Governor?"

"Definitely one at a time. And I don't want any of them to know I'm chit-chattin' with the others."

"Any particular order for these little chit-chats?"

"Let's start with Alexa King. See that this little chit-chat is strictly after-hours, right here in my office. And make sure security has top secret clearance for her."

3

Bo Swaggart was a native West Texan. He was born and raised in the little West Texas town of Alpine, Texas. The population the year he was born, 1965, was just north of 5,000.

At the time, Sul Ross University was still called Sul Ross Normal College. His mother, Beatrice Swaggart, taught English at the college, so the Swaggarts lived on campus in family housing. His father, Satchel Swaggart, was a traveling salesman for a local appliance store. Bo mostly saw his dad on weekends and holidays. His mom he saw every day, and she left a lasting impression on him, sometimes with a willow switch cut from a tree in their tiny backyard.

On Sundays, Bo was typically glued to his family's sole television set watching his uncle, an evangelist and would-be messiah, spout his religious rhetoric. Sadly, he was photographed entering a motel in a seedy section of New Orleans with a known prostitute. His career quickly went downhill from there. But man, could that man preach!

Bo attended Alpine Elementary School, where he tended to hide in the back of the classroom and goof off. It got a little harder to hide in middle school, where his teachers were on to his antics. Harder still at Alpine High School, Home of the Fightin' Bucks, where he tried out for and made the football team as a utility player. Bo was a safety on defense, and once in a great while, a backup quarterback on offense.

The Bucks never won a State 2A title, but they did go to the district semi-finals while Bo was playing. From that point on, Bo would tell anyone who would listen that he was the star quarterback on the District Championship team, which was roughly the same time that Bo started putting a little hair on his stories.

With his mother's connections, Bo was accepted to what had by then become Sul Ross University. That's where he first met King Ranch heiress Alexa King.

Bo's Sul Ross days were a whirlwind of activity. Too small to play college football, Bo tried out for baseball, tennis, and golf, and failed miserably at all three sports. Seems Bo was best suited for drinking, which he quickly mastered. Then one day he spied Alexa King sauntering across the Sul Ross campus, and he knew right then and there that his fate was sealed. He would woo and marry this gorgeous creature, even if it meant he'd have to go easy on the sauce.

At first, Alexa wasn't particularly interested in this West Texas hayseed. But Bo had a keen sense of humor, and soon they were laughing and drinking and eventually "doing the wild thing," as Bo liked to call it. Turns out, Alexa knew considerably more about doing the wild thing than Bo, but he was a quick and enthusiastic learner.

Then one day in their senior year, Alexa confided in Bo that she was pregnant.

"That's great!" Bo gushed. "Now we can get married, buy a house, have kids, and figure out what we're going to do with the rest of our lives!"

"Hold your horses, cowboy!" Alexa said. "I know exactly what I'm going to do with the rest of my life, and it doesn't include buying a house, having kids or, frankly, marrying you, Bo Diddly!"

That was her nickname for Bo, since she was convinced he didn't know diddly about friends with privileges.

"Privileges?" Bo had asked her.

"Sexual privileges."

Bo giggled. "Oh, right! I've never considered myself privileged until now!"

As soon as they graduated, Alexa headed back home to Dallas. Bo had licked his wounds and set about figuring out what he was going to do with the rest of his life.

Somehow, Bo got interested in politics. It all started when he made a run for the Alpine City Council. He lost, but he learned a valuable lesson. It's not so much what you say, it's how you say it.

In short order, Bo was running a friend's campaign for Mayor of Alpine.

"Let *me* do most of the talkin', and I guar-on-tee you'll be our next Mayor," Bo told his friend. Wonder of wonders, Bo's raucous rhetoric helped his buddy win the mayor's race. Suddenly, other politicians were noticing this firebrand from the hinterlands.

4

Alexa King stared at herself in the mirror, something she did on a regular basis.

"Why would the Governor of Texas possibly want to see me?" she asked herself for the umpteenth time.

Sure, they were friends, acquaintances at least, and had been since their college days at Sul Ross University, a public university in Alpine, Texas, named for the former Texas governor and Civil War Confederate general Lawrence Sullivan "Sul" Ross.

Alexa was a descendant of the famous Richard King of King Ranch fame. The ranch, between Corpus Christi and Kingsville, is the largest ranch in Texas.

Alexa was rich. And a troublemaker. Which is why her parents sent her from Dallas out to West Texas. To get closer to the land, they told her. She soon discovered the land was smack dab in the middle of the Chihuahuan Desert. Hailing from Big D, a city of well over a million people, Alexa found herself in a one-horse town of just under 6,000 hicks, as she called them.

True, Alpine, at an elevation of 4,475 feet, has vistas that stretch on forever, and the surrounding mountain peaks are over a mile high. The area had been a campsite for cattlemen tending their herds between 1878 and 1882. Eventually a town of tents was erected by railroad workers and their families. Since that section of the railroad was called Osborne, that was the name they gave the community for a brief time.

Alexa, or "Alex" to her friends, entered Sul Ross University in the early '80s and quickly made herself known to her fellow students as both smart and terrifying. Her temper was legendary. You crossed Alexa at your own peril. She was either your friend or your sworn enemy.

During those four long years, she met a fellow student named Bo Swaggart. Bo was ruggedly handsome and it seemed to Alexa he was on some kind of quest. They dated off-and-on, made out off-and-on, and in her senior year Alexa got a quick and quiet abortion in Luling, Texas. Bo begged her to keep the baby. Alexa had much grander plans for her life.

Upon her return to Big D, Alexa found herself estranged from her parents, who had banished her to the hinterlands of West Texas "for her own good." Alexa wasted no time elbowing her way into Dallas' snooty high society. In short order, she married a millionaire fast food magnate who was 40 years her senior. Alexa opted to keep her maiden name, King.

Less than a year later, her sexagenarian husband died abruptly *in flagrante delicto,* which is to say, doing the wild thing with his hyper-sexed bride. A grieving Alexa inherited the bulk of her late husband's estate, and coupled with her own sizable trust fund, she suddenly found herself on every Dallas high society A-list.

Alexa never remarried, although she often found herself in the company of a lot of pretty boys that she called friends. Alexa was clearly on a mission, and that mission simply didn't include a husband.

Instead, Alexa shrewdly volunteered her talents to Dallas' highest profile civic, social, and humanitarian organizations, avoiding politics like the plague. Ten years later, she was awarded the prestigious Linz Award, the Dallas area's highest form of recognition of individuals whose civic or humanitarian efforts over the last decade or more have bestowed the greatest benefit to their beloved city.

A year later, the crème de la crème of Dallas society urged Alexa to run for mayor. Alexa politely yet firmly refused, but her benefactors would hear nothing of it. Alexa reluctantly agreed to run, assuring she would be a shoe-in. She won.

Alexa wasted no time bending the Dallas City Council to her forceful will. If council members crossed her, they quickly found themselves ignored at best, more often removed from office on strictly scurrilous charges.

Alexa was enjoying her role as Mayor of Dallas, but she secretly longed for more.

5

By dictionary definition, a pentagram is a five-pointed star,

The Lone Star, which appears in white on a blue field on the Texas flag, is five-pointed. Outside the Bullock Texas State History Museum in Austin, a huge faceted bronze Lone Star has become something of a photo destination unto itself.

When the Bullock Texas State History Museum asked how they might shorten the ponderous name of their new edifice, Texas author Max Sinclair suggested they nickname the museum "The Story of Texas." To Max's surprise and delight, The Story of Texas was carved in pink granite on the building's architectural crown.

"Five-pointed Lone Star, five Texas states. Hell, this is a no-brainer!" Governor Swaggart chuckled as he drew a crude, faceted star on a napkin one afternoon at his private table in the Cloak Room dive bar.

Then he flipped the napkin over and redrew the faceted star, this time separating the five facets. Above each facet, he scrawled a letter: N, E, C, S, and W. He glanced around to make sure no one was watching. Then he discreetly pulled his newly acquired Bowie knife from the scabbard beneath his suit jacket and stabbed it into the heart of Central Texas.

"That's mine. Let those other governors fight over what's left."

There were other stars on the Texas horizon, they just didn't know it yet. Dallas mayor and socialite Alexa King was one of them. So was Houstonian Jeremiah Jones, a prominent African American political kingmaker who hoped to be a king himself one day. Likewise, Laredo kingpin Estevan Barrero, rumored bastard son of the late Colombian drug lord and narcoterrorist Pablo Escobar. Rounding out this constellation was El Paso native Ponce Ponzio, fifth son of a Sicilian father and a Mexican mother, who vaingloriously called himself a Sicilican.

They would soon receive a private, personal invitation from Governor Swaggart. None of them would ignore the Governor's summons. As they were all aware, one ignored Bo Swaggart at one's own risk.

6

"Do you have proper identification?" the gun-wielding State Trooper asked Alexa King as she reached the top of the impressive pink granite steps that lead to the main entrance of the Texas State Capitol building.

Alexa glared at him. "Do you know who I am, Trooper?"

"Well, Ma'am, given that it's after hours and there's only one name on the Governor's special guest list, I have to assume you are Mayor Alexa King."

"Didn't your daddy ever tell you that when you assum*e*, you make an ass out of you and me, Tex?"

"Well, actually, yes ma'am, he did."

"Not ma'am, *Mayor*, Cowboy," Alexa said. "And if you want to be working here tomorrow, I suggest you allow me to pass."

"Just following the rules, ma'am, er, Mayor."

"Didn't your momma ever tell you that rules are for fools, Son? No, I guess not. After all, you weren't raised on the King Ranch."

"No ma'am, Mayor. But nearby, in Sarita, the county seat of…"

"Kenedy County. Yes, I know. The one county Captain King and Gideon Lewis chose not to make part of their ranching empire.

I can see why. You can swing a dead cat and not hit anyone of consequence in that godforsaken place!"

"May I see please see some identification, Mayor King?" the trooper asked politely, changing the subject.

Before she could take the trooper down another notch, the grand doors of the Capitol swung open and Governor Bo Swaggart himself greeted his guest.

"Alex! Long time, no see! Is everything in order, Trooper?"

"Perfectly, Sir," the trooper replied.

Brushing his gatekeeper aside, the Governor of Texas invited the Mayor of Dallas upstairs to his private chambers. Like a spider to a fly.

"I brought you a little housewarming present, Bo."

"A present? Whatever for, Alex? After all, you're my guest in this little pink palace."

"Neither you nor your pink palace are little, as I recall, Bo."

The Governor just smiled. He and Alexa went way back together.

"May I pour you an adult beverage?" Bo prodded. "Champagne? Wine? Something a bit stronger?"

"You may recall I only drink bourbon, Bo. Straight. Three fingers."

"How could I ever forget three fingers?" Bo said, pouring them both a double highball of Maker's Mark Private Reserve. "Now, what's this little gift you've brought me?"

"We just finished this year's stud breeding down at the ranch, and I thought you might enjoy seeing how wild things do the wild thing, Governor."

"Please, inside these walls, just call me Bo."

"Bo. Short for Beauregard, if memory serves. And I seem to recall you always threatened to kick anyone's ass who called you by your given name, am I right?"

"Right you are, Alex. And I hear you've been kickin' some ass up in Dallas these past few years."

"That I have, Bo. Would you mind pouring me another stiff drink before we watch this stud breeding video? You do have a projection screen in this fancy office, don't you?"

Bo simply pressed a button on the wall of his private reception area and an enormous screen slid down from the ceiling at the end of the room.

"Like I've always said, everything's bigger in Texas, Governor."

New drinks poured, Alexa handed Bo a flash drive, which he slid into a slot in the wall behind him. Immediately, the rousing strains of the Magnificent Seven theme filled the room, accompanied by the famous King Ranch Running W logo on-screen.

Alexa smiled her devilish smile. "I think you're gonna enjoy this."

"I bet you're right!" Bo responded, noticing Alexa's sheer white blouse and deeply slit black silk skirt.

On screen, a magnificent King Ranch stallion sniffed at the rear haunches of an ebony Arabian thoroughbred mare.

"I do believe she's got his attention, Bo!" Alexa observed. Indeed, it was hard to miss the prodigious red penis that had suddenly unsheathed itself beneath the stallion.

As Alexa leaned over the end of Bo's massive conference table, it was hard for him to miss that she didn't appear to be wearing any undergarments.

As Bo began clumsily unzipping his trousers, Alexa glanced over her shoulder and remarked, "My, my, Mr. Governor. I seem to have your attention, as well!"

Marina Alvarez rarely stayed late to clean up the Governor's office, but she had been lured away to catch a glimpse of the Senate in session earlier that day. As she approached the Governor's private chambers, she thought she heard a woman scream.

"That's it! That's it, you stud, you! Show that stallion how *we* do the wild thing!"

Marina gasped when she peeked through the door to the Governor's private conference room. The Governor of Texas and the Mayor of Dallas were giving the two *caballos* on the screen a run for their money.

Marina discreetly videoed the tryst on her cell phone, then silently slipped away into the shadows.

"*¡Madre de Dios!*" Marina muttered under her breath.

7

"Let me get one other thing straight, Bo. You plan to divide Texas into five separate states?" Alexa asked as she straightened her wardrobe after horsing around.

"That's about the size of it," Bo replied.

"No, *that's* about the size of it," Alexa said, pointing to the bulge in the Governor's Italian suit pants.

"Ready for another round, filly?"

"Nope. I'm one-and-done. Let's chat about why you invited me here today, Bo."

"How'd you like to be Governor of the State of North Texas, Alex? I intend to introduce legislation to take advantage of one of the Union's 1845 Annexation Agreements, giving me the legal right to divide Texas into five states."

For a moment, Alexa couldn't breathe. Mayor of the third largest city in Texas was one thing. But the governor of what she figured might be one of the largest states in Bo's New Texas was beyond her wildest expectations.

"Nothing could please me more, Governor Swaggart."

Bo winked. "Nothing?"

"Absolutely nothing, stud. Now, how about another bourbon so we can toast to our bright future together."

"As you wish, Madam Governor," Bo said, bowing deeply.

When Alexa's private jet landed back in Dallas, she was still beside herself.

Was she dreaming, or had the Governor of Texas just offered to make her the Governor of the as-yet imaginary State of North Texas?

True, she had lured him into showing her his cards when she showed him her backside. And the sex hadn't been half bad! She might have to watch footage of stud breeding with some of her other pretty boys.

But something was nagging at her, and she couldn't quite get her head around it. Bo had mentioned five states of Texas. Assuming he would name himself governor of one of those states, who would Bo coronate for the other three? After all, if Bo Swaggart could somehow pull off this miracle, Alexa figured he would have a hand in who else got elected governors.

She'd have to reassess her opinion of Bo. He might have once been a West Texas hayseed, but he'd evolved into a very powerful man. A man to be feared. A man to be, what was the word, handled.

Alexa's burgundy Bentley Flying Spur was waiting for her when she deplaned. Her pretty boy chauffeur, Randall, was waiting for her in his usual tailored black suit, no cap. He opened the rear door, illuminating the rich leather interior, crafted from flawless matched hides from the King Ranch and sporting the King Ranch Flying W logo.

"Good trip, Mayor?"

"Great trip, Randy. Life-changing, I dare say."

"Didn't you go to school with the Governor, Mayor?"

"School. Bed. You name it. Which reminds me, do you have any plans for the rest of the evening?"

"None I can't change," her chauffeur quickly replied.

"Good! Let's you and I take the rest of the night off. I got some thinking and drinking and wilding to do."

Randall simply nodded and gently closed the self-latching door on the Mayor's bespoke motorcar.

"Life is good," Randall thought to himself as he opened the driver's door and slid in behind the rich wood-and-leather-wrapped steering wheel. "Life. Is. Good."

While Alex King was making her evening plans, Governor Swaggart was making plans to meet with his next prospective governor.

Sitting at his vintage desk, he admired the blade of his prized Bowie knife before settling down to type an email to his chief of staff:

Next week I want to meet privately after-hours with Houston kingmaker Jeremiah Jones. Same routine as the Mayor of Dallas. Only this time, make sure the bar is stocked with Courvoisier XO. Since I know you don't drink, that's cognac. Nothing but the best for my African American friend Jeremiah. We both should probably have been preachers. But now, we may both be governors, instead. Be sure you end it with "God Bless Texas!" And Jules, no one, and I mean no one, is to know about this meeting!

Bo reread the email, then hit SEND. He knew his chief of staff only slept a few hours a night. She'd hear the *ding* when this arrived on her computer and would probably be typing his invitation to Mr. Jones before he hit the hay himself.

Truth was, he was tired. Very tired. Alex King had a knack for draining a bourbon and draining a man. Just like old times.

8

If you look up "mover and shaker" in the dictionary, you might discover a photo of Jeremiah Joshua Jones in the margin.

His close friends called him 3-J. But Jeremiah didn't really have many close friends. He had believers. People in high places who believed Jeremiah Jones was the reason they got there in the first place.

Jeremiah Jones was a political kingmaker. He'd helped elect a mayor of Houston, a state representative from Houston, a U.S. senator from Houston, and, some say, the 44th President of the United States.

Little was known about Jeremiah Jones, save for a brief bio on the Internet. According to that bio, Jeremiah Jones was a "fixer." He fixed things, apparently including elections.

According to his birth certificate, Jeremiah Joshua Jones was born in Sugar Land, Texas, one of the most affluent and fastest-growing cities in Texas. Sugar Land traces its roots back to the original Mexican land grant to Stephen F. Austin.

Jeremiah's grandfather had worked for the Imperial Sugar Company, but it was his father who pulled Jeremiah aside when the Voting Rights Act passed in 1965.

"Son, this changes everything," his father told him. "If you can harness the power of the Black vote, you can change the world."

That's exactly what Jeremiah set out to do, first in Sugar Land and then in the sprawling, oil-rich city of Houston an hour northeast.

"I don't rightly know what the Governor of Texas wants with me, but it can't be good," Jeremiah admitted to his wife, Grace, whom he insisted would one day be the first female African American President of the United States.

"Can't hurt to go see the man, 3-J." It was a nickname he hated, which is precisely why she goaded him with it occasionally. "You've caught bigger fish than him," Grace reminded him. "Besides, how many brothers do you know who have a master's degree in political science from Harvard?"

His wife had a point. He was one of the best-educated, best-looking, most influential politicos on the planet, and he had the track record to show for it.

"Aight," he answered, "I'll go see da man at da Big House. But if he thinks dat I'm-a kiss his cracker ass, he's dead wrong."

"Jeremiah Jones, you look at me. Look at me!" Grace scolded. "Governor Beauregard Swaggart knows a winner when he sees one. Besides, the future first female African American President of these United States has got your back."

9

Jeremiah Jones strode up the pink granite steps of the State Capitol building three at a time. A veritable superman at six-foot-seven, he probably could have done it in a single bound.

"I'm…" he started to introduce himself to the black State Trooper at the landing.

"Oh, I know who you are, Mr. Jones," the trooper interrupted him.

"But how…"

"Let's just say that your reputation precedes you, Sir. I'm originally from Houston, and where I come from, you hung the moon, maybe the stars, to boot!"

"To whom do I have the pleasure of addressing, trooper?"

"State Trooper Tobey Terrence, sir, at your service."

"Pleasure to meet you, Trooper Terrence," Jeremiah responded in his signature *basso profondo*. People often compared his booming voice to that of American actor James Earl Jones.

"The pleasure is all mine, Mr. Jones."

"Right. Well, I'm here to see…"

"…Governor Swaggart. Yes, I have you on his after-hours Special Visitors list. No need to wand you, is there? I trust you're not packing?"

"My wife might disagree," Jones chuckled. "But no, my brain is my weapon of choice."

"Jeremiah Jones, as I live and breathe!" Governor Swaggart bellowed as he strutted through the massive south entry doors to the Capitol.

"Bo Swaggart! Ain't you a sight for sore eyes!" Jeremiah bellowed back good-naturedly.

"Step inside this house, my man!" Governor Swaggart said, holding the door for his guest.

"It's an honor, Bo. To what do I owe the pleasure of this visit, old friend?"

"We'll get to that soon enough, Jeremiah. First things first: I believe Courvoisier is your drink of choice if memory serves!"

At five-foot-eight, Governor Swaggart trailed in the shadow of the man he had invited to his office. Swaggart considered himself a bit of a clothes horse. His tastes leaned toward Italian suits and Lucchese boots. But if the Governor was dressed to the nines this evening, Jeremiah Jones was dressed to the elevens.

Reverend Jones, as both friends and enemies alike often referred to Jeremiah, was sporting a bespoke navy pinstripe Saville Row suit this evening over brown double monk-strap Ferragamo dress shoes. His crisp white linen Brioni dress shirt provided a tasteful canvas for a spectacular orange silk Trumbull & Asser power tie and matching limited-edition silk pocket square.

Bo was clearly no match for his guest's sartorial splendor. But he did have *one* thing Reverend Jones would likely kill for. The governorship of the second largest state in the Union.

"I took the liberty of pouring us two cognacs when I saw you headed up the steps, Jeremiah. As you can see, I've been gently warming both snifters over a flame to release the bouquet.

"I'm duly impressed, Bo. You know, I've learned a lot watching your meteoric rise to the top of the political heap these past few years."

"More like a dung heap, if you ask me, Jeremiah. But you know what they say, 'Turds always rise to the top.'"

"Yes, well, if it takes being a turd to be Governor of Texas, you are definitely the shit! Cheers, Governor!" Jeremiah toasted his host. "Now, let's cut *through* the shit, shall we?"

"Certainly, Jeremiah. But first let me show you around the place. My God, if these walls could talk, right?"

After a brief tour of his impressive offices, Bo got down to brass tacks.

"Jeremiah, how would you like to be Governor of Texas?"

"I'm a kingmaker, not a king myself, Bo. Besides, this office isn't big enough for both of us."

"Oh, I'm not talking about this office, Jeremiah. I'm talking about you becoming Governor of East Texas," the Governor said, pausing a moment to enjoy the befuddled look on Jeremiah Jones' face.

"But Governor, East Texas isn't a state," Jeremiah said, clearly confused.

"That may be true today, Jeremiah. But if I have anything to say about it, East Texas is about to become one of the five states of Texas. And it's going to need a governor. Are you interested in the job?"

"Hell yes, I'm interested, Bo!" Jeremiah said, cocking an eyebrow. "Who do I have to kill?"

"No one this time, Jeremiah," Bo said. "All you have to guarantee is that, when the shit hits the fan, I'm elected Governor of Central Texas in a landslide. Think you can handle that?"

"Is the Pope Argentinian?" Jeremiah replied.

Bo wasn't sure. But he was pretty sure it didn't matter. With Jeremiah Jones running his campaign, he couldn't lose.

10

Pablo Emilio Escobar made infrequent, clandestine trips across the border between Nuevo Laredo, Mexico, and Laredo, Texas, during his glory years as one of the world's best known and most feared Colombian drug lords and narcoterrorists. His cartel supplied an estimated 80 percent of the cocaine smuggled into the United States at the height of his career, earning him billions in personal income.

Pablo was known far and wide as "The King of Cocaine," and one of the wealthiest criminals in history. By the early 1990s, he had an estimated net worth of $30 billion, making him one of the wealthiest men in the world in his prime.

His notoriety didn't stop Pablo from making very dangerous border crossings into Texas. Flaunting his disdain for both countries, he would fly from Columbia on his private jet with his close personal friends for a little *descanso y relajacion.* Rest and relaxation.

Pablo typically crossed the border incognito. His *hombres* handed the border guards large stacks of pesos on the Nuevo Laredo side and U.S. dollars on the Texas side. He had a strange affinity for a local bar and restaurant called *Siete Banderas,* Seven Flags, which he would rent *en todo* for his and his *compadres* personal pleasure.

Everyone in Laredo knew what was going on. Nobody complained. After all, Pablo Escobar was a hero on *both* sides of the border and throughout the Americas. His large, anonymous contributions to the communities of Nuevo Laredo and Laredo spurred their economies in hard times.

On one of these secret forays, Pablo met a drop-dead gorgeous young *Siete Banderas* bartender by the name of Valentina Rosario. True, a 27-year-old Pablo Escobar had eloped with Maria Victoria Henao, who was 15 at the time. But that did not distract Pablo's *mirada distraída,* his wandering eye, as he grew rich and infamous. Valentina pretended to ignore Pablo's advances, but ignoring Pablo Escobar was akin to ignoring a hurricane. One did so at one's own risk.

A year later, Valentina gave birth to a baby boy at Doctors Hospital of Laredo. On the birth certificate, Valentina was listed as the boy's mother. The father was recorded as Estevan C. Barrero, Sr., no known address. Coincidentally, Doctors Hospital received an anonymous grant of $1 million on the very day the child was born.

Estevan Colombia Barrero II was a beautiful baby boy. Long, curly brown hair, bright green eyes just like his mother, and a curious laugh that bordered on sardonic. He and his mother lived in a large compound by Laredo standards, surrounded by a high wall strung with razor wire, and guarded around-the-clock by men who only spoke Spanish.

Estevan received private tutoring in his mother's palatial home. He and his mother were rarely seen outside the compound and always escorted by an ominous fleet of black Chevy Suburbans sporting mud-splattered Mexico license plates.

Anywhere else, all this fanfare might have drawn some outsider's interest. But the mayor of Laredo made it clear to the citizenry that Señora Rosario and her son were never to be disturbed, under penalty of law. Or worse.

On very rare occasions when Valentina and her son visited a market, library or restaurant, the facilities were temporarily closed to all others.

Valentina and her son made annual visits to Nuevo Laredo, often remaining for several weeks before returning. Young Estevan was fluent in both English and Spanish and would charm family and friends on both sides of the border with his knowledge of both countries' histories.

"History," Estevan told them at a relatively early age, "is written by the victors. I intend to be a victor."

When his mother died in 2005, Estevan was devastated. At her funeral, a man in a dark suit handed Estevan a worn leather tube at her funeral. Inside were a series of crude, hand-drawn maps depicting various remote locations in Colombia and South America. No further explanation was given.

Years later, in 2015, Estevan binge-watched the American television crime drama series, *Narcos*. Set and filmed in Colombia, it told the story of Pablo Escobar, a multi-billionaire from the production and distribution of cocaine.

Narcos chronicled the life of Pablo Escobar from the late 1970s, when he first began manufacturing cocaine, until July 1992. Colombian soldiers found Escobar and his entourage outside *La Catedral* but are too terrified of the legendary drug lord to make an arrest. The United States dispatched a new ambassador from their Colombian Embassy, partnered with the CIA.

Estevan, now one of the richest, most successful real estate developers in South Texas, would invite his closest friends to his Laredo mansion to binge-watch the series with him. Vehicles filled with handsomely dressed men and scantily women were patted down and admitted to his mother's former compound. These *fiestas* often lasted for several days, where non-stop music and wild poolside banter would sometimes breach the walls of neighboring compounds. Not surprisingly, no one ever complained.

11

Estevan Colombia Barrero chuckled when he received the invitation to visit the new Governor of Texas, Bo Swaggart.

He and Swaggart went back a few years to Swaggart's unlikely bid for governor. If elected, Swaggart could offer something Estevan lusted after. A toll road stretching from Laredo, north to San Antonio, and eventually all the way to the state capital, Austin.

Estevan made a calculated donation of $10 million to Bo's campaign. If elected, Bo promised to post a contract for a Texas toll road that would stretch some 235 miles at an estimated cost in the billions of dollars. Bo further promised that Barrero Construction would be the low bidder, by hook or by crook.

Estevan was already a billionaire several times over. Once he turned 21, he began searching for the Xs marked on the maps of Colombia the mysterious *consejero* had handed him when his mother died. What he discovered boggled his mind. In rusty barrels, wrapped in black plastic garbage bags, were millions, maybe even billions, in moldy U.S. currency.

Estevan knew that only one man could have amassed such a fortune. The man depicted in the *Narcos* television series. Pablo Escobar.

Before she passed away, Estevan's mother had drawn him to her breast. She confided her liaison with the notorious drug lord years before.

"You are Pablo's legacy, Estevan. One day you must use your great wealth only for good, my son." Which was like Adolf Hitler's mom telling her son to use his artistic talent only for good.

"Mi amigo, Estevan," the Governor of Texas had written. "I have not forgotten your generous contribution to my campaign for governor. While I cannot, at this time, keep my promise of building a toll road from Laredo to Austin, I can promise something bigger. Much bigger. Meet me at the Cloak Room next Sunday afternoon at 2 p.m. The joint is closed on Sundays, except by special request of the Governor of Texas, which is me."

Estevan grimaced. Was the governor going back on his word? He had killed men for less. But he had to admit, he was intrigued by Bo's offer of something much bigger. He'd fly to Austin in his private jet, a golden Gulfstream G600, after church on Sunday. Estevan never missed church on Sunday at Laredo's San Martin de Porres Catholic Church. It was, after all, where he conducted many of his business dealings.

Estevan arrived punctually at the downstairs door of The Cloak Room adjacent to the State Capitol in Austin. A huge, black-suited Hispanic security guard wearing a white Stetson hat, dark glasses, and a coiled security device in his ear took one look at Estevan and slowly moved aside, opening the door, and welcoming him in Spanish. "*Bienvenidos*, Señor Barrero."

"*Gracias*," Estevan replied. "Nice hat!"

"Would you like it, sir?"

"No thanks. You don't wear a hat when you've got hair like mine or Jack Kennedy's. Estevan's shoulder-length brown mane made most women swoon.

The security guard spoke with military precision. "The governor's at his private table, Mr. Barrero. I have instructions not to admit anyone else for any reason."

"Special Forces? Estevan asked in passing.

"Sir, yes sir!" the guard replied.

"*Bueno*. I have several of your comrades on my security staff. Is it true that any one of you can kill a man…"

"Sir, I'd rather not discuss our paramilitary tactics. The governor will see you now."

"Estevan! Steve! Why, aren't you a sight…"

"…for sore eyes? Let's cut to the chase, shall we, Bo? You promised me a Texas toll road. Are you reneging now?"

"What? I'm not exactly sure what you mean by reneging, but I'm going to make you a deal you can't refuse."

"Try me."

"How would you like to be governor?" asked Governor Swaggart, sipping on his third double Bourbon & Branch.

"I've already made you governor as a gift, Bo. But my risks come with non-negotiable rewards. You owe me, plain and simple. I'm here to collect."

"And what I have in mind will make you richer and more powerful than you already are, Estevan. How would you like to be Governor of South Texas?"

12

"How ARE YOUR chats going, Governor?" chief of staff Julie Truman asked when the Governor rolled into the office around 10 a.m. the following Monday.

"Great!" Three down, one to go. Set up a meeting at the Cloak Room with Ponce Ponzio."

"Aren't you forgetting one other little chat you'll need to have, the one with 30 million Texans?"

"Good point, Jules. Guess I'll have to convince my fellow Texans that dividing our Great State into five good states will make us the most powerful coalition in the Union. But first, I've gotta get 'El Popo' on the hook."

"El Popo" was also the nickname of Mexico's ominous active volcano, Popocatépetl.

Popocatépetl has erupted at least 15 times since the arrival of the Spanish in 1519. Suffice it to say, Popocatépetl is a catastrophe waiting to happen.

"El Popo" was also the nickname of one of the most volcanic forces of nature in El Paso, Texas. Ponce Ponzio. Ponce was the fifth son of his Sicilian father and his Mexican mother. He believed his nickname "El Popo" instilled both fear and respect among his friends and enemies. El Pasoans had other names for Ponzio, but they tended to keep those names to themselves.

For a border town with a Spanish name meaning "The Pass" or "The Way," El Paso has a wayward political history. A full 80 percent of the population is Hispanic or Latino. Yet the West Texas city has largely been run by rich white men for as long as anyone can remember.

El Paso has long had a strong federal and military presence. William Beaumont Army Medical Center, Biggs Army Airfield, and Fort Bliss all call the city home. Fort Bliss is one of the largest U.S. military complexes and the largest training area in the United States.

In 2012, El Paso received an All-American City Award. El Paso had recently been ranked The Safest Large City in the U.S. for four consecutive years, an honorific that Ponzi considered a bad joke. He often pointed out bullet holes in the walls of the County Courthouse from shots fired from AK-47s across the border in Ciudad Juárez.

But Ponzio had a dream. With all El Paso's vast military might, he felt El Paso deserved a much larger role in state government. Little did he suspect that his dream might just become a reality.

"Governor Swaggart would like to meet with you privately, Mr. Ponzio. Next Sunday at the Cloak Room, just west of the Capitol," the governor's chief of staff informed the El Paso strongman.

"I know the Cloak Room well, Ms. Truman. I never miss a chance to sip cocktails and rub elbows with the legislators when the Legislature is in session. To what do I owe this honor if I may ask?"

"That's way above my pay grade, Mr. Ponzio. But I can assure you that Governor Swaggart speaks very highly of you, especially after you helped deliver the West Texas vote for him in the election."

"Felt it was my duty, Ms. Truman. After all, I'd like to think that the West Texas vote is what pushed Bo over the top."

Think what you will, Mr. Ponzio, Julie thought to herself. True, Bo Swaggart had rallied the Hispanic vote with his cry for Texas secession. True, El Popo had delivered, with the caveat that the new Governor wouldn't forget him or his West Texas stronghold. But Julie didn't like Mr. Ponzio. Didn't trust him.

"May I tell the Governor that you accept his invitation, Mr. Ponzio?"

"Tell him I'll be there with bells on, Ms. Truman!"

Hells bells, Julie thought to herself.

13

THE CLOAK ROOM is an interesting establishment. It is the closest thing Austin has to an authentic speakeasy. Located just across the street from the westernmost Capitol grounds, a short flight of stairs down to the subterranean bar clearly qualifies it as a dive.

The historic drinking den is known for under-the-table political dealings and other potentially unsavory activities. The joint opened in 1970, and long before Las Vegas touted its infamous slogan, it went without saying that what happened in the Cloak Room stayed in the Cloak Room.

The Cloak Room's notorious bartender was a no-nonsense woman named Brenda Prendahl. If you were a regular, Brenda greeted you warmly and placed your favorite poison on a napkin in front of you as you climbed aboard a well-worn barstool. Before your drink was empty, Brenda poured you another round.

The vintage jukebox pumped out the hits of Johnny Cash and Otis Redding. There was no rap music on the playlist. The Cloak Room was strictly old school. If that didn't float your boat, there were always plenty of other bars in and around Austin.

The doors opened at 3 p.m. and closed at 2 a.m. weekdays, 8 p.m. to 2 a.m. Saturdays, closed Sundays. Unless, of course, you were the Governor of Texas.

A large white 1964 Lincoln Continental convertible rolled up in front of the Cloak Room at precisely 2 p.m. the following Sunday afternoon. Word on the street was that it had once belonged to Lyndon B. Johnson, one of two associated with his presidency. The more famous of the two was the stretched 1961 Continental known as the X-100, which Johnson's predecessor was riding in when he was assassinated.

Ponce "El Popo" Ponzio slid smartly out of the driver's seat in a white linen suit, snapped his cufflinked cuffs, straightened his Windsor-knotted tie, and headed toward the steps leading down to the bar below street level.

"Who goes there!" a gruff voice bellowed.

In the shadows, Ponzio could barely make out a figure dressed in a dark suit, Stetson hat, mirrored sunglasses, and a security guard's pigtail earpiece snugged in his ear.

"Ponce Ponzio's the name. The Governor is expecting me."

"On a Sunday? Not likely!"

"Just tell him 'El Popo' is here to see him."

"Tell him yourself!" the shadowy figure replied, pulling off the mirrored sunglasses to reveal his identity. The Governor of Texas himself.

"Damn Bo, you had me going there for a minute."

"Never thought I'd be able to pull a fast one of the likes of you, El Popo." Fiddling briefly with the lock on the door, Governor Swaggart turned back to Ponzio.

"Buy you a cocktail, Ponz? Just name your poison, *mi amigo*."

Once inside, Ponzio recognized the familiar face of Brenda Prendahl.

"Doesn't the Governor give you a day off, Brenda?"

"Usually. But I'm here for him, day or night. He pays me well for such privileges. The usual, Mr. Ponzio?"

"Diablito Extra Añejo, with a Corona back," Ponzio replied. "Salt and lime, and keep 'em comin', *por favor.*"

"Bourbon & Branch, Governor?"

"Need you ask, Brenda?"

"No, sir. Just wanted to make sure you didn't want to slip over to the dark side with El Popo, here."

Both men chuckled, clinked glasses, and began their lively negotiation.

"How long have we known each other, Ponz?"

"Long enough to get you elected governor, Bo. And we both come from West Texas. You're from Alpine as I recall. I was born and raised in El Paso. By the way, do you know that when you leave Austin heading for California, when you get to El Paso…"

"…you're halfway to Los Angeles," Bo finished his sentence. "Yep, this is one big ass state, Ponz. Not the biggest anymore…"

"…but if you melt all that ice, we'd be bigger than Alaska! I seem to remember writing that line for one of your stump speeches, Bo."

"That you did, Ponz. But let's get down to business, shall we?"

"Shoot!"

"I know that you're the unofficial King of El Paso, Ponz. But would you be willing to accept a promotion if it made you even more powerful than you already are?"

"What do you have in mind?"

"How would you like to be Governor of West Texas?"

"But West Texas isn't a state, Bo."

"Not yet. But it soon will be."

Behind the bar, Brenda Prendahl busied herself polishing bar glasses and pretending not to overhear the conversation between these two Texas titans. But her ears perked up when the Governor of Texas mentioned something about a State of West Texas.

PART II:
BATTLE LINES

14

THE STREETS OF DOWNTOWN Austin mirror the major rivers of Texas, running south to north. Rio Grande, Nueces, San Antonio, Guadalupe, Colorado, Brazos, Trinity, Neches, Sabine, and Red River.

When dividing Texas into five states, those rivers and the county lines would play a large role in the battle lines secretly being drawn by Governor Beauregard Swaggart. Bo's first inclination was to enlist the help of Texas author, songwriter, and amateur scientist Max Sinclair. But Bo wasn't sure that Sinclair could be trusted with the assignment. Max had, after all, uncovered a plot in San Marcos, Texas, a couple of years before involving a nefarious landfill owner, an American traitor, and a Russian spy. Sinclair might just spill the beans.

Instead, Bo turned to a high-profile Texas political advisor, reform advocate, media columnist and television producer named Mitchell Marks. Marks' recent claim to fame was co-hosting the popular political television series, *Trick or Tweet?*

Bo had no illusions. Marks was a straight shooter. So Bo figured he'd throw him a curve ball. He scheduled a meeting in the Governor's office, a place with which Marks was familiar, given that he had once orchestrated the campaign of the second woman to govern Texas.

"Howdy!" Swaggart greeted Marks, who shook the Governor's hand vigorously while looking him dead in the eye, a Marks trademark.

"Governor Swaggart, it's an honor, sir."

"The honor is mine, Mitch. May I call you Mitch? And you can just call me Bo."

"With all due respect, Governor, I prefer to call you by your title. You've earned it."

"Whatever floats your boat, Mitch," the Governor replied, pulling down a map of Texas from a slot in the ceiling beside his weathered oaken desk. Marks couldn't help but notice deep gashes in the desktop, as if someone had taken a large knife to it.

"You're familiar with the map of Texas, I take it?" Bo asked.

"If you're asking if I can name every county and county seat in the Lone Star State, the answer is yes, Governor. If you're asking if I can name every governor of Texas, starting with James Pinckney Henderson all the way up to you, Number 49, the answer's the same."

"Good! Good!" the Governor beamed. "That's why I invited you here, Mitch. I'm guessing you're also familiar with the terms of the Annexation Agreement between Texas and the Union, am I right?"

"In general terms, Governor. Most of the fine print has never been enforced. Terms like our right to fly the Lone Star flag at the same height as the Stars and Bars, our right to secede..."

"...and the right to divide Texas into as many as five states," Bo prompted.

"That's probably the least likely term to ever be acted upon, Governor."

"Funny you should say that, Mitch. Let's play a little game together, shall we?"

Realizing Governor Swaggart seemed deadly serious, Marks decided to play along.

The Governor extracted a laser pointer from a drawer in his desk. He began tracing some imaginary dividing lines on the huge map.

"Gotta start with the rivers, wouldn't you agree, Mitch? Texas is defined by its great rivers, south to north."

"Rio Grande, Nueces, San Antonio, Guadalupe, Colorado, Brazos, Trinity, Neches, Sabine, and Red River," Marks recited from memory. That'll inform some boundaries in the north, east, and south. But it's a different can of worms out west. Out west, the Pecos and the Rio Grande have done your work for you.

"Here, this might make our little game a little easier," the Governor said, pulling down an acetate overlay depicting the 254 counties in Texas. "Here, take this marker and carve up the state into five states any way you see fit, Mitch."

It was a game Marks might have preferred not to play, but it was a game, after all. Nobody in his right mind would seriously consider divvying up the Lone Star State.

The sun was setting when Marks stepped back and glanced at the governor. There was something in the gleam in the governor's eyes that troubled Marks, but he chalked it up to typical political gamesmanship.

"Of course, Texans would never buy it, Governor."

"Of course not!" Bo assured him. "But speaking of buyin', can I buy you a drink?"

The Bourbon & Branch the governor handed him left a peculiarly unsavory taste in Marks' mouth.

15

CHIEF OF STAFF Julie Truman arrived at the Capitol the next morning, and there was a crudely drawn map of Texas on her desk. Someone had taken a highlighter and divided the state into five proportional sections. There was a scribbled note attached with a paper clip.

Work your magic, Jules. I'd like a finished version of this map on my desk in a Top-Secret folder FOR MY EYES ONLY by the end of the day. Don't bring any of our map folks in on this. Use those computer skills you've told me so much about. Mum's the word! ~Your Governor

The governor's chief of staff assumed this was some kind of joke, but she knew better than to assume anything about Governor Beauregard Swaggart. After clearing her desk of the usual mail and documents to sign, she opened her computer and googled Texas Maps. There were geographic maps, geologic maps, city maps, county maps, road maps, interactive maps, maps of Texas rivers, you name it.

Sipping her second cup of black coffee, Truman settled in for a long day's work.

This assignment would clearly require all her computer skills. *He can't be serious, can he?*

The afternoon turned into evening, and still there was no sign of the governor. Truman took a break at 7 p.m. and grabbed an egg salad sandwich from the refrigerator in the kitchen.

Turning the Governor's crude highlights into actual county-by-county demarcations was no easy task. One thing was obvious. Texas rivers had delineated many of the counties and would now form some of the borders of the five areas the Governor imagined. Was he really dividing up the state for a run at a second term? Seemed like it would be much easier to just use the Congressional District map, which had gotten him elected in the first place.

Around midnight, Truman slipped the finished product into a leather folder marked "Top Secret: Governor's Eyes Only" and slid it into the secret compartment in the governor's vintage oak desk. Only she and the Governor had keys to that hidey-hole. She picked up the worn velvet pouch that allegedly contained the original Bowie knife and placed it on top of the leather folder before closing and locking the hidden cabinet.

Surely the Governor has better things to do than redraw the map of Texas. Truman grabbed her purse and headed toward the North exit, where a State Trooper would probably want to inspect her purse before allowing her to pass.

Texas, My Texas, All Hail the Mighty State! she hummed beneath her breath as she flicked off the lights and headed toward the elevators.

The Governor of Texas rarely arrived early to his oak-paneled office, but this morning was an exception. Reaching into his coat pocket, he extracted the skeleton key that opened the secret compartment where he had instructed his chief of staff to leave her handiwork.

Lifting his precious relic and sliding out the folder beneath it, the Governor marveled at Julie's proficiency. Sure, it might need a bit of tweaking, but that could wait until the next scheduled meeting with his secret sharers. His governors.

Pouring himself a strong cup of coffee and spiking it with a generous splash of bourbon, Governor Beauregard Swaggart began a day that would, to paraphrase President Franklin Delano Roosevelt, live in infamy.

Spreading the map out before him on his desk, Governor Swaggart had to admit that never in his wildest dreams had he ever imagined what he was about to propose to his fellow Texans.

"Not one, but *five* Great States of Texas!" he said, practicing a speech that he planned to deliver before the next election. "Not two, but *ten* Texas Senators in the Senate!"

Swaggart paused when he uttered those last few words. If he could pull this off, Texas and Bo Swaggart could one day quite literally rule the Country.

"Did my computer-generated map meet with your approval, Governor?" Chief of staff Truman asked when she arrived at the office promptly at 8 a.m.

"Just a passing fancy, Jules. Pay it no mind. But yes, you did a fine job, as always. I hope you weren't up too late working on it."

"Beats trying to teach a pig to sing."

"What's that's supposed to mean?" asked the Governor.

"Oh, just something my daddy used to tell me," Truman answered. "Never try to teach a pig to sing. It wastes your time, and it annoys the pig."

Governor Swaggart spit coffee all over his fancy new map.

"Sorry, Jules. Guess you'll have to print out another copy for me."

"Your wish is my command, Governor," Truman said, barely stifling a laugh.

16

THE HEADLINERS CLUB, which commands the 21st floor of the Chase Bank Tower in downtown Austin, enjoyed unparalleled views of Austin and the surrounding cityscape.

Step off the elevator and to the right, past the Shivers Room, was the Main Lounge & Bar, where luncheon was served to members and their guests in the Parliament Room, overlooking I-35 to the east and Lady Bird Lake to the south.

Turn left, and one was greeted by the smiling countenance of an elegant receptionist. She would stamp your parking ticket and politely direct you to your appointed destination. Continuing down a long hallway past the Press Box and the Green Room was the Gentlemen's Restroom, one of Governor Swaggart's favorite haunts.

"You can stand there at the urinal, with a waterfall cascading down in front of you to get your juices flowin' while you gaze out the chest-high windows and piss all over those West Austin elitists," Bo was fond of saying.

The Headliner's Club is where Governor Swaggart decided to call a meeting of the minds to discuss collectively what he had discussed only individually. Dividing Texas into five states. He instructed his chief of staff to reserve and cordon-off both the Press Box and the Green Room for the occasion and to station a State Trooper outside of the entrance to The Nash & Read II Meeting Rooms on the west and south-facing corners of the Club. The trooper was further instructed to time the duration of any uninvited male guest taking a leak in the Gentleman's Restroom, knock on the door and summon the poor bastard if he overstayed his welcome. A second State Trooper was stationed at the doors leading from the elevators to the cordoned-off Brown Room and Read Room I, barring entry.

The stage was being set for one of the most important and covert meetings of the new Governor's term in office. Perhaps one of the most important and covert meetings in Texas history.

The engraved invitations with the Governor's embossed gold seal went out on a Tuesday.

"Everybody's still too hung-over after the weekend to pay attention to mail on Mondays," the Governor said to his chief of staff, "and once hump day rolls around, they're already makin' plans for the weekend."

The invitations left no doubt about either the importance or the secrecy of the meeting to which only four VIP guests were invited:

The Governor
Of The Great State of Texas
Cordially Invites you to join him
For a Private Summit
At the Headliners Club,
21st Floor of Chase Bank Tower,
Austin, Texas,
Friday, March 15th,
Six o'clock in the Evening

It only required a second glance for Jeremiah Jones to register the significance of the appointed date.

"That sonuvabitch wants us to meet on the Ides of March!" he told his wife, Grace.

☆

"Everyone has responded in the affirmative, Governor," chief of staff Truman reported.

"Meaning they have all accepted my little invite, Jules?"

"Affirmative, Governor." Truman could barely contain her chuckle at her own little private joke.

"Perfect!" the Governor replied, somehow failing to see the humor in his chief of staff's repartee. "Make sure my Bowie knife is in attendance, as well, Jules."

"Duly noted, Governor. Will there be any other surprises?"

"Of that I can assure you, Jules. Too bad you can't be a fly on the wall. But remember to wire the meeting room. I want this recorded for prosperity."

"I believe you mean *posterity*, Governor," Truman said, stifling another chuckle.

The Governor quickly recovered. "That too!"

17

HOLLY WORTHINGTON WAS no shrinking violet when it came to rooting out the story-behind-the-story when the topic was Texas-style shenanigans.

As an investigative reporter at LONE STAR magazine, Holly refused to accept the police report when three Houston prostitutes were found dead in as many months. Holly dug up the truth when two love-struck teenagers buried the third lover in their sordid *ménage à trois*. Holly also fingered a small-town Texas funeral home director who hid the body of a local widow in his freezer.

When Holly asked the new Governor of Texas for an interview, he seemed happy to accommodate her. Perhaps a bit too happy. After all, Holly had been doing a little research on The Man Who Would Be Governor, and what she discovered wasn't all on the up-and-up.

Holly had driven out to Alpine one weekend and chatted with a few locals who had gone to grade school and high school with Bo Swaggart.

"The first day of fifth grade, the teacher called him Beauregard," one of his grade school buddies recalled.

"Name's Bo!" the scrawny fifth grader had corrected her.

"Well, I like the name 'Beauregard,' young man. So that's what I intend to call you in my classroom," his teacher told him.

"Well, I like the name 'Cunt,' Teach. So that's what I intend to call you in your classroom," Bo fired back.

That was the first of many trips Bo made to the principal's office, his buddy recalled with what seemed like an inordinate amount of glee.

"Principal Parks blistered Bo's butt with a paddle drilled with holes to avoid air pressure from slowin' down that WHACK! We could hear it all the way down the hall. But I gotta hand it to Beauregard," his school chum admitted, "He would always slink back to homeroom red-faced. But we never saw a tear.

Holly had dropped by Sul Ross University for a visit with the President, Mr. Barnard Skye.

The conversation began cordially enough, with President Skye priding himself in reminding Holly that the new Governor of Texas was a Sul Ross Lobo-for-Life.

"I kind of get the sense that Governor Swaggart might be a lobo-in-sheep's-clothing, President Skye," Holly said.

The President feigned shock. "Bo Swaggart? No way! Bo's the real deal!"

"Then why can't I find any record of him graduating from Sul Ross, Mr. President?" Holly said.

"That's preposterous!" the Governor replied. "Bo Swaggart was one of our most decorated graduates, as I recall."

"And I recall that you weren't president back when he graduated. Am I correct, Mr. Skye?"

"Right you are, Ms. Worthington. But I met Bo Swaggart at his 25th college reunion. He even invited me to his Inauguration up in Austin!"

"So you could put your hands on his college records if I asked you to?"

"You can ask all you want, little lady. But our students' records are subject to the privacy rights of the great State of Texas. I hereby declare this meeting adjourned!"

"And I hereby declare you on-notice, President Skye. LONE STAR magazine has resources to retrieve information we deem important to a story."

"I'll be sure and let Governor Swaggart know you'll be snooping around his personal records, Ms. Worthington. And may I offer you some personal advice, off-the-record?"

"If you wish, Mr. President."

"Don't fuck with Bo Swaggart!"

When Leviticus Gingrich, publisher of LONE STAR magazine, called Holly into his office, she naturally assumed it was to heap more praise on her investigative skills.

"Do you like working here, Holly?" Gingrich began the conversation.

"Of course I do," Holly replied. "I can't imagine working anywhere else!"

"Then back off the Governor or your imagination may get the better of you."

"What? Are you telling me to stand down on my story on Governor Swaggart?"

"I'm telling you that Texas is full of stories. Stories that might one day win you a National Magazine Award, maybe even a Pulitzer. But this isn't one of them."

"I don't believe what I'm hearing," Holly stammered.

Gingrich grimaced. "Then believe this. Governor Swaggart is off limits. Do I make myself perfectly clear?"

"Very," Holly replied, standing up and storming out, slamming the door to Gingrich's office and almost shattering the pebbled glass etched with the single word PUBLISHER.

There was a reason Gingrich's employees called him "The Grinch" behind his back. He took great joy in squelching everyone else's spirits.

18

Max Sinclair was in Austin on a wild hare. He was in the middle of writing a new novel about a devil of an earthquake. He wanted to get some first-hand knowledge of geology from the school where his all-time favorite professor, Dr. Fred Bullard, had once thrilled him with his encyclopedic knowledge of the geologic sciences.

Professor Emeritus Bullard had died in 1994, but his legacy lived on. One of Sinclair's old college roommates, William "Wild Bill" Rickey, had gotten his undergraduate, graduate and PhD degrees in Geology from UT and had gone on to teach at his alma matter in true Bullard style.

"What brings you back to the Forty Acres, Sinc?" Rickey asked when Max appeared at the door to his office one morning.

"I need some earth-shattering answers, Wild Bill."

"Still working on that earthquake novel of yours?" Rickey asked.

"As a matter of fact, I am. Professor Bullard always taught me to look for the cause-and-effect when things get shaky."

"Are we still talking about earthquakes here, Max?"

"Well, yes and no. I could really use your help on that whole after-shocks thing. But the truth is, I'm still shocked over that rascal Beauregard Swaggart getting elected Governor of Texas."

"You're not the only one, Max. But if a minority of Americans and a few Russian hackers could elect someone like Donald Trump, it shouldn't surprise you that even a state as great as Texas could elect someone like Bo Swaggart."

"Yeah, I guess you're right. Still, something doesn't seem quite right about the election. Especially when some of his school records turned up missing in the middle of the campaign."

"I'm guessing it happens all the time. Kids these days can hack into any computer, anywhere, anytime they want. Heck, my credit card has been hacked three times this year alone!"

"I feel your pain, Wild Bill. Guess I best stick to my knitting, as my momma used to tell me. Can you loan me a textbook or two on earthquakes while I'm here in town?"

"Can a Longhorn kick an Aggie's ass?"

"Not since they moved to the SEC. The biggest mistake in college football history. All because the UT Athletic Department got dollar signs in their eyes when ESPN pitched 'em that Longhorn Network deal back in 2010."

"Yeah, well word has it that the UT-A&M rivalry may be coming back, if the Athletic Department can get their horns out of their asses!"

Max just shook his head. "I'll believe it when I see it. In the meantime, thanks for the textbooks. And Hook 'em, Horns!"

"Hook 'em, Horns!" Rickey replied, flashing him the Longhorn wide-fingered salute.

☆

Max had intended to slide on down to San Marcos to visit his daughter Sunny and his new grandson Jackson. But this Swaggart burr was lodged firmly under his saddle. He was intent on extracting the pesky irritant.

He had scanned the textbooks his old roommate had loaned him. He now had a better feel for what caused a Force 7 or greater earthquake. But his earthquake novel would have to wait. Who did he know who might have the goods on Beauregard Swaggart?

And just like that, Max found himself crooning the Neil diamond classic, 'Holly Holy.' Humming that tune, Max decided he'd stop by the Cloak Room and trouble Brenda Prendahl for a double Old Fashioned.

Brenda Prendahl smiled broadly. "Max Sinclair, as I live and breathe! May I ask why you've darkened my door this fine day?"

"I couldn't imagine taking another breath without inhaling your seductive perfume, Lady Prendahl. Chanel, isn't it? Coco Mademoiselle?"

"Max, you could charm a diamondback out of its rattle, you scoundrel!"

"Happy to debate that possibility, m'lady, but mind if we do it over double Old Fashioneds?"

"Templeton Rye?"

"Aye, aye, Cap'n!

Brenda winked. "Mind if I join you, mate? I've got a feeling you've got something important on your mind. And I've got nothing but time on mine."

"Only thing holding us back is gravity," Max said. "Cheers!"

19

Celeste Veronica Swaggart was often ribbed by her friends about being a stand-alone pharmacy. Having the initials CVS didn't help.

Veronica was their first call for their pharmaceutical pleasures. Uppers. Downers. Pills for anxiety or depression. Even opioids.

The hospital gave Veronica opiates after the birth of her only child, Beauregard Swaggart, Jr. "Li'l BoBo," she and her husband had nicknamed him. Li'l BoBo earned his mother an extreme episiotomy.

"You're going to require the Güttentite Procedure, Veronica," her doctor and Bo's golf buddy had joked, winking at Bo. "Your baby is a big-un, and his daddy is going to want your nether regions good'n'tight once this is all over!"

Veronica was not amused. And the post-op pain down there was agonizing. Hence her first, but certainly not her last, prescription for opioids. And so it was that Veronica joined the legions of Americans, both rich and poor, who were hooked on opioids. It was, some politicians and doctors had to admit of late, a national epidemic.

"Starting a little early, are you, Vee?" Bo said to his wife as he slipped on his suit coat before heading to his office over in the capitol.

"Don't press me this early in the morning, Beauregard!" Veronica answered, sipping on the first of what might be several Bloody Marys before her workout in a couple of hours. Veronica was one of those women who willed themselves thin, working out several hours a day before settling in with a martini or two in the evening. She was also the only person on the planet who could get away with calling her husband Beauregard.

"Maybe you should hold off on the sauce until you've dropped Li'l BoBo off at kindergarten, is all I'm sayin', Sweetheart."

"And maybe you should kiss my tight little ass, Beauregard!"

Bo Swaggart knew when to pick his battles. This wasn't one of them.

"I'll be a little late this evening, Hon. No need to wait up for me."

"What would be the point, Beauregard? If I wanna smell like liquor and sex, I'll pour myself another stiff one and cuddle-up with my vibrator."

The Governor just shrugged and gently closed the front door to the Governor's Mansion. A State Trooper accompanied him on the short walk to the capitol.

"Jules, why don't we go over my secret map of New Texas one more time before this little shindig at the Headliners Club," Governor Swaggart suggested to his chief of staff.

Julie Truman had fine-tuned Mitchell Marks' quick sketch dividing Texas into five states. The result was a bit Frankensteinish for her. But the Governor seemed hell-bent on carving up the Lone Star State.

Julie had to admit that Mr. Marks' approach was rather ingenious. He let the rivers determine some trickier boundaries, but also understood that existing counties should not be split apart. Granted, not everyone would be happy with the result. But that's where the governor and his salesman skills would come into play.

"Not to worry, Jules. I've got this. Besides, my hand-picked governors will have their hands full just trying to decide where to build their capitol buildings."

The governor was right, of course. Where would the five new Texas governors build their capitol buildings? Truman was pretty sure no one was going to opt for a new capitol building for what might soon become Central Texas. After all, the impressive Texas Capitol in Austin was 130 years old, constructed of precious pink granite, added to the National Register of Historic Places in 1970, and recognized as a National Historic Landmark in 1986.

"I'm willing to bet that Alexa will want a grand capitol for North Texas," Swaggart said. "But I'll be damned if her capitol will outshine mine!"

"No, Governor, I'm sure it won't."

"Now as for Jeremiah, I figure he'll want his East Texas capitol in Houston to reflect Petro Metro's reliance on the oil bidness."

"I suspect you're right, Governor."

"There's actually no tellin' what Estevan will conjure up for Laredo, given that he's got billions of his own money to toss around. One thing's for sure. San Antonio is gonna be majorly pissed that they aren't the capital of South Texas!"

"Majorly," Truman agreed.

"And I can't wait to see what El Popo comes up with for El Paso. I'm guessing he'll want a bullet-proof building, no matter what he builds for West Texas!"

Chief of staff Truman simply nodded. Hard to believe that Swaggart was serious about splitting Texas into five states. Particularly given that he hadn't asked Texans for their blessing yet.

20

Max Sinclair could barely believe his ears.

According to his favorite bartender, Brenda Prendahl, there had been a secret meeting between the Governor of Texas and the infamous Ponce "El Popo" Ponzio right there in the Cloak Room.

Max and Brenda didn't have many secrets, but this is one he wished she'd kept to herself.

If what Brenda overheard was true, the Governor was contemplating the unthinkable. Carving up Texas into two states. Maybe more!

Max asked if there were cocktails involved. Brenda confessed that both men had been drinking heavily.

Swaggart got elected by promising Texas would secede from the Union. Now he was talking, not about secession, but about dividing the great state of Texas into five smaller entities.

Max found he couldn't sleep. He thought about calling his reporter friend Holly Worthington. But it was after 2 a.m. Instead, Max grabbed his big-bodied Taylor guitar and began slowly strumming "The Eyes of Texas" to calm his nerves.

Max finally fell into a fitful sleep about the time the sun was rising. *Maybe it was just all a bad dream,* he tried to persuade himself as he dozed off.

☆

Julie Truman told herself that the governor's Headliner Summit was too important to miss. Besides, she might pick up on some nuance that the governor might otherwise miss. After all, the future of Texas hung in the balance. She would just have to figure out some way to convince the governor that she would merely be a fly on the wall.

The opportunity unexpectedly presented itself the next morning.

"Jules, I'd like you to attend my little shindig at the Headliners Club. I need an extra pair of eyes and ears around this bunch of thieves," Swaggart explained.

"Honored to join you, Governor."

The Governor's chief of staff spent the rest of the day going over the plans for the big event. The bar would be stocked to her exacting specifications. Bourbon & Branch for the Governor. Maker's Mark Private Reserve straight up for Alexa King. Courvoisier XO for Jeremiah Jones. Estevan Barrero preferred tequila, any top shelf would do, as long as it was *añejo*. And Ponce Ponzio was very picky. Diablito Extra Añejo for the devil himself. With a Corona Extra back.

The menu for the evening was fit for four Texas kings and a Texas queen. For starters, Gulf Coast Oysters Rockefeller, followed by a Texas Caesar Salad. Romaine lettuce seasoned with cilantro, red wine vinegar, freshly grated Parmesan cheese, chopped shallots, anchovy fillets, garlic cloves, fresh lemon juice, extra virgin olive oil, jalapeño chilies seeded and chopped, sweet white corn, and sun-dried tomatoes.

The main course would make any Texan's mouth water. For the carnivores, a choice of herb-marinated, pan-seared Angus Ribeye steak or Pretzel-dusted Schnitzel with Sweet Onion Caraway Noodles. For the herbivores, Alexa King was likely the only one, a choice of grilled Portobello Tacos with Salsa Verde or baked Chiles Relleno with Smoky Tomato Sauce. Regardless of one's choice, there would be a steaming side of Texas Caviar, aka Black-Eyed Peas, for good luck.

The dessert course was the *coup de grâce.* Warm Texas Pecan Chocolate Fudge Pie from the legendary Collin Street Bakery in Corsicana, topped with a generous scoop of Blue Bell Homemade Vanilla ice cream from the little creamery in Brenham. After dinner drinks would include a staggering selection of Amaro, Sherry, Grappa, Brandy, and Ouzo. For any smokers, Honduran-leaf Texas-rolled cigars.

Once properly sated, smoked and sotted, the five new potential governors of the five potential new states of Texas would get down to 'bidness,' as Bo called it.

The governor insisted that all the bartenders and waiters be Texans, representing the racial identities of his special guests. Absolutely none of them were to remain once the after-dinner meeting got underway.

Chief of staff Truman was also charged with bugging the room for 'prosperity,' another Bo Swaggart malapropism. She interviewed several security companies before finally settling on BlackOps Security. They assured her that there would be no copies made of any conversations. And no BlackOps personnel attending the governor's private dinner.

BlackOps would, nonetheless, be covertly listening-in. It was, after all, how they had built one of the most successful security forces in the country. Top secret information was the new currency. And BlackOps was rolling in it.

21

SISTER MARY CECILE, as was her habit, locked eyes with her accuser.

Six months before, during the last days of the former administration, she had been accused of aiding and abetting a peaceful protest at Planned Parenthood in Austin. Today was her day in court, and she planned to make the most of it.

"Is it true, Sister Cecile…" the prosecutor began.

"Sister *Mary* Cecile," she corrected him.

"Right. Is it true, Sister Mary Cecile, that you knowingly aided and abetted pro-choicers at a Planned Parenthood rally in the fall of last year? September the 22nd, to be exact."

"Please define 'aided and abetted,' Counselor."

"Aided and abetted, as I'm sure you know, Sister, is a legal doctrine related to the guilt of someone who aids or abets a commission of a crime. It exists in several different countries," the smarmy lawyer continued, "and generally allows a court to pronounce someone guilty for aiding and abetting in a crime, even if they are not the principal offender."

"The principal offender, in my opinion, Counselor, is, or at least was, Governor George Tolbert."

"May I remind you that you, not former Governor Tolbert, are on trial here today, Sister."

"And may I remind you that Governor Tolbert, not me, might be on trial here today if he had remained in office, Counselor."

The prosecutor simply shook his head and addressed the judge.

"Your honor, I believe Sister Mary Cecile's response speaks for itself. No further questions."

"Defense, do you care to examine the witness?" Judge Margo Olivier asked the defense attorney.

"No, Your Honor. The defense calls Texas Governor Beauregard Swaggart."

A hush fell over the crowd as the huge oak doors opened and the Governor of Texas sauntered into the courtroom.

"Your Honor, this is outrageous!" the prosecutor stood and shouted.

Judge Olivier slammed down her gavel. "Order in the court! One more outburst like that, Mr. Prosecutor, and I will hold you in contempt of court!"

The prosecuting attorney sat down, tail tucked figuratively between his legs.

"Please raise your right hand, Governor," the bailiff instructed. "Do you promise to tell the truth, the whole truth, and nothing but the truth, so help you God?"

"Hell yes!" Governor Swaggart said.

"A simple yes will suffice, Governor Swaggart," the judge admonished him, barely concealing a smile behind her cupped hand.

"Yes, Your Honor," said Governor Swaggart, who then paraphrased, "You shall know the truth, and the truth shall set Sister Mary Cecile free!"

"Objection, Your Honor!" shouted the prosecutor.

"Overruled. Please just stick to the facts, Governor."

"Of course, Your Honor."

The defense attorney slowly approached the witness stand and observed the governor for a long moment.

"Governor, do you know Sister Mary Cecile?"

"I know she's innocent!"

"And why is that, Governor Swaggart?"

"Because she was simply standing up for basic women's rights."

"With all due respect, Governor, that's not how your predecessor saw it."

"What my predecessor tried to get away with was downright criminal!"

"Objection, Your Honor!" shouted the prosecutor.

"Sustained," agreed the judge. "Governor, please remember that Sister Mary Cecile, and not former Governor Tolbert, is on trial here today."

"Roger that, Your Honor. I'm just saying that arresting a woman of the cloth for standing up for what she believes is right in the eyes of God is unpardonable."

"No one is suggesting a pardon!" the prosecutor shouted angrily.

The governor simultaneously skewered the prosecutor and butchered the French language with his retort. "*Oh contraire, Monsewer Prosecutewer.* It is completely within my power to pardon Sister Mary Cecile. Which I hereby do!"

There were audible gasps from the crowd. From the back row of the courtroom, a small gathering of Catholic nuns began quietly singing 'Amazing Grace' *a cappella.*

"Order in my courtroom!" Judge Olivier gaveled, but not without a sly grin to Governor Swaggart, who winked back at her.

"Case dismissed! If there is no other business, this court is hereby adjourned," the judge announced, then promptly retired to her chambers.

22

Iain Clarkson McClain, the new Lieutenant Governor of Texas, was tall, movie-star handsome, Harvard-educated, family trust-funded, and gay.

The office of the Lieutenant Governor is part of both the executive and legislative branches. According to the Texas Constitution, the Lieutenant Governor is the Constitutional President of the Senate, also known as the President Pro Tempore.

Lt. Governor McClain was Governor Swaggart's bone thrown to the growing Human Rights and LGBTQ communities in Texas. The two of them campaigned together, appeared together, and won together.

The Texas Tea Party, of course, gravely objected, and pulled out their famous Bag of Dirty Tricks, arguing that electing Iain McClain would place his blasphemous gay feet one step closer to the governor's office. It didn't work.

Texans, Republicans and Democrats alike, were so enthralled with Swaggart's secessionist rhetoric that they simply didn't care who ran on his coattails. Swaggart and McClain both won by the narrowest of margins, with their rivals losing by less than 200,000 votes. But as they say in Texas, "Close only counts in horseshoes and hand grenades!"

Where Swaggart was a bit of a blow-hard on the campaign trail, McClain was exceedingly erudite. Swaggart proclaimed it was time for the Great State of Texas to become a Nation again. McClain countered, suggesting it was time for Texas to regain its rightful place among the most prosperous states in the Union.

The Texas Governor, Lt. Governor and Secretary of State have functional offices in the Capitol, as well as some additional offices in neighboring buildings.

Lt. Governor McClain's office was in the east wing of the second floor of the state Capitol, in Room 2E13. While some might consider the number 13 unlucky, McClain considered it very lucky. A paean to his recent unlikely victory.

Governor Swaggart's office matched his bluster. Dark-paneled oak walls replete with early Texas flags, famous Texas battle scenes, and a stuffed longhorn.

McClain's office looked like it might have been decorated by Jacqueline Bouvier Kennedy herself in earlier times. The crisp, white walls showcased original contemporary paintings by David Hockney, Keith Haring, Andy Warhol and Robert Mapplethorpe. The carpet was contemporary yet arabesque. His desk, a chrome-and-glass masterpiece. His desk chair, an ergonomic feat of sculpture.

One made appointments with Lt. Governor McClain through his chief of staff, a stunningly handsome Black man named Rory Minton, a Texas-born actor. Minton had opted to trade his acting career for the political arena. Senators and Congressmen alike gave the pair a wide berth when McClain and Minton roamed the halls of the Capitol, out of respect mixed with a fair amount of primal fear.

Lt. Governor McClain harbored no misconceptions. He would never be elected Governor of Texas. But, as he sometimes reminded himself in reflective moments, election wasn't the only path to the highest office in Texas.

For the moment, McClain's office was embroiled in a fierce battle to alter the course of Texas' do-nothing Congress. Under former Governor Tolbert, the Texas Senate and Texas House were dominated by Republicans.

Texas, buoyed by a growing number of liberal Texas voters, had elected decidedly more Democrats, reminiscent of the Republican Backlash of 2018. This did not mean, however, that Governor Swaggart and Lt. Governor McClain would have an easy go of it. Quite the contrary. The Congressional battleground was strewn with dead bills. Swaggart and McClain had successfully resurrected two bills ravaged by the previous administration. Planned Parenthood and Redistricting.

McClain was particularly proud of his hard-fought battle to re-establish Planned Parenthood, health centers that promoted birth control to help in the both the prevention of and planning for pregnancy. Morning-after pills safely prevented pregnancy up to five days after unprotected sex.

McClain's first congratulatory call came from a Sister Mary Celine, who was under investigation for aiding and abetting a not-so-peaceful protest by Planned Parenthood deniers. Five months later, she would be exonerated by Governor Swaggart's pardon.

23

THE FIRST LADY of Texas had expansive offices in the underground Capitol Extension, beneath the street level north wing of the Capitol itself. Officially, this was known as the Office of the First Lady & Governor's Appointments.

Celeste Veronica Swaggart was the new First Lady of Texas. FLOTEX, as the Texas press often called her.

The First Lady hated the moniker. "Sounds like Kotex!" she complained to her friends. "Is Veronica ever *not* on the rag?" her BFFs tittered privately.

First Lady Swaggart prided herself in her expansive offices and staff. At taxpayers' expense, the new First Lady figured she had more than earned a large staff and an even larger redecorating budget. Veronica had long considered herself a fashion designer. She wasted no time spending several million dollars transforming what she considered her threadbare offices.

When asked who had approved her budget by the Ways & Means Committee chairman, she flashed him her right palm and declared, "Either talk to the hand or talk to the governor. I've got more redecorating to do."

The First Lady was particularly fond of the after-hours parties she threw for her friends in her lavish new digs. There was no short supply of exotic canapés, top shelf liquors and French champagnes, pharmaceutical-grade cocaine, live music, and buff boys flown in first class from male burlesque clubs.

Husbands, of course, were not invited. These quarterly events were billed as 'High Fashion Flings,' with an emphasis on the word 'high.' A dozen or so women in risqué cocktail dresses and six-inch heels were often seen slinking out of the Capitol just as the janitorial crew arrived pre-dawn. Yet no one spoke a discouraging word. Hell hath no fury like a First Lady scorned.

There was just one problem: The First Lady's escapades were beginning to draw the attention of the conspicuous minority of female members in the Texas House and Senate.

One of them, a distant relative of the first African American elected to the Texas Senate after Reconstruction, was incensed by the late-night charades behind closed doors in her beloved State Capitol.

Bethany Jordan finally gave up trying to garner an engraved invitation to one of the First Lady's flings. She figured she'd find another way to skin that cat, as her daddy was fond of saying.

Senator Jordan was a favorite of the Capitol custodial staff. It didn't take long for her to trade two floor-level seats to a Texas Longhorn women's basketball game for a borrowed capitol staff server uniform and apron. A wig would complete the ruse.

The stage was set. All she had to do was wait until the next after-hours soirée.

It was a busy Spring, and for one reason or another, the First Lady decided to postpone her next High Fashion Fling until early May. If she waited any later than that, most of her girlfriends would be long gone, flying off to Colorado to avoid the dreadful Texas summer heat.

Veronica often joined her friends for long weekends in Aspen. She was a very popular guest. These days, marijuana was legal in

Colorado. Veronica's treats, which she carried in a crocodile-skin diplomatic pouch, were still on the Controlled Substances list.

No TSA agent ever dared to search the legendary 'Dragon Lady of Texas.'

24

THE LIMOUSINES BEGAN arriving outside the Headliners Club at precisely 7 o'clock in the evening on March 15th.

The first stretch limo revealed its lone occupant. A tall, regal Jeremiah Jones, the firebrand politico from Houston. Jones considered this a State Dinner and dressed accordingly in an elegant black Brunello Cuccinelli tuxedo and Ferragamo velvet loafers emblazoned with his trademark JJJ logo.

Chief of staff Julie Truman met him curbside and directed him to the elevators inside. At the express elevator to the 21st Floor, a tall, no-nonsense state trooper greeted him by name.

"Good evening, Mr. Jones. The governor is expecting you, sir."

"Why thank you, my good man," Jones replied, stepping into the elevator and snapping the cuffs on his Canali dress shirt before pushing the elevator button. "Going up!" he winked at the trooper.

The following two limos arrived simultaneously. One white, one pink.

Ponce 'El Popo' Ponzio of El Paso exited the white limo sporting a white dinner jacket. Alexa King slid seductively out of the pink limo in a clingy pink evening dress. Neither had ever met the other.

"Good evening, Ms. King, Mr. Ponzio," Julie Truman welcomed the odd couple. "The governor is pleased you could both join us this evening."

"As if we had a choice!" Ponzio muttered under his breath. Alexa King simply ignored the little man beside her and strutted toward the entryway on her pink Louboutin stilettos.

When Ponzio and Ms. King waltzed into the waiting elevator, she noticed that Ponzio, at a mere 5-foot-6, was leering unapologetically at her ample décolletage.

"Do you mind?" she said.

"Oh, I don't mind at all, Ms…"

"King. Perhaps you've heard of the King Ranch?"

"I've hunted quail there many a season, Ms. King. But I've never had the pleasure of meeting the King's Queen!"

Alexa smirked at Ponzio's sad attempt at a pick-up line, then turned away as the elevator door opened.

"Good evening, Ms. King, Mr. Ponzio. The Governor is expecting you. Right this way please," said a second state trooper as he escorted them down the corridor towards the Nash Room, where yet a third state trooper stood guarding the door.

Ponzio motioned for Alexa to enter first, no doubt so he could get one last look at her curvy derrière. He winked at the state trooper. The trooper simply refused to acknowledge Ponzio's crude chauvinism.

The fourth and last limo was a vintage, fully restored ghost grey 1935 Rolls-Royce originally built for Lady De Frece, who once owned the Mayfair Hotel in London.

Julie Truman gazed longingly as a uniformed chauffeur opened the rear door of the Sport Salon and stood aside as billionaire Estevan Barrero slowly stepped from the gleaming coachwork.

Barrero extended his right hand to Truman, then bowed and lightly kissed her hand before looking into her eyes appreciatively.

"Julie Truman, you are as beautiful as ever!"

"Why thank you, Mr. Barrero. You're very kind."

"Please, call me Estevan. Steve, if you prefer. I trust the governor is treating you well?"

"You know the governor, Mr…Estevan. He treats everybody well!"

Until he doesn't need them anymore, Barrero thought to himself.

"You're the last invitee, Estevan. The others have already headed upstairs to the Headliners Club. A state trooper will meet you at the elevators. And may I say, I've never seen an automobile quite as impressive as yours."

"The Grey Lady? She's my pride and joy. As a friend of mine once reminded me, 'We're not here for a long time, we're here for a good time!' Perhaps I can take you for a spin in her one of these days, Julie. Do you ever get down to Laredo?"

"Oh, I have a feeling I'll be seeing plenty of Laredo in the months ahead, Estevan. Thank you for your kind offer."

"It would be my pleasure, I assure you, Julie." And with that, Estevan Barrero swept inside Chase Tower and up the elevator to whatever destiny might await him.

The door to the adjoining Read Room II opened and in pranced Governor Swaggart, warmly welcomed by his four special guests.

A string quartet struck up "The Eyes of Texas," signaling the beginning of an evening that would long be remembered.

25

DRINKS WERE POURED, formal introductions were made, and the evening got off to an auspicious start. None of the four guests had ever officially met, yet all four knew the others by reputation.

There was a single, large white linen-clad round table in the middle of the room, lit by a crystal chandelier. Five heavy silk-cushioned chairs were spaced evenly around the table with engraved place cards, one marked by a place card that simply read, The Governor.

"I learned this trick from a visit to a United Nations conference in New York City," Governor Swaggart told his guests. "At a round table, everyone's equal."

Eyeing the governor's thrown-like chair, Alexa King stifled a chuckle. *Although some are more equal than others,* she reminded herself.

The governor tapped his crystal double old-fashioned glass. "Another round of drinks before we dig in?" Swaggart circled his hand above the table. Another round of stiff drinks was promptly served.

The private Summit Dinner was nothing short of sumptuous. Alexa King, as expected, requested a vegetarian serving. The gentlemen grazed on rare Angus ribeyes and pecan-dusted schnitzel. Some had both. Vintage wines refilled bottomless wine goblets, and a lively conversation ensued.

"I've spoken with each of you individually," Swaggart began, politely dabbing his wine-stained lips with his linen napkin, "but I think it's high time we put all our cards on the table. You've each been chosen because of your unconditional loyalty and unbridled support of my election. Without you, I might still be jackin' my jaws on the peas-and-carrots circuit. Thanks to y'all, we've won the governorship of the greatest state in the Union!"

Here, Swaggart paused, gauging the response to his soliloquy. Everyone nodded agreeably.

"Tonight, I want to repay your largesse with something mere money can't buy. The governorships of what I propose will become the five States of Texas!"

While each of his guests had heard his proposal in strictest confidence, they were clearly taken aback by the governor's audacity.

Alexa King raised her hand. "Should we be having this conversation here and now, Governor?"

Swaggart slid back his chair and stood, holding his wine glass in his hand. "Why the hell not? As you can plainly see, the wait staff has been excused for the evening. The only other ears in the room belong to my chief of staff, Julie Truman. Think you can keep a secret, Jules?"

Embarrassed by him calling her out, Truman simply nodded discreetly.

"So what say we enjoy some after-dinner cordials before we dive into this, pardon the pun, divisive discussion. Jules, would you please do the honors? And gentlemen, there are some Monte Cristo No. 2 cigars from the future fifty-first State of Cuba on the bar. Light 'em up, boys!"

"Mind if I join you boys in a Monte 2?" Alexa King interrupted seductively. "I was smokin' stogies on my granddaddy's porch while you were all probably still wettin' your beds."

Estevan Barrero slipped an aluminum tube off a Cuban cigar and expertly bit off the torpedo end with his perfect white teeth. He toasted the business end with his solid gold lighter, then handed the banned cigar to a clearly impressed Alexa King.

"I bet you do just about everything well, Estevan," Alexa cooed.

"I trust I will live up to your expectations, Ms. King." Barrero smiled, letting his eyes drift to the deeply plunging neckline of her pink silk cocktail dress.

Governor Swaggart interrupted the revelry, clinking his crystal brandy snifter. "My fellow Texans, please finish up your Cubans and cordials. It's high time we got down to bidness!"

Cordials quaffed and stogies expended, the potential candidates for governors of the five states of Texas reconvened around their host's round table.

"Jules, please see that we're not disturbed," Swaggart whispered to his chief of staff. "For any reason," he added. Truman nodded and headed toward the door to speak to the state trooper on duty.

"Lady and gentlemen," Swaggart said theatrically, swirling his index finger in the air, "Let the games begin!"

26

CHIEF OF STAFF Julie Truman returned to the table, wheeling a large easel bearing a Texas flag draped chart.

The governor gestured broadly. "Jules, if you'll please do the honors,"

Truman responded by ceremoniously lifting the flag of the Lone Star State, revealing a map of Texas divided into five states. North, East, Central, South, and West.

Gasps echoed through the private room.

"Now wait just a damn minute!" Ponzio bellowed, beating the others to the punch.

"No, *you* wait just a damn minute, El Popo! And that goes for any of the rest of you scalawags, at least until I've had my say. The lines you see drawn here are the handiwork of many a long evening spent with one of Texas' foremost political minds. I believe y'all know Mitchell Marks?"

The governor's guests had to agree. Mitchell Marks knew his stuff.

"Let's start with North Texas, shall we? Obviously, it will encompass the Panhandle, and Dallas will be its capital. I recommend that Ms. Alexa King be our nominee for Governor of North Texas. All in favor, say 'aye!'"

This was clearly a rhetorical vote. Four 'ayes!' quickly followed.

"Next up, East Texas. You'll notice that the line delineating the borders of East Texas run north and southeast beyond Houston. That means the cedar-choppers and coon-asses will have to join hands with the oil field rednecks and roustabouts. As for the capital, Houston wins hands-down. And it is my recommendation that Mr. Jeremiah Jones be our nominee for Governor of East Texas. Can I get an amen?"

"Amen," came the measured response.

"No question who holds an iron grip on South Texas," Swaggart continued. "Hell, my amigo Estevan Barrero could probably buy South Texas if he chose to! Anybody got a problem with Estevan being our nominee for Governor of South Texas or Laredo being its capital?"

When no one objected, Swaggart fist bumped Barrero before moving on.

"Now West Texas is a can of worms," Swaggart said. "Those richy-riches over in Midland probably think they deserve to be the capital. And they'll get some serious pushback from Odessa. Well fuck 'em both! I say we make El Paso the capital of West Texas. With your blessing, I'd like to see Ponce Ponzio in the governor's mansion there."

The silence was deafening.

"I'll take that as a yes!" Swaggart said. "Furthermore, I trust there's no doubt about me being Governor of Central Texas. And I've already got the perfect capitol."

"So Austin will be the capital of Central Texas, am I correct, governor?" Jones asked.

Hell yes! Swaggart wanted to say. Instead he settled on "Hallelujah! Now, if all that's settled, I suggest you all head back to your prospective new states and start figurin' out where to build your capitol buildings."

"Where will the funds come from?" Alexa King asked.

"From your taxpayers, of course!" Swaggart said.

"Are there any rainy-day funds available to us?" Jeremiah Jones chimed in.

"Hurricane Harvey wiped out every last dime and then some," Swaggart replied. "You might just have to raise some new taxes in your new states to pay for your new playhouses."

Estevan Barrero glanced around the table. "That could make getting us elected a bit problematic."

"Look, y'all! I'm handing you the governorships of sovereign Texas states on a platter. If you can't figure out how to raise the money to build your state capitols, maybe I've picked the wrong people."

"Oh, you've picked the right people, Bo. But you seem to be forgetting one little hitch," the King Ranch descendant offered.

"Yeah, and what might that be, Alexa?"

"Registered Texas voters will have to agree to split their precious Lone Star State into five smaller states. In a state where everything's bigger, that dog might not hunt."

Bo stood again, signifying the meeting was over. "Leave that to me, lady and gentlemen. If there's no other business, this meeting is hereby adjourned. Safe travels back to the soon-to-be five states of Texas!"

Part III:

Capitol Ideas

27

THE NORTH TEXAS Capitol would make Dallas the financial hub of Texas. The envy of the five new states. Of that, Alexa King was certain.

For openers, her capitol would be one of Dallas' largest and most distinctive buildings. Alexa had her eye on Infomart, the information technology and data center built in 1985 and modeled after the Crystal Palace, a huge iron-and-glass building originally erected in Hyde Park in the 19th Century to house Britain's Great Exhibition of 1851.

Alexa's proposed new capitol would also feature a stunning reproduction of the Crystal Fountain. There was only one problem. How would Alexa convince the more than 110 technology and telecommunications companies to abandon their landmark offices?

"That's child's play," Alexa told her close confidantes. "When you're a star, you can do anything. Just ask our former pussy-grabbing President."

Indeed, Alexa had already contacted her friends in the property management sector about relocating the Infomart Data Centers to Las Colinas, an upscale second-city development in the Dallas suburb of Irving. Her idea made some sense. Las Colinas was centrally located between Dallas and Ft. Worth. Due to its proximity to DFW Airport, it was an attractive destination for corporate and business relocation. An upscale planned community with many corporate offices, luxury hotels, landmark office towers, luxury townhomes, expensive single-family homes, private country clubs, gated enclaves and urban lofts.

"What Alexa wants, Alexa gets!" was Alexa's mantra.

Alexa had already busied herself with grandiose plans of converting Infomart into her own personal Crystal Palace. It would be known far and wide as the North Texas State Capitol. But Alexa preferred to think of it as *her* state capitol. That would, of course, necessitate a great deal of capital. Alexa had already begun priming the pump among her Dallas political backers. But in her humble opinion, this was bigger than Big D. The Crystal Capitol, as she preferred to call it, would become a global destination, visited by kings and queens, presidents and prime ministers.

Alexa had also privately retained the services of a world-famous architect to begin drawing up plans to deconstruct the interior of her Crystal Capitol and reconstruct it in a manner befitting the original Crystal Palace.

"Money is no object," she assured him. "Everything's bigger in Texas, including our architectural budgets!"

But Alexa didn't stop there. She also hand-picked one of the world's foremost landscape architects. One of his most recognized projects of late was the national 9/11 Memorial, a forest of oak trees forming the core of the rebuilt World Trade Center in New York Center.

"I want people driving by to see an infinite sea of trees, gardens and fountains, reflected in the grand windows of my Crystal Capitol," Alexa explained. "And I don't want them to see hundreds of parked cars. We must figure out a way to build underground parking."

Alexa stamped her foot when her architect argued that her Crystal Capitol might collapse into the underground parking cavern, given the immense weight of what he privately called the Crystal Monstrosity.

And while no one could confirm its veracity, rumor had it that Alexa was in negotiations to procure sculptor Benjamin Waterhouse Hawkin's circa 1854 Crystal Palace dinosaur statues to roam the grounds of her Crystal Capitol.

Of course, Alexa had no intention of discussing her ambitious plans with any of the other potential four Texas governors. She wisely surmised that she couldn't build her Crystal Palace noticeably larger than Austin's state capitol building. But Alexa could and would build it grander. After all, she and Bo Swaggart had what some in polite company referred to as history together. She knew she could charm the new Governor of Texas out of his knickers. Alexa smiled as she recalled their little Texas tryst in the Governor's office when she suggested they watch her King Ranch stud doing the wild thing. Thankfully, nobody had caught them *in flagrante delicto*. That certainly wouldn't sit well with those holier-than-thou Texas Baptists!

That reminded Alexa that she needed to personally thank Bo's Mexican chambermaid Marina for cleaning up after them. She seemed nice enough and suitably discreet, although loyal Mexican housekeepers were a dime-a-dozen where she came from.

Alexa would, of course, need an entirely new wardrobe for her role as governor of one of the five new states of Texas. She began picturing herself in a royal blue Armani suit with a white silk Dolce & Gabbana blouse, a custom-designed scarlet Hermes scarf, and navy Jimmy Choo Viper stilettos. She'd show those other Texas governors how a true Texan dressed to impress!

28

THE EAST TEXAS Capitol would be a different affair altogether, if Jeremiah Jones had anything to say about it. And he would.

Houston had recently weathered its latest superstorm, Hurricane Harvey, which dumped nine trillion gallons of water on Texas. What the 150 mile-per-hour winds didn't demolish, the storm surge and the rising waters from Houston's bayous had inundated. Former Governor Tolbert guesstimated the damage to Texas in the hundreds of billions of dollars. In an optimistic effort to raise $200,000, Houston Texan football star J.J. Watt had instead raised more than $30 million. Houston-born Austin technology billionaire Michael Dell and his wife pledged $36 million.

But raising money to repair the damage caused by Hurricane Harvey didn't solve the inherent problem. Houston is perennially flood prone. In the wake of Harvey, global scientists suggested that Houston consult with experts from the waterlogged Netherlands, where climate change is considered neither hypothetical nor a drag on the economy. Instead, the Dutch insist, it's an opportunity.

The Netherland's globe-trotting salesman-in-chief for Dutch expertise on rising water and climate change offered to share his expertise with Houston's politerati post-Harvey. Houston politely declined.

Jeremiah Jones, the potential new governor of the new state of East Texas, knew what he had to do.

"Higher ground!" he preached to his wife, Grace. "I'm not building my capitol in a hurricane's path, no way!"

"So you're going to build it on top of a landfill instead?"

"I'm gonna build my capitol on Sugar Hill, the highest hill in Houston. No hurricane will ever swamp me!"

The highest hill in Houston does, in fact, rise above the 3rd Ward in flat-as-a-board Houston. Depending on wind direction, one might notice a not-so-polite stench in the air. One might also hear some unusual pressurized air releases in the area.

Sugar Hill sits atop the McCarty Road Landfill, which processes 7,200 tons of waste a day. The eighth largest landfill in the United States has a remaining life expectancy of 35 years. It is one of the largest producers of the region's landfill biogas. Landfill biogas, created when organic material in a municipal solid waste landfill decomposes, consists primarily of roughly 50 percent methane. San Marcos, Texas recently experienced an explosion of catastrophic proportions when a drifter extinguished then relit the biogas burn-off flames at Lone Star Disposal.

Unlike San Marcos, the captured gas from Houston's McCarthy Road landfill was carried through a six-mile pipeline to the Anheuser-Busch Budweiser brewery to help generate steam energy for the brewery's power plant.

None of this seemed to bother Jeremiah Jones, who would rather his new capitol be high-and-dry, not wetter-than-an-otter's-pocket.

"Worst case, as Governor of East Texas, I'll simply shut down the McCarty Road landfill and move it someplace else," Jeremiah told himself. "I bet those fine folks over in Pasadena would welcome a landfill if it came with minimum-wage jobs."

Besides, Jeremiah had bigger fish to fry. What, exactly, should the capitol of East Texas look like? After all, Houston was the most populous city in Texas and the fourth-most populous city in the United States. Founded on the banks of Buffalo Bayou in 1836 and named after General Sam Houston, Houston was now the home of the Texas Medical Center, the world's largest concentration of healthcare and research institutions. Then there was NASA's Johnson Space Center, where Mission Control Center resided on the city's perimeter. The whole world listened as astronaut Neil Armstrong recited those five famous words in 1969. "Houston, the Eagle has landed."

Should the capitol of East Texas reflect Houston's pioneering cotton and oil days, or its pioneers in space? Jeremiah had the answer: Why not *both?* After all, the Bob Bullock Texas State History Museum in Austin had giant reliefs on its façade recounting the state's rich history, from the early settler days right on up to the dawn of the Space Age. The Bullock also boasted a gigantic bronze star that has become one of the most photographed images in Texas.

Jeremiah knew that the Johnson Space Center had a few leftover Saturn V rockets. Perhaps one of those giant rockets could be the centerpiece of his new capitol. Perhaps with a giant syringe beside it to honor Houston's medical expertise.

"You have got to be kidding me, 3-J!" Grace said.

"Just thinkin' out loud, Gracie."

"I'm not sure there's any thinkin' goin' on in that thick skull of yours, Jeremiah."

"First things first, Gracie. I gotta get East Texas declared a state. Then I gotta get myself elected governor."

Gracie just smirked. "And if a frog had wings, it wouldn't bump its ass when it jumps!"

Jeremiah didn't know yet what he would nickname his new state capitol. That was more Grace's thing.

For the time being, he would simply refer to it privately as The Sugar Shack.

29

THE SOUTH TEXAS Capitol, unbeknown to the rest of the country, was already well underway.

Estevan Barrero, billionaire developer and likely new governor of the proposed new state of South Texas, had been working on the largest construction project in the region for several years.

Originally, Estevan had deemed it The Laredo Miracle, given that the construction project encompassed 10 acres, making its footprint more than three times the size of the Texas Capitol in Austin. Like the Texas Capitol Annex, Estevan's dream also had a massive underground component. He assured visitors to the site that the massive hole in the ground was primarily for parking for the many Fortune 500 companies he would soon be attracting to Laredo.

Curiously, Estevan had recently purchased several hundred tons of railroad track manufactured in South Korea. When the steel rail arrived in port in the United States, it was inspected and rejected on the basis of U.S. International Trade Commission requirements for core steel strength.

Instead of shipping it back to Korea to be recast, Estevan had purchased it for pennies on the dollar, explaining that he planned to melt it down and bring it up-to-code for the structural steel in his massive Laredo project. Nobody blinked an eye at Estevan's clever solution.

Truth was, Estevan had no intention of melting down the railroad track. Cloaked in secrecy, Estevan began building his own private underground railroad.

His entire project was surrounded by a 20-foot chain link fence topped with razor wire and guarded around the clock by armed mercenaries. No outsiders ever inspected his covert railway. But if they had, they might have been surprised to learn it ran south toward the Mexican border.

In Estevan's mind, it was an easy transition to go from building and developing Laredo's first monolithic commercial and residential center to what he had now decided to call *Casablanca del Sud.* The White House of the South.

Estevan's plans for the South Texas capitol were mindboggling. For one thing it would be one of the largest capitols in the United States. He would be careful not to make it the tallest, so as not to get Governor Swaggart's panties in a knot. But if you were to count the floors beneath Casablanca del Sud, it might be one of the tallest capitols in the world.

Construction had already been proceeding nicely on Estevan's groundbreaking project in Laredo. However, most of it went unseen by passersby. Most of the current construction was happening beneath street level in a huge subterranean cavern two blocks long, two blocks wide, and 100 feet deep. The uppermost level contained enough parking for every car in Laredo and then some. But no one spoke of the other three levels, primarily because only a handful of Estevan's closest associates knew anything about what was happening belowdecks.

If someone had managed to scale the razor wire capped chain link fence and somehow evaded the around-the-clock heavily armed paramilitary guards, they would still have found access to the lower three levels impenetrable. Giant case-hardened steel doors required complicated digital codes and retinal scan technology before opening.

Only three irises on the planet could open those doors. Estevan, his chief contractor and enforcer, and his son Estevan III. Estevan trusted his chief contractor and enforcer, 'Diablo' del Porto, with his life. Not his son, however, who had a wandering eye for the ladies and an insatiable addiction to cocaine.

Estevan's railroad workers ate, slept, and worked in the bowels, the *intestinos,* as they called them, of what was now destined to become Casablanca del Sud. Bowels was accurate, since Estevan refused to waste money on a proper sanitary system for his underground work crew. The way Estevan saw it, none of his railroad workers would ever make it out of the bowels alive.

There was just one problem. But it was a huge one. One hundred fifty miles north of Laredo lay the city of San Antonio, the second-most populous city in Texas and the seventh-most populous city in the United States.

Rhett McCullum, nephew of the legendary Red McCullum, was about to pull off something that his famous uncle had always said was patently impossible. Rhett was going to bring an NFL team to San Antonio. Rhett was not a politician. He had neither time nor passion for politics. Instead, he fancied himself King of San Antonio.

Rhett McCullum was not yet aware that Governor Swaggart was conspiring to make Laredo, not San Antonio, the capital of the proposed new state of South Texas. Such a decision would not go unchallenged by his majesty, King McCullum.

30

The West Texas Capitol would be an enigma unto itself. Ponce Ponzio had decided that his capitol would be built entirely underground.

Furthermore, Ponce had decided to build his new capitol on the grounds of Fort Bliss, one of the largest military complexes in the United States. Named in honor of Lieutenant Colonel William Bliss, a mathematics genius who was the son-in-law of Zachary Taylor, Ft. Bliss encompassed an area of roughly 1,700 square miles, including sections of Texas and New Mexico. The portion of the post located in El Paso County was a census-designated area with a population fluctuating near 10,000. Ft. Bliss provided the largest contiguous tract of restricted airspace in the continental United States. It was used for missile and artillery training and testing.

None of this was lost on Ponce, who knew full well that there would be serious gamesmanship among the new governors of the new states of Texas. When push came to shove, Ponce figured being on the delivery end of military might was preferable to being on the receiving end.

The inspiration for the underground capitol Ponce envisioned was the Deep Underground Command Center, a United States military installation that was proposed in 1962 to be a very deep underground center close to the Pentagon. Protected to withstand direct hits by high-yield weapons and endure at least 30 days in a post-attack period. According to the Pentagon, the Center was never built, while the Cheyenne Mountain Complex in Colorado Springs was further fortified as a nuclear bunker in the late 1960s.

Where Ponce's precious underground capitol would differ would be in the aesthetics. Ponce imagined a 20-acre slab of polished black granite, the only thing rising above it being a towering flagpole bearing an immense State of West Texas flag. Massive black granite stairways would lead down into the futuristic capitol below. Ponce privately admitted to a bit of jealousy over Steve Jobs' dream campus, The Mothership, in Cupertino, California.

Damn! I wanted to build a spaceship, but Jobs beat me to it! Ponce lamented. And when a few of his colleagues joked that his capitol concept looked more like a mausoleum, Ponce quickly replaced them with a new brace of colleagues. "We will bury you!" he told his former friends, borrowing a phrase from the former Soviet premier Nikita Khrushchev.

A former President of the United States had hurled similar threats at North Korea, Iran, and China at the Meeting of the General Assembly of the United Nationals in 2017. That hadn't turned out so well.

But Ponce was patient. He knew that Governor Swaggart had to convince 30 million Texans that dividing their Great State into five smaller states was in their best interest. Only then might Swaggart be instrumental in getting his five governors elected. Until then, new capitols for the five new states were little more than a pipe dream.

Speaking of pipe dreams, a few tokes on his handmade Hindu hookah had inspired Ponce to build his capitol underground. Texas was slowly but surely making marijuana legal for its citizens.

Ponce was simply speeding-up the timetable by importing some choice ganga from Ciudad Juárez, across the border from El Paso.

That very same evening, Ponce had yet another epiphany. If marijuana was soon going to be legal in Texas, why not get a jump on other like-minded entrepreneurs and designate the new State of West Texas as the Cannabis Capital of North America?

Not to be outdone by the pompous governors of the other four proposed states, Ponce contacted two famous contemporary Mexican architects to design his groundbreaking underground capitol.

Both architects were at first critical of the idea. Still, once they considered the immense energy-savings of such a structure, they were hooked. "This could earn us a coveted LEED Platinum rating, the architects mused. In fact, LEED might have to create a new, even higher rating for energy-savings, Ponce suggested. Ponce's ego swam along the currents of his brilliant thinking.

Meanwhile, the other governors were quietly planning their own capitols, unaware that Governor Swaggart had a scheme in mind that would make his pink granite capitol the envy of every capitol on Earth.

31

THE CENTRAL TEXAS Capitol was a *fait accompli.*

Completed in 1888 in downtown Austin, the Italian Renaissance Revival-style capitol contained the offices and chambers of the Texas Legislature and the Office of the Governor. Designed in 1881 by architect Elijah E. Myers, it was constructed from 1882 to 1888, largely by convict labor under the direction of civil engineer Reuben Lindsay Walker.

At the time, Texas was land rich and cash poor. Hence, in one of the largest barter transactions in recorded history, John V. Farwell and Charles B. Farwell, the builders of the capitol, were paid with more than three-million acres of public land in the panhandle region of Texas. Three million acres was roughly the equivalent of three Rhode Islands. This titanic tract eventually became one of the largest cattle ranches in the world. The legendary XIT Ranch.

A $75 million underground extension to the Texas State Capitol was completed in 1993. Once completed, Texans were invited to a Grand Reopening of Every Texan's Second Home.

Bo Swaggart knew that he dared not tinker with the beloved pink granite Capitol of Texas. That didn't prevent him from imagining a mindboggling addition to the existing edifice. Something he called 'The Dome Over the Dome.' His grand plan was to build a vast acrylic dome over the current capitol grounds.

To be perfectly honest, Bo had gotten the idea from horror author Stephen King in his novel, *Under the Dome.* In King's bestseller novel, the small Maine town of Chester's Mill was abruptly separated from the outside world by an invisible, semipermeable barrier of unknown origin.

As outlandish as it seemed, what Bo was contemplating was turning the existing State Capitol of Texas into the 21st Century equivalent of a snow globe!

"I know, I know, it never snows in Austin, Jules," Bo confided to his chief of staff. "But just imagine if we could heat and air-condition the environment around the entire capitol grounds year-round. The Capitol of Central Texas would become a year-round destination! We could have picnics on the lawn in the middle of the freakin' winter!"

Truman simply replied, "Warm in the chilly Texas winter, cool in the blazing Texas summers? Why don't we just add a water feature like the one at Schlitterbahn and charge admission, Governor?"

"I like the way you think!" Bo replied, failing to recognize her sarcasm. "And while we're at it, why not add one of those artificial ski slopes like they've got in Minnesota!"

"If you'll excuse me, Governor, I've got some important work to do," Truman said, interrupting the governor's dizzy daydream.

Perhaps Governor Swaggart's Dome Over the Dome idea wasn't as crazy as it sounded. Back in 1995, Las Vegas unveiled The Fremont Street Experience. The $90 million experiment included a five-block section of Fremont Street that was permanently closed to automobile traffic. An LED display canopy runs along a promenade from Main Street to Fourth Street.

One section, comprising one-fiftieth of the total canopy, equaled the size of the world's largest electric sign. Over 12 million LED lamps illuminated the overhead canopy in a dazzling display that never failed to elicit oohs-and-aahs from Vegas visitors.

"By God!" Bo thought to himself, "The stars at night could be big and bright, deep in the heart of Texas!" He punctuated his theory with the requisite *clap-clap-clap-clap* that accompanies the singing of the nostalgic tune, 'Deep In The Heart Of Texas.'

"While my Legislature is getting nothing done inside my capitol, visitors from all over Texas and beyond can be having a high ol' time outside my capitol."

Satisfied that he had dedicated sufficient brainpower to his harebrained idea, Bo tapped the button on his desk that electronically closed the massive oak door to his office, kicked off his boots, and nestled into his saddle-leather sofa for a nap.

32

"Why have you never asked me about my name?" Lev Gingrich asked his favorite investigative reporter.

"Leviticus?" Holly answered. "Third book of the Jewish Bible and the Old Testament. The instructions of Leviticus emphasize ritual, legal, and moral practices. You clearly have your rituals here at the magazine. You've got a law degree from The University of Texas and your morals are above reproach. I'd say it's a pretty good name for you, Chief."

"And I'd say that's why you're my favorite investigative reporter, Holly. Speaking of investigations, I heard through the grapevine that Governor Swaggart is planning some cockamamie addition to our beloved State Capitol."

"You mean his insane Dome Over the Dome idea?"

Gingrich frowned. "Is that what he's calling it? Has the man finally gone batshit crazy?"

"If you ask me, it's simply a diversion. My spidey-sense tells me that Swaggart's got something far more sinister up his sleeve."

"Then I want you on this full time, Holly. Hand off your other assignments to some of my minions. Swaggart and his dome are Priority One until I tell you otherwise."

"I thought you told me to leave Swaggart alone."

"Things have changed."

"Copy that, Chief. Swaggart won't know what hit him," Holly said as she exited her notorious publisher's office sporting a Cheshire grin.

Holly was more than happy to give up her somewhat boring assignments. She was currently working on an exposé on the drug trafficking going on behind the scenes in many of the bars down on Dirty Sixth Street. Plus a deep dive into burying nuclear waste in West Texas. But there was one story she simply refused to stop sticking her nose into. Sul Ross University's bogus explanation about Beauregard Swaggart's ersatz graduation. Bo Swaggart wouldn't be the first politician to fudge his college credentials. But he might be the latest. Once confronted with the truth, most politicians opted to resign from office. Holly had no misconceptions about the Governor of Texas resigning. At least not without a prolonged and dirty fight. But one thing Holly loved was a knock-down, drag-out fight.

Elsewhere in the political universe, Governor Swaggart's chief of staff had been given a puzzling task.

"Get me everything, and I do mean everything you can find on the current mayors of Dallas, Houston, Laredo and El Paso, Jules. And leave no stone unturned. Particularly if any of those mayors have been stoned lately."

"You didn't mention the mayor of Austin, Governor."

"No need, Jules. I have no intention of making him the Governor of the State of Central Texas."

Hearing the words State of Central Texas made Julie Truman's skin crawl. Surely the Governor didn't intend to go through with his crazy idea of splitting Texas into five states, did he? That was simply a diversion, wasn't it?

"How deep would you like me to dig, Governor," Julie asked. "Do I go through the usual channels? Or is this a job for one of our fixers from the campaign days."

"Good point, Jules. Let's give Jeremiah Jones this assignment. 3-J can uncover dirt that most people are content to sweep under the rug. If he gives you any pushback, tell him I might want him to run for Mayor of Houston before he runs for Governor of East Texas. He'll get the message, loud and clear."

Julie winced at the mention of Jeremiah Jones' name.

"What's the matter, Jules? Getting' too hot in this kitchen for you?"

"Not at all, Governor. It's just that we have some pretty important issues on the docket these days…"

"I'll decide what's important and what isn't, Jules," the governor interrupted, slamming his fist on his desk, a sure sign that the conversation was over.

"Roger that, Governor. I'll get Mr. Jones on the phone right away. Would you like to speak with him personally?"

"Plausible deniability, Jules. Look it up if you're not familiar with the term."

"Oh, I'm familiar, Governor. It's pretty much how we run things around here these days."

Governor Swaggart squinted at his chief of staff, measuring her for any sign of disloyalty. Which he simply wouldn't tolerate. Nope. Julie was a keeper. At least for now.

"Give Jeremiah my regards, Jules. Along with that hot wife of his, Greta."

"I believe her name is Grace, Governor."

"Grace, Greta, whatever. I just remember that spread that Vogue magazine did on her a few years back. She's smokin' hot, if you catch my drift."

"Drift caught, Governor. I'll ring Mr. Jones and tell him we have a job for him."

"Not *we*, Jules. *You.* Tell him the Attorney General is looking into a few rumors about some of our Texas mayors. Strictly hush-hush, of course."

"Of course, Governor. By the way, the Cloak Room called a few minutes ago. Said something about a young lady waiting impatiently to meet with you."

"You tend to your work, Jules, and I'll tend to mine," the Governor said, running his fingers through his hair in front of an antique mirror on his office wall and straightening his tie.

"Cancel the rest of my afternoon and evening appointments."

33

Governor Beauregard Swaggart had no intention of following through on his pledge to build a dome over the Capitol dome. It was simply his way of diverting Texans' attention away from his real plan. Dividing the Lone Star State into five states.

Bo Swaggart was, if nothing else, a master manipulator.

When Democratic opponents demanded his tax returns, a former U.S. President promised he'd get around to it. He never did. When his presidential opponents suggested he had no experience for the job, he berated them with nasty nicknames. And promised racist American voters that he'd Make America Great Again. A dog whistle for Make America White Again.

When hurricanes pummeled the Caribbean, causing catastrophic damage to Puerto Rico and its United States citizens, instead of helping them, the former president went on a Twitter rampage about NFL players taking a knee during the national anthem in protest of police brutality and racial discrimination.

"Nobody protested when Tim Tebow took a knee!" Governor Swaggart scolded the press. Privately, Bo admitted to himself that this deflection thing was a powerful weapon if used properly.

True to form, Bo began dropping not-so-subtle hints about the seriousness of his latest boondoggle, the Dome Over the Dome. He flooded the airwaves with architectural drawings of what he was now calling The Ninth Wonder of the Modern World. No one was quite sure what the eighth wonder of the modern world was. But that didn't stop Bo's proselytizing.

"Let America fight her own battles! Let's make Texas Great Again!" the governor bellowed at rallies.

The Texas Attorney General was somewhat flummoxed when he got a call from Houston politico Jeremiah Jones.

"Let me get this straight, Mr. Jones," Attorney General Haggard responded to Jones' odd request. "The Governor wants me to dig up dirt on the mayors of Dallas, Houston, Laredo and El Paso?"

"Not the Governor, Mr. Attorney General. Never use the governor's name or office when you are conducting this intel."

"I understand, Mr. Jones. But I'm afraid I don't get it. What does the Gov…er, the Attorney General's office care about what goes on behind the closed doors of four Texas mayors?"

"Let's just say the Party has some concerns about collusion between these mayors to fix the prices on certain city services, for starters. And the Party believes there may have been some nefarious goings-on at some of their fundraisers, if you know what I mean."

"No, sir, I'm afraid I don't know what you mean."

"Hanky-panky, Haggard. A bit of the old in-and-out, if you catch my meaning."

"Are you suggesting extramarital sex, Mr. Jones?"

"Extramarital, intramarital, kinky, you name it. We can't have wife beaters and pedophiles representing our fair cities, can we?"

Attorney General Haggard was speechless.

"Do you have a problem with this request, Mr. Attorney General? You have a re-election campaign coming up soon. I trust this assignment won't prevent you from running a good, clean race in the fall."

"Are you threatening me, Mr. Jones?"

"I don't threaten, Mr. Attorney General," Jones hissed. "Threats are for politicians. I'm a fixer, and I'm fixin' to open up a 50-gallon drum of whup-ass if you don't get busy investigating four city mayors!"

"I'm on it, Mr. Jones. And if you happen to run into the Governor, please give him my best regards."

"You had best regard your assignment, Mr. Attorney General. Think of it as job security."

The line went dead before Attorney General Haggard could muster a reply.

Mitchell Marks was beginning to wonder privately if he'd been hornswoggled by Governor Beauregard Swaggart.

Thinking back on their impromptu meeting in the governor's office, Marks shuddered as he recalled the governor's casual suggestion that he carve up a map of Texas into five states. At the time, it seemed like fun and games. But as Marks well knew, "It's all fun and games until somebody loses an eye," as his mother used to say.

What in the hell have I done? Marks pondered his fate over a cold mug of beer at the Mean Eyed Cat bar on 5th Street. Almost as if intuiting his pain, bartender Matt Welty asked him if he wanted another round.

"Oh, what the hell," Marks replied, chugging his third Shiner. "I may have just unwittingly sold Texas down the river!"

34

Marina Alvarez was scared shitless, as Anglos were fond of saying.

She had told absolutely no one what she had witnessed late one night a year or so ago in the Governor's office. There he was, the Governor of Texas himself, pants down around his knees, matching the stud on the television screen stroke-for-stroke as Alexa King, the Mayor of Dallas, moaned and groaned with every thrust.

She locked the door to her cramped studio apartment and looked once again at the video she had captured on her cell phone that fateful night.

"*Madre de Dios!*" she repeated. Marina couldn't afford to lose her job at the State Capitol. She was 55 years old. All it would take was one word from the governor and she would never work in this city, much less this state, ever again. In fact, she would probably be rounded up by U.S. Customs and deported to Mexico.

She considered, for the third time, simply deleting the video. But a thought stirred within her. "This is my *seguro,* my insurance," she reminded herself.

Tomorrow she would buy a new cell phone. One of the cheaper models. But she would not trade in her old phone or try to sell it on the Internet.

It was, after all, her *proteccion.*

Meanwhile, Senator Bethany Jordan had somehow managed to pull off the impossible. She had convinced one of the staff servers to let her borrow a uniform and name tag for First Lady Veronica Swaggart's Spring Fling. It had cost the Senator six tickets to the Lady Longhorns' volleyball game against Tennessee's Lady Volunteers. But it was well worth it.

FLOTEX had postponed her annual Spring Fling until May, which gave Senator Jordan more time to prepare for her little charade. With her hair pulled back in a bun, she looked a lot like the staff server she would be replacing for the event. Her fellow conspirator had already greased the palms of the rest of the wait staff with future Lady Longhorn tickets. They had eagerly agreed to turn a blind eye to Senator Jordan's prank, which was just what she had convinced them it was. A silly prank. No harm, no foul.

But harm was conceivable if Senator Jordan could confirm the rumored goings-on at the First Lady's upcoming party. According to rumor, there was never a lack of young, virile men in attendance to entertain the First Lady's guests.

Senator Jordan would wear no makeup, don a wait staff uniform, hide behind a pair of thick glasses, and affect a slight limp. She would only speak if spoken to, with a slight lisp to further confound the partygoers.

It was a flawless plan. Until it wasn't.

Brenda Prendahl, the vintage bartender at the infamous Cloak Room Bar, locked the door after her last customer left, lit a cigarette and poured herself a double Old Fashioned.

It had been a long night. The Legislature was in session and the usual suspects had begun slinking into her subterranean bar around dusk. As usual, Brenda had dimmed the lights and turned up the juke box. Representatives and senators of both stripes mingled with the real power in the legislature. The overpaid, overprivileged lobbyists.

This was where the deals got made. The lobbyists didn't take long to break out Cuban cigars for their political partners-in-crime. The governor knew better than to be seen in public with these charlatans, and the Lt. Governor wouldn't be caught dead in the Cloak Room. The Attorney General, on the other hand, was already well into his cups and slurring, "'Nother round for me and my friends, Brenda, and put it on the governor's tab."

"Now General, you know I can't do that, darlin'," Brenda cooed as she placed another round of The Macallan 18 single malt scotch in front of him. Truth is, one rarely addresses the Attorney General as General. But it always seemed to please Attorney General Haggard. And he always managed to leave a big tip.

"I know where you can find an even bigger tip, darlin'," Haggard winked at the end of another hard-drinking evening, casting his eyes towards the fly of his pants.

"So I've heard, General!" Brenda teased back. "I believe I heard it from your wife, Corinne, if I'm not mistaken."

The mention of the Attorney General's wife always seemed to deflate any notion the AG had of hooking-up with Brenda after-hours. That was a good thing, considering that Brenda was a lesbian. And damn proud of it.

The Attorney General and his colleagues were long gone and dawn was breaking when Brenda finished cleaning up the Cloak Room bar. That's when she remembered the private meeting Governor Swaggart had with El Popo all those months ago.

Something about a State of West Texas, she recalled. Bleary eyed, Brenda turned out the lights, set the alarm, locked the door, and climbed the stairs to street level, where her Dodge Ram pickup waited patiently curbside.

"Time for some shut-eye, old girl!" Brenda said as she slid behind the wheel and lit up a doobie for the lonely drive home to Pflugerville.

35

When asked about Governor Swaggart's outrageous plan to build a dome over the Texas Capitol's dome, Lt. Governor McClain responded by commenting on the current statue perched atop the Capitol dome. Something he called the Dome Gnome.

"Have you ever gotten a good look at that beastly creature atop our beloved Capitol building?" McClain provoked the press.

"The Goddess of Liberty?" they would gamely respond.

"Goddess? More like the Golem of Liberty!" he egged them on.

In 1881, architect Elijah Myers designed the Goddess of Liberty as the crowning element of the Texas Capitol. Likely inspirations were the State of Freedom on the National Capitol, the Statue of Liberty, and perhaps even Pallas Athena, Zeus's daughter from ancient Greek folklore.

But surveyed up close, a goddess she was not. To be kind, her countenance was shockingly gruesome. Which led McClain to refer to her as a monster.

In 1888, metal contractors created a foundry in the basement of the Capitol to prepare the Goddess of Liberty for her exalted perch atop the dome. Using plaster molds from Chicago, they cast 80 separate pieces in zinc. They welded these parts together into four major sections. The torso, the two arms and the head of the statue. A crew then hoisted each section to the top of the dome and used large screws to put the nearly 16-foot-tall statue together.

In 1915, Texas hired steeplejack 'Cyclone Jack' McCarthy to paint the Goddess white. Several years later, an unidentified painter provided the Goddess with black hair, pink skin, and a blue robe with a gold sash.

Alas, no amount of colorization seemed to improve her ghastly visage. In 1939, workers returned the Goddess to her original pallor.

In 1983, workers painting the dome noticed extensive cracking along the arms, right hand, and sword of the Goddess. A study of the statue revealed corrosion, lost fasteners and missing pieces. Impurities in the original zinc alloy, along with atmospheric pollutants, lightning, temperature changes, and high winds all contributed to the deterioration of the iconic symbol.

In 1985, the State Preservation Board voted to install a replica of the Goddess on the dome and place the original in a controlled environment. Ultimately, the Bob Bullock Texas State History Museum. Workers placed the Goddess in a structural support with nylon strapping and removed the upraised arm and sword. A Texas National Guard helicopter then lifted the Goddess from the dome and placed her on the Capitol grounds for temporary viewing.

That's when a young University of Texas government major named Iain McClain first beheld the Goddess, and an idea was born. It would be another several decades before McClain's bright idea came to light. Neon light.

Now, in his new role as Lt. Governor, McClain had a brainstorm: Why not reconceive the Goddess as the Cowgirl of Liberty? And instead of a long flowing robe, why not dress her in cowgirl boots, denim skirt, checkered shirt, cowgirl hat, twirling a neon lariat lassoing a lone star! A tribute to beautiful University of Texas alum and American actress Farrah Fawcett.

This was, of course, all a diversion of Swaggart's diversion. A deflection of Swaggart's deflection. It would take an act of God to convince the Texas Legislature to approve McClain's plan. Which is precisely why the Lt. Governor decided to sidestep the Legislature and go straight to the people of Texas.

McClain personally contacted and paid a renowned American sculptor to create an eight-foot half-sized miniature of the Cowgirl of Liberty, and then persuaded a local neon artist to attach a neon lasso to his half-scale model.

During the week, Lt. Governor McClain would wheel his Cowgirl into the hall outside his office for all Capitol visitors to see. At night, McClain would roll her over to one of the large plate glass windows in his office and light her up so all the passengers and pedestrians on Congress Avenue could admire his creation.

None of this made Governor Swaggart particularly happy. But Swaggart had bigger fish to fry. Namely dividing Texas into five states.

36

HOLLY WORTHINGTON COULDN'T believe her luck. She'd somehow managed to get an appointment with Governor Swaggart to discuss rumors of his notorious Dome Over the Dome.

"The Governor will see you at 3 p.m. sharp," Swaggart's Chief of staff advised her over the phone. "You'll have precisely 20 minutes unless the governor is called away on more urgent state business. Do you agree to those terms, Ms. Worthington?"

What was she going to say? "Could we make it 3:30 p.m.? I've got a hair appointment. And let's say one hour unless I'm called away on more urgent magazine business."

No, of course not.

"Of course, I agree. And thank you very much, Ms. Truman."

"So good of you to see me, Governor," Holly began the conversation.

"Always a pleasure to meet with one of my supporters, Ms. Worthington," the governor replied. Holly let the governor's assumption slide.

"As I'm sure you're aware, Governor, there are rumors that you intend to build a dome over the Capitol dome. Can you verify that rumor, Sir?"

"Verify it, I can. Dignify it, I will. My Dome Over the Dome initiative will ensure that Texans and Texan wannabes can visit the Capitol and its magnificent grounds any time of the year."

"Forgive me for asking, Governor, but do we really need a dome over the dome? After all, sir, the average temperature in Austin is 69° Fahrenheit. Our average high is 80°F. Our average low is 59°F. And our average rainfall is considered moderate when we're not in a drought.

"I see you've done your homework, young lady. Very impressive. But you obviously missed one very important statistic."

"Sir?"

"You failed to note the average Texan's tolerance for messin' with his or her travel plans."

"I'm afraid I don't follow, Governor."

"Obviously. Consider a family of four from Beaumont who gets one chance all year to visit Austin and tour the Capitol. They show up late Saturday morning with a picnic lunch they've packed to enjoy on our beautiful capitol grounds. Then it starts to sprinkle. Their picnic is ruined and they can't bring their lunch into the building. Dad schleps back to the parking garage in the rain while the kids whine that they're starving. Mom texts Dad and tells him just to pick them up and they go hang out in their el cheapo motel. And just who do you think gets the blame for all that, missy? Me, their governor, that's who!"

"But Governor Swaggart…"

"And another thing: Are you aware that my Dome Over the Dome concept includes entertainment for their little brats? A gigantic water slide in the summer and a man-made ski slope in the winter?"

"But Governor, it doesn't snow in Austin…"

"So we just let that family drive to Colorado instead of visiting their State Capitol? Over my dead body!"

"Speaking of bodies, Governor, are you aware of Lt. Governor's plan to replace the Goddess of Liberty with what he's calling the Cowgirl of Liberty?"

"I've heard rumors, Ms. Worthington. But I'd like to see him get that past the Texas Legislature!"

"What if he called for a statewide referendum, Governor? From what I hear, his Cowgirl of Liberty idea appears to be resonating rather well with voters."

"It'll be a cold day in hell when the Great State of Texas replaces our beloved Goddess of Liberty with a frickin' cowgirl, Ms. Worthington. I trust you're familiar with the average temperature in hell?" With that, he tapped a button under his desk.

Before Holly could answer, there was a knock on the door and Chief of Staff Truman entered the room and handed the governor a note.

"I'm afraid the governor has been called away on important business, Ms. Worthington."

"No worries. I think I have what I need for my story," Holly replied, gathering her things.

The governor lit up. "Your story?"

"That's correct, Governor. And with any luck, it might even make the cover of LONE STAR in a couple of months."

"Chief of staff Truman can assist you if you need a photo of me," the governor beamed.

"Oh, I think I have everything I need for now. Good day, Governor."

37

THE FIRST LADY's Spring Fashion Fling was shaping up to be quite an affair.

Twenty-five engraved invitations found their way to twenty-five of Austin's hoity-toity millionaire and billionaire wives. One did not miss one of the First Lady's private Spring Flings. Unless one had a death in the family. Presumably one's own.

The First Lady's expansive conference room was being completely transformed for the upcoming event. A stage was being constructed at one end of the room, the same height as the room's massive conference table. The table would be draped with a white satin tablecloth. Vintage French dining chairs upholstered in white Belgian linen would seat the fashionable attendees. Crystal chandeliers would be hung with upside-down fresh white roses by Austin's primo event florist, Curious David.

Official State of Texas bone china, sterling silverware bearing the state seal, and Waterford crystal stemware would grace each coveted place at the imposingly long table. The stage itself would be curtained with enormous Lone Star flags. No expense would be spared on a high-end sound and lighting system.

The year's Spring Fling menu was over-the-top sumptuous, thanks to Austin's finest guest chefs. The appetizer course would include Fried Milk, Wagyu Beef, and Yellowtail Sashimi. The *amuse-bouche*, Prawn Sambai Bostador. The main course, one's choice of Maine Lobster Thermidor or Wild Boar Ravioli. For dessert, Baked Alaska a la Texas topped with a Texas flag and two crisscrossed flaming sparklers.

Nothing but the finest wines and champagnes, of course. This year's favorite was Roederer Cristal Rosé.

The stage was set. Cocktails at 7:30 p.m. Dinner at 8:30. Spring Fashion Show at 10. And a Special Surprise at 11.

Twenty-four RSVPs arrived within days of delivery. Sadly, one billionaire's wife would be out of the country on business. Said business being a facelift and boob job in Brazil by one of the finest *médicos* money could buy.

Three days before The Big Event, contractors were putting the finishing touches on Veronica's Spring Fling. The huge conference table was sidled up to the stage at one end, allowing models to strut right down the center of the table once it was cleared of dinnerware.

The hanging white roses would be one of the final touches. A sound and lighting check insured that the systems were performing to Veronica's exacting standards. Texas state troopers would man all the entrances and exits.

Two days prior, Veronica conducted a taste test of the various menu items. She personally deemed the appetizers and the *amuse-bouche* perfect. She spat out the Prawn Sambai Bostador, declaring it unfit to serve, and demanded a suitable replacement within 24 hours. She rejected Thumbelina Carrot and Golden Raisins with an Orange Glaze and ultimately settled on Hot Potato, Cold Potato, a cold potato-truffle lapping against a butter-poached Yukon gold potato, parmesan, black truffle, and sea salt.

The day before, the models arrived from New York and California. Veronica put them through their paces, promptly rejecting two of the models as simply too pudgy.

On the day of the Spring Fling, the First Lady's offices were closed for official business, stocking the caterer's kitchen, the massive bar, and cooling the room to a chilly 66 degrees. "Cold makes guests pert and alert," Veronica reasoned. "And believe me, there will be plenty of reasons to stay pert and alert tonight!"

With that, Veronica headed home to the Governor's Mansion to take a long, luxurious bath before shoehorning herself into her form-fitting designer cocktail dress.

Veronica had her own definition of a dresser. A dresser, she explained to her girlfriends, was the cocktail you have as you prepare for the evening. "My preference is Pimm's No. 1 Cup."

Veronica placed a slice of cucumber in her Pimm's Cup before slipping into her claw-footed bubble bath, placing a slice of cucumber over both eyes.

"Girlfriends, you need to bring your A-game tonight," Veronica said aloud, sipping her chilled cocktail and luxuriating in her copper cauldron.

"If only Momma could see me now!" she giggled, feeling the first buzz from her second Pimm's Cup. Her mother still lived in Marfa, Texas. Forever searching for those mysterious Marfa Lights.

38

THE FIRST GUESTS began arriving in chauffeured limousines at 7:25 in the evening. One did not want to be fashionably late to the First Lady's Spring Fling.

Each guest was met at ground level by a Texas state trooper, her name carefully checked against the guest list, and then escorted to an elevator leading to the First Lady's underground office and party suite.

As they arrived downstairs, each guest was offered a crystal flute of Louis Roederer Cristal Rosé or her choice of cocktail. This seasoned band of sisters was trained to appear unimpressed by glitz and glamor. Nevertheless, upon entering Veronica's Hideaway, everyone gasped with delight.

Each guest found her name in flowery calligraphy on a cream-colored card at the elegant dinner table. No one questioned the seating arrangements. Nor did anyone one make the mistake of sitting in Veronica's bespoke throne at the head of the table.

Once they were all generously sated with champagne and properly seated, dinner was served, carefully orchestrated by Becky Walford, Veronica's favorite Austin caterer and keeper of secrets.

Ms. Walford conducted the serving of the various courses like a Bolshoi ballet, timed down to the second. The main course was delivered to the table, each covered with a sterling silver dome.

Once all were placed in front of Veronica's guests, all twenty-five domes were lifted simultaneously. Oohs-and-aahs were clear affirmation that her guests were duly impressed.

Fine wines were served, and no crystal goblet ever went empty. Baked Alaska a la Texas arrived for dessert, complete with blazing sparklers, accompanied by a round of Sandeman Cask 33 Limited Edition Very Old Tawny Porto.

Afterwards, guests were invited to powder their noses in the First Lady's private, candle-lit bathroom. Veronica had even provided the powder. Pharmaceutical-grade cocaine.

When they returned, the room had once again been transformed. Gone was the elaborate dinnerware. The imposing table was now a fashion runway, leading from the stage draped in billowing Lone Star flags.

Veronica's guests once again took their appointed seats as cool jazz wafted over the hidden speakers. From behind the curtains, a lone, willowy model appeared, wearing a bespoke evening gown created by one of France's premier fashion houses. She was followed by a parade of fashionably disinterested models, each wearing designer evening attire that would eventually be sent home with each of Veronica's guests.

"Let me know if you see something you like," Veronica told her girlfriends. "And don't be surprised if it shows up in your closet in the morning. After all, what are friends for?"

Veronica's girlfriends knew the score. Upon leaving, they would each discreetly leave a sizeable donation in the crystal vase by the door in appreciation for all they'd shared. Typically, these donations ranged in the six figures. A few guests were known to leave seven-figure checks, signed on their husbands' off-shore bank accounts.

From time to time, a guest would retire to Veronica's private bathroom, ostensibly to check her makeup, but more likely to powder her nose. Veronica's Spring Fling fashion show continued unabated for an hour.

Off to one side of the room, Becky Walford pretended to be completing her caterer's checklist on her Apple iPad. Her staff had already left, and it was not unusual for her to discreetly ask Veronica if there was anything else she needed before departing.

But Becky was secretly taking a video of the fete underway. It was her private pleasure to pretend to be one of the invited guests at Veronica's annual events. She would, of course, never share the video with a living soul.

Unbeknown to Becky Walford, a cleverly disguised server during the festivities was anxious to verify her suspicions about the First Lady's over-the-top galas. Senator Bethany Jordan, masquerading as wait staffer Lucille according to her nametag, had not been disappointed. Now all she had to do was slip out unnoticed with the rest of the staff.

But Senator Jordan was curious. Why had so many of the guests taken so many trips to the First Lady's private loo? She decided to verify her suspicions on her way out.

She was startled by a voice behind her.

"Would you care for some makeup?" the First Lady asked pleasantly enough. "After all, a senator has a certain reputation to uphold."

Bethany gamely attempted to pull off her charade. "No ma'am. I must've opened the wrong door."

"What you opened, Senator, is a can of worms!" Veronica hissed. "If any word of this ever reaches the press or the voters, I'll see that you are summarily dismissed from the Senate for felony trespass on state property. And that won't be the worst of it, Bethany. I have a dossier on you going back to your high school days before you realized that you had a family legacy to uphold. You were quite close with some of your girlfriends, weren't you, sweetie? Some might even say, a little too close, if you catch my meaning. Now get out of my sight before I call one of my troopers!"

39

A CHASTENED SENATOR Jordan hurried to the elevator, blotting her tears on her apron.

"Damn!" she muttered under her breath as the elevator rose to street level. "I had that bitch dead-to-rights. Now no one will ever know."

As she stepped out of the elevator, a state trooper directed her curbside to wait for her ride. "I'll just walk from here," she told the trooper, "I don't live far."

A loud siren captured her attention as she hung her head and began to plod away. As she looked on in disbelief, a huge black Suburban screeched to halt at the curb, disgorging five policemen dressed in black riot gear, complete with helmets and tinted shields.

Senator Jordan couldn't believe her eyes. As the cops approached the state trooper, he saluted them and stepped aside, allowing them to pile into the elevator and disappear underground uncontested.

"What the hell?" Senator Jordan pondered. "Maybe I'll get some justice after all!"

"Move along, ma'am. Nothing to see here!" the trooper barked.

Shaking her head, the senator slowly ambled away. Maybe there was a God after all.

"What is the meaning of this?!" Veronica shouted as the black-clad SWAT team rushed into her private party. Without a word, the five cops quickly handcuffed the First Lady and four of her girlfriends and pushed them toward the steps leading up to the stage.

When the fashion show had ended, the models had left five colorful silk Hermes scarfs hanging from five hooks on a rolling dressing rod on-stage. On orders from the cops, Veronica and her friends dutifully draped their handcuffs over the hooks as the cops blindfolded them with the silk scarves.

Unable to move or see, the five women nonetheless raised their collective voices in pointless protest.

"Shut the fuck up!" the lead cop shouted at them. And with that, the five cops began slowly unzipping their slinky dressing gowns. As their dresses slipped to the floor, revealing their scanty Victoria's Secret undergarments, reggae music suddenly blasted over the speakers:

As Veronica and her cohorts began to writhe to the music, the five cops began unbuckling their riot gear. Slipping off their helmets, it was clear that these were no ordinary cops. They were too handsome. And as they began removing their uniforms, the guests realized that they were also too muscle-bound for ordinary cops.

It took a moment, but Veronica's guests finally caught on. These weren't cops. They were sexy male models. And they were here for the guests' pleasure.

As if on cue, Veronica's other girlfriends began slipping out of their evening attire and joining the party on stage. That's when the Lone Star Flags parted, revealing an oversized jail cell, complete with cots and a table overflowing with ice buckets bearing open bottles of Dom Pérignon champagne. To the beat of the music, each guest grabbed her own bottle of bubbly and began gyrating with the nearly naked male dancers.

"I don't think you'll ever be able to top this par-tay, Vee!" one of her girlfriends slurred.

"Never fear. The night is young!" Veronica grinned. And with that, she unsnapped her bra and flung it toward one of the male dancers, who caught it in his perfectly whitened teeth. This was a Spring Fling for the record books. The criminal record books.

"I just hope they all got what they deserved," Senator Bethany Jordan comforted herself as she unlocked the door to her condominium across from the Capitol. Entering her foyer, she glanced up at the portrait of her hero.

"I guess I blew it tonight, Babs," Bethany confided. "I went into politics to right some wrongs, just like you. Seems like all I've managed to do is screw things up royally."

Her famous aunt was no longer around to console her brave relative. But if she was, she'd probably say something like, "We human beings must be willing to accept people who are different from ourselves."

Bethany was willing to accept people like Veronica Swaggart existed. But as she trudged upstairs to her bedroom, she was clearly unwilling to forgive and forget how the First Lady of Texas had threatened her this night.

PART IV:
THE RACE IS ON!

40

THE RACE FOR Mayor of Dallas was a no-brainer. No one in their right mind would oppose incumbent mayor Alexa King. Precisely why an Independent by the name of Geoffrey Friedman chose to run. He literally had nothing to lose.

Geoffrey was, by his own reckoning, The Last Hippie in Dallas. Geoffrey was also a Jew, although a thoroughly reformed Jew. Geoffrey was fond of quoting his hero and infamous Texas musician Richard "Kinky" Friedman, who once famously sang, "They ain't makin' Jews like Jesus anymore!"

Where Alexa reportedly had a war chest exceeding twenty million dollars, Geoffrey's war chest lagged far behind, at roughly twenty thousand dollars. But what Geoffrey lacked in campaign funds, he more than made up for in chutzpah.

Geoffrey also had a hole card. Although he had no proof, he was pretty sure there was some hanky-panky going on between high-tone Mayor Alexa King and low-brow Governor Bo Swaggart.

Alexa King wasn't worried, and for good reason. Early polls showed her winning re-election as Mayor of Dallas by a landslide. Respected pollsters were predicting a win by 80-85 percent of the vote. Turns out, the typical turnout for a mayor of Dallas race rarely exceeded ten percent of eligible voters. Not surprisingly, rich white, Republican voters traditionally elected Dallas mayors.

On the other hand, Dallas has one of the largest Jewish communities in the state. German Jews arrived in Dallas as part of the mid-nineteenth century immigration to Texas from the German principalities following their revolutions.

Early Jewish merchants contributed substantially to the growth of Dallas. Local newspapers received most of their income from advertising from Jewish merchants, enabling them to remain independent and impartial in their reporting, unlike European newspapers which were often funded by a particular political party. Jewish merchants were also often among the largest bank depositors and frequently sat on the boards of Dallas banks.

Alexa's supporters included many of Dallas' most prestigious business and community leaders, including a Dallas cosmetic icon whose three husbands were, respectively, a Catholic, a Protestant, and a Jew.

For a brief time, Alexa had even considered converting to the Jewish faith, purely for economic reasons. Upon returning to Dallas after graduating from Sul Ross University, she had married a Jewish sexagenarian fast food magnate. As fate would have it, sex was what killed her first and only husband and set her on her quest to take Dallas by storm.

Unbeknown to Alexa, a new storm was brewing in Texas. But its name wasn't Geoffrey. A storm of Texas-sized proportions was gathering strength in the Texas capital. Its name? Hurricane Beauregard.

Geoffrey Friedman was an anomaly. A massive head of curly brown hair fell to his shoulders. His preferred wardrobe included tie-dyed tee shirts and bellbottom jeans. He called his Mexican sandals 'Jesus boots,' and his wire-rimmed glasses 'Lennon specs.' In the beginning of the 21st Century, Geoffrey was clearly a throwback hippie in an Age of Hipsters.

This was precisely why Dallas hipsters adored Geoffrey. That was the good news. The bad news, Dallas hipsters were loath to vote in either local or national elections. The Dallas Morning News didn't give Geoffrey a chance in hell of defeating incumbent mayor King.

41

THE RACE FOR Mayor of Houston was a different ball of wax. For one thing, the current mayor was rather popular. While his predecessor had made a mess of things, Anderson Whitliff was the city's golden boy.

In the aftermath of Hurricane Harvey, the former mayor received criticism for his decision to deny any form of evacuation. He responded by pointing out the deaths in the 2005 Hurricane Rita evacuation.

Houstonians figured that was reason for treason, and Anderson Whitliff was elected in a landslide. Whitliff kept his promise to consult with scientists from the Netherlands, and when he proposed bonds to pay for massive levees to control future flooding, Houstonians reluctantly funded his grand plan.

But Jeremiah Jones knew what to do. Convince Houstonians that some of those funds found their way into the new mayor's pocket. He invited Mayor Whitliff to lunch, where Jeremiah would spring his hidden agenda.

"You thinkin' about runnin' for another term, Brother Whitliff?" Jeremiah asked the mayor over lunch at Brennan's Steakhouse.

"Since when did you get all brotherly on me, 3-J? That's mighty down-home for a Harvard man such as yourself."

"C'mon, Andy, we both know how to appeal to the people of Houston, Bro. Give 'em what they wanna hear and they'll be eatin' outa your hand."

"Knock it off, Jeremiah. We both know why you're here. The way I hear it, you might even be thinking about running for mayor yourself someday. Maybe sooner than later."

"Let's cut the crap, Andy," Jeremiah said, pausing to take another bite of his rare filet. "You've had a good run, my man. But folks in Houston think some of that money you raised to control flooding might have made its way into your campaign coffers. It wouldn't be the first time some rich white guy profited from scaring the bejesus out of his constituents.

Mayor Whitliff took a long sip from his glass of Paso Robles Grenache before answering. "I know what you're up to, 3-J. And it won't work."

"What won't work is you callin' me 3-J, Mayor. Name's Jeremiah Joshua Jones. And you better get used to hearing it pronounced properly and often in the upcoming mayoral race."

"Are you threatening me, Jeremiah?" Mayor Whitliff asked, wiping his mouth with his white cloth napkin.

"I don't threaten people, Andy, I…"

"Excuse me, gentlemen," their waiter interrupted, "Did either of you save room for dessert?"

Mayor Whitliff licked his lips. "I'll have a slice of your Chocolate Hazelnut Cake."

Jeremiah baited him. "That's funny, Mayor, I sorta figured you for the Fluffy Cheesecake, given your flood control plan was more fluff than substance."

"On second thought, just bring Mr. Jones the check, waiter. I'm sure he can expense this meal on one of his lobbyist accounts. Right 3-J?"

Before Jeremiah could react, the Mayor abruptly stood up and stormed off, stopping at several tables to shake hands with several well-heeled diners.

"Put the bill on the mayor's tab." Jeremiah instructed the waiter. "And bring me a bottle of Paso Robles Treana Red Blend to go. Let's see the Mayor explain a $450 lunch tab to the very people he's bilking for campaign funds. And give yourself a $100 tip, while you're at it!"

Anderson Whitliff wasn't about to be intimidated by the likes of Jeremiah Jones. He hadn't gotten elected mayor of the largest city in Texas by pussyfooting around the issues that truly mattered to Houstonians, chief among them flooding.

On the other hand, Jeremiah Jones was known for winning at any cost. Yes, he was a successful kingmaker. And yes, he was a celebrity in the loftiest Houston social circles. But the kings he had made and the celebrity he enjoyed might be the very things that would ultimately bring about his fall from grace.

Mayor Whitliff would bide his time. He didn't trust Jones. He relied heavily on Ronald Reagan's dictum, "Trust, but verify."

You've picked the wrong opponent this time, 3-J, Whitliff told himself. *This time, the good guy is going to finish first.*

It was a noble, if not a prescient notion.

42

THE COVER OF LONE STAR magazine wasn't particularly kind to Governor Swaggart.

True, it was a life-like enough bust of the governor. But a clever artist had replaced the top of his head with the Capitol dome, then placed a huge acrylic dome over his cocked eyebrow. A gleaming sparkle on one of his canine incisors rounded out the message:

"DOD, or DUD?" read the headline of the story featured inside. The author was none other than Lone Star investigative reporter, Holly Worthington.

"Get that little bitch on the phone, Jules!" Governor Swaggart yelled from his office. "Better yet, get her here, in my office. Today!"

Chief of staff Truman knew that was a bad idea. When Governor Swaggart had a burr under his saddle, he would often fly off the handle, only making matters worse.

"Worthington is just rattling your cage, Governor. If you ask me, she wants you to summon her so she can confirm her suspicions. She's one smart cookie, that one."

"Maybe you're right, Jules," Swaggart said, calming down a bit. "And maybe this isn't all bad. Texans will read about my Dome Over the Dome plan and decide for themselves if it's a dud or not. And you don't see McClain's face or his idiotic Cowgirl of Liberty on the cover!"

"Lt. Governor's Cowgirl is in the article, too, Governor. You might want to read it before you dismiss what McClain's really after."

"And what would that be, Jules?"

"Well, some say he's got his eye on the Governor's office."

"Over my dead body!" Swaggart bellowed, his face suddenly flashing bright red.

"Might be time to fight fire with fire, Governor. Why don't you consider speaking at the upcoming HRC convention?"

"What's HRC?"

"The Human Rights Campaign, Governor," Truman replied. "It's the largest LGBTQ civil rights advocacy group and political lobbying organization in the United States. They focus on protecting and expanding rights for LGBTQ. Advocating for marriage equality, anti-discrimination, and HIV/AIDS advocacy."

Swaggart smirked. "I'm sure Lieutenant Gay-vernor McClain will be making an appearance."

"Not if you agree to speak first, on the condition that you are the only spokesman for the state government, Governor."

"I like the way you think, Jules. Hell, you might even make governor one day! If that big-haired Ann Richards could get elected…"

"Easy does it, Governor. You need to speak for all Texans."

"Speak for all Texans. Yeah, that has a nice ring to it, Jules. Dome be damned! Cowgirl be screwed! Bo Swaggart speaks for all Texans, whether they wear cowboy boots or tap shoes!"

"That's the spirit, Governor!" Truman said, perhaps a bit too enthusiastically. *Oh my God, now what have I gotten us into?* she worried to herself.

☆

"Have you seen the latest copy of LONE STAR magazine, Rory?" Lt. Governor McClain asked his Chief of staff.

Chief of staff Minton grinned broadly. "Hard to miss, Iain. It's plastered on every newsstand and magazine rack in the city and across the state,"

"If this doesn't kill his ridiculous Dome Over the Dome idea, nothing will!"

"Swaggart's dome is just a diversion, Iain. Chances are, he's got a much bigger plan up his sleeve."

"Like what?"

"I'm not sure. But I've got some folks looking into it. People we can trust."

"In the meantime, did you see where Holly mentioned my Cowgirl of Liberty idea?"

"Word on the street is that Texans are beginning to cotton to the idea of replacing the Golem with the Cowgirl."

"What does 'cotton to' mean, exactly, Rory?"

"Just a figure of speech. A Texas colloquialism. Means to like or approve of something. Although my ancestors didn't exactly cotton to pickin' cotton."

"Your ancestors are one of the reasons we're the Great State of Texas, not the Good State of Texas, Rory. Cotton played an outsized part in that greatness. So did oil. And putting the first man on the Moon."

"Yeah, well, good thing there ain't no cotton on the Moon."

"Something much more valuable, Rory. A rare, non-radioactive isotope of Helium with two protons and one neutron called Helium-3. My NASA buddies tell me that one shuttle load of the stuff could power Texas for an entire year."

"Keep talking like that and you'll either wind up in the loony bin or the governor's office, Iain."

Iain grinned. "That's my plan, Rory."

43

THE RACE FOR Mayor of Laredo was a lead pipe cinch.

Current Mayor Franco Spinosa was merely a figurehead. Billionaire Estevan Barrero ran the city like a well-oiled machine. Spinosa would step aside, no questions asked, and pocket a substantial stipend from the new mayor when the time was right.

The time was right. An unnamed ailment threatened Spinosa's health. In the best interest of the City of Laredo, he touted Barrero as his successor. Not surprisingly, no one openly challenged Estevan Barrero, save for one ill-advised attempt by a city councilman who accused Barrero of building his empire on the backs of immigrants.

The poor bastard awoke before dawn one morning to the smell of something cooking in the kitchen of his humble home. Was his wife Gloria making holiday tortillas this time of year?

When he padded into his dimly lit kitchen, he spied a large pot boiling on the gas stove. Curious, he grabbed an oven mitt off the counter and slowly lifted the lid.

"*Madre de Dios!*" he screamed. But it was not the mother of God in the caldron. It was the couple's pet Chihuahua. In shock, he failed to detect another odor overpowering the smell of boiling meat. Natural gas.

GAS EXPLOSION DESTROYS COUNCILMAN'S HOME. NO SURVIVORS.

The headline in the Laredo Morning Times recorded a massive explosion in the suburban home of Councilman Hermanez. The gory details included mention of the remains of their pet dog. Both she and her husband's remains were also discovered in the home, victims of an unexplained gas leak. So quick was the explosion over that the neighboring homes survived relatively unscathed.

A grief-stricken Estevan Barrero paid for the couple's funeral, their burial, and an impressive cemetery monument in their honor. He also set up a scholarship fund in their name for the city's students.

It was as if the untimely and unfortunate deaths of two of Laredo's esteemed citizens had been something of a godsend. The Morning Times applauded Barrero's selfless generosity, and openly endorsed his unopposed run for mayor.

Meanwhile, construction of Barrero's massive downtown project, the Laredo Miracle, continued unabated. The massive structure was beginning to rise skyward, sheathed in classic adobe.

"I gotta admit, Estevan, your little project is catching the attention of the rest of Texas," Governor Swaggart told Mayor Barrero on an unscheduled visit to Laredo one Saturday afternoon. "Mind if I take a little tour?"

"That wouldn't be wise, Bo. The construction site is still quite hazardous. One of the underground parking floors partially collapsed recently, and we've had to shore it up with temporary timbers. But if you'd like to see an architectural rendering, I've got one in my on-site construction office."

Barrero's on-site construction office looked more like the security area of a large Las Vegas hotel, complete with around-the-clock video monitoring. Some of the screens were conspicuously dark when the governor entered the elaborate fortress.

"Damn, Estevan, this must require a shitload of capital!"

"Capitols require a lot of capital, Governor."

"For all anyone knows, your Laredo Miracle is a mixed-use development. When the time comes, there'll be plenty of time to convert it, along with public opinion."

"Whatever you say, Bo. But just so there are no misconceptions, the real miracle is that you're looking at the future *Casablanca del Sud*. The White House of the South.

"My momma always told me, 'Don't count your chickens before they hatch.'"

"And my mamacita always told me, 'Estevan, dream big. And make sure nobody who opposes you survives their worst nightmares.'"

"Wise words, Estevan. And what did your father tell you?"

"Let's leave my father out of this, Bo."

"Of course, Estevan, of course. I'm not even sure I've ever heard his name spoken."

"Some things are best left unsaid. May I offer you a shot of Gran Patron Burdeos Añejo tequila to celebrate, mi amigo?'"

"Don't mind if I do, Mayor Barrero," Swaggart replied, clinking shot glasses with Estevan. "Here's to the future Governor of the State of South Texas!"

44

Senator Bethany Jordan was deeply depressed. What had ever possessed her to think that she could pull off masquerading as a server at the First Lady's annual Spring Fling?

Her intentions may have been honorable, but her plan was deeply flawed. Sneaking under Veronica Swaggart's radar was a fool's errand.

Even worse, the First Lady had threatened to bring up rumors from Bethany's high school days. True, she and one of her friends had gotten high a few times and messed around. What budding teenage girl hadn't? If the First Lady did have a dossier on her, what else might it contain?

Bethany turned a chair in her foyer around backward, poured herself a generous glass of wine, plopped down and began a conversation with the portrait of her famous aunt Barbara.

"Okay, I screwed the pooch. So what should I do now, Babs?"

The portrait of her famous aunt simply stared back at her, all-knowing. After a moment or two, Bethany was almost certain she saw her late, great aunt wink.

"Ahhh, of course!" Bethany smiled. "Two can play the dossier game! All I need to do is find some rich Austin bitch who didn't get invited to the Spring Fling, invite her for drinks and dinner, and start a dossier of my own that will make Tammy Faye Bakker look like Mother Teresa. Thanks, Babs!"

Across town, Marina Alvarez was babysitting her grandchildren. But her mind was elsewhere. It had been months since she'd even thought about the short video she took of the governor and the Dallas mayor.

She had mentioned it to no one. If she showed it to her friends, they'd probably suggest she blackmail the governor for better pay and shorter hours. Or maybe blackmail Mayor King for mucho dinero.

But that wasn't the way Marina was raised. She was taught to accept her position in life. And to be thankful for the small things her hard work provided for her family and her grandchildren.

More than anything, she wanted her grandchildren to get good educations and graduate from college. Which was a stretch on her salary. She had managed to send her children to college. But they had incurred student loans that they were struggling to repay. Which meant they both still lived at home with her.

Maybe she could sell the video to some television station, with the promise that her name would never be mentioned. She glanced at the LONE STAR magazine on her kitchen countertop, the one with the unflattering picture of the governor on the cover. She wondered if they would be interested in posting the video for every Texan to see.

"Enough, Marina!" she scolded herself. "You have a good job that pays the mortgage and provides food for your family. Don't risk everything you've worked so hard for!

Brenda Prendahl surveyed her Cloak Room domain and sighed.

How many more years are you going to spend pouring drinks for these political junkies? she asked herself. She had started bartending here when she was 30. Now she found herself on the wrong side of 50. She had witnessed enough back-stabbing sessions to last her a lifetime. And not once had she spilled the beans to family or friends, much less the press. Only a few months ago, she thought she'd picked up on something about Texas being carved up.

Sure, plenty of Cloak Room regulars had offered to marry her, not realizing that she played for the other team. But lately, she was content to drive home late at night in her trusty pickup, roughhouse with her German Shepherd, and occasionally invite one of her girlfriends over to spend the night.

Her daydream ended abruptly when who but Senator Bethany Jordan walked through the door, sidled up to the bar, winked, and quietly said, "Girlfriend, I need some advice."

Veronica Swaggart paused from removing her makeup to count the checks again. If her math was right, she had netted over five million dollars from her Spring Fling guests.

True, there had been that awkward moment when she recognized Senator Jordan pretending to be a member of the caterer's staff. But she had quickly squashed that feeble attempt at blackmail.

Five mil would buy some nice trips to Aspen this summer, along with jaunts across the pond for the Paris fashion shows in the fall on one of her besties' private jets.

If Bo didn't get too big for his britches and managed to get re-elected next term, the high life would go on for another four glorious years. That would give her time to seriously consider divorcing the rat bastard.

45

THE RACE FOR Mayor of El Paso would require split-second timing. The current mayor was the darling of the rich white establishment that had typically elected El Paso's mayors for the past 150 years. Mayors with names like Austin. Jackson. Duke. There had been a smattering of Hispanic surnames. Salazar. Ramirez. Caballero. But they were few and far between.

El Paso's newest mayor was fond of showing visiting VIPs the bullet holes in the City Hall building, reportedly fired from across the border in one of the infamous drug skirmishes that periodically interrupted the peace and quiet in The Second Safest City in America.

The mayor was scheduled to show the brass from Ft. Bliss around his fair city in a few weeks. The bullet-riddled wall of City Hall would be included in the tour.

"Chicago's got its St. Valentine's Day Massacre site in Bugs Moran's warehouse on North Clark Street," the mayor would regale visiting VIPs. "El Paso has our Magic Bullet site right here at City Hall. Nobody knows who fired the shot, and no one has ever fessed up to the crime," the mayor often emoted. "The only person who claims to have insider information is our colorful mayor pro tem, Mr. Ponce Ponzio."

"Maybe it was drug smuggling gone bad," the mayor pro tem would tantalize the mayor's guests. "And the odds of that ever happening again, especially from that distance, are a million-to-one."

The last time the Army sent three of its top people to Ft. Bliss was back in 2009 to announce the Year of the Non-Commissioned Officer.

This year, the Secretary of the Army and the Army chief of staff were scheduled to tour the downtown sites and announce the Year of the Transgender Soldier.

Midway through the day, the military entourage arrived at City Hall and the mayor began his yawner of a soliloquy he called The Tale of the Magic Bullet.

"From a mile away, a magic bullet sped at almost 4,000 feet-per-second across the Rio Grande, between the reinforced steel bars of the border wall, before striking our beloved City Hall. Perhaps one of you soldiers can tell us the precise caliber of the bullet?"

The Army Chief of Staff leaned closer and surveyed the bullet's signature pockmark.

"Looks to me like a 12.7x99mm NATO round."

The chief of staff's interpretation was abruptly interrupted by the mayor's head exploding, spraying a ghastly gout of blood and brain matter against the wall of City Hall.

Military security immediately threw their commanders to the ground and formed a cordon around the gathered dignitaries and press.

A military helicopter gunship from Ft. Bliss swooped low over the border wall, searching for a hidden sniper. In the attendant confusion, five migrants were slaughtered by .50 caliber gunship fire on the Ciudad Juarez side of the border.

"What are the odds?" a clearly shaken mayor pro tem, now acting Mayor, asked a CNN reporter later that evening.

Mayor Ponzio played to the press. "Ballistic experts now believe that the bullet fired years ago was just a test. Somebody was planning to kill one or more of our dignitaries, although it's uncertain whether that was the Army Chief of Staff or our congressman. It's unlikely that the bullet was intended for our beloved mayor."

When asked if he intended to run for mayor in a special election, Ponzio simply answered, "I'll leave that to the will of the people of El Paso."

"The people of El Paso appear to either revere or fear Ponce Ponzio, depending on who you ask," a CNN reporter noted at the end of the interview. Either way, the choice for the next mayor of El Paso is likely to be the man they call El Popo."

Ponzio picked up the phone on the first ring, hardly needing to glance at the Caller ID to know who would be calling him at midnight that fateful evening.

"Governor Swaggart, how good of you to call. It's been quite a day here in The Second Safest City in America! How soon should I announce that I'll be running for mayor?"

"Hold your horses, Ponz. Better to let things simmer down before you start firing them up. For one thing, the Army will conduct a full-scale investigation. Apparently, the round that killed your mayor is identical to the bullet hole in the wall of your City Hall. Like someone was taking target practice a few years ago."

"I can only imagine what the conspiracy theorists will do with this, Governor."

"Don't just imagine it, Ponzio. Make it happen."

46

THE RACE FOR MAYOR of Austin really didn't matter. Texas already had a governor, and Bo Swaggart wasn't going anywhere. Except maybe to a higher office. All in good time.

Austin's mayor had stood his ground on some key issues. Locally, he had shut down the rants over the For Women Only screening of the movie *Wonder Woman*. Nationally, he had fired back at the President over the transgender military ban. Bo wasn't sure where the mayor stood on Code Next, the first major rewrite of Austin's Land Development Code in 30 years. But it appeared he supported it, pitting him against Old West Austin. That was his fight, not Bo's.

Bo had bigger fish to fry. He was, after all, one of the most popular governors of Texas in recent times. Sure, liberals missed Ann Richards. Conservatives missed George W. Bush. But they'd never had a governor quite like Bo Swaggart.

Here was a guy who ran on Texas seceding from the Union. Now it looked like he had swerved toward a bigger prize. Dividing Texas into five states.

Texans weren't aware of his Project Pentagram just yet. They were still reeling over his announcement that he planned to put a dome over the iconic Texas Capitol. A good number of Texans preferred Lt. Governor McClain's idea of replacing the Goddess of Liberty with the Cowgirl of Liberty.

"Let sleeping dogs lie," was Governor Swaggart's answer to the race for mayor in Austin. Nobody of consequence was challenging the current mayor, and that was fine with Bo. Bo simply needed to make sure no one ran against him for his second term as governor.

Lt. Governor Iain McClain had to admit that, given the attention his Cowgirl of Liberty campaign was getting, running for governor was tempting. Perhaps too tempting. It was as if Governor Swaggart himself was tempting him to run. Did Swaggart know something he didn't? Sure, there were rumors about Swaggart dividing Texas into five states. But that was a pipe dream, wasn't it? Texans would never agree to that, would they? Did Swaggart have something else up his sleeve, something even more sinister?

As he did at the end of each workday, Lt. Governor McClain rolled his miniature Cowgirl of Liberty in from outside his office in the Capitol and rolled her over to the window overlooking Congress Avenue. The Cowgirl had become a regular fixture in Austin, and a must-see attraction for visitors to the Live Music Capital of the World.

He plugged her in and switched her on. Above her head, a neon lasso encircled a glowing Lone Star. As people drove past the Capitol, they slowed down to honk their approval. Not long ago, McClain had commissioned HONK IF YOU LOVE THE COWGIRL bumper stickers. Now more and more were showing up every day on Austin cars, pickups, and SUVs. He'd even seen them plastered on a few of the city's Metro buses.

The way McClain saw it, he might not have to run for governor at all. It might just fall into his lap. Swaggart was clearly overstepping his bounds. While secession was only a ploy to win the election, McClain wasn't so sure about Swaggart's secret plan to divvy up Texas into five independent states. That was ludicrous. The problem was that Texans had a long-standing affection for breaking the rules.

Chief of staff Rory Minton was nothing if not loyal. He had supported Iain McClain from the get-go when most pundits predicted McClain, a gay man, didn't have a chance in hell of riding on Beauregard Swaggart's coattails. But that's where the pundits had been wrong. Swaggart knew that the way to win over Texans was to offer them something new. Something controversial. Something that rattled the cage of the status-quo. Sensing a growing tolerance for LBGT, Swaggart attended a few rallies with Lt. Governor candidate McClain. It was a calculated risk that earned Bo the governor's job.

Texans were clearly ready for a change and Swaggart promised them one. Texans didn't realize that Swaggart was envisioning a bigger change than they could ever imagine.

If Swaggart had an end game in mind, it deftly escaped Texas' finest political minds. That's probably because Swaggart's end game wasn't just dividing Texas into five states. Five states meant ten senators. Ten senators could determine a presidential election.

47

Races for Mayor in Texas are staggered over two years.

Not surprisingly, Dallas Mayor Alexa King was re-elected for a second term. She thanked her constituencies profusely, then reached out to her opponents and welcomed them to City Hall to help chart the course for the future of Dallas.

"Whether you voted for me or not, you have a stake in the future of our great city," she told them. I welcome your opinions as we work together to make Dallas one of the greatest cities in America. Those folks over in Houston," she winked, "will just have to wait their turn."

Alexa had won in a landslide, something she and her handlers had carefully orchestrated. But she was careful not to share her loftier goals with her constituents just yet. First, she had to cement her widespread support into something approaching religious fervor. She allowed, hell, she demanded citizens call her "Alexa," shirking her official title as Mayor. And why not? Who wants to be remembered as mayor when one day you might be heralded as governor?"

Jeremiah Jones was the newly elected Mayor of Houston. The race had been closer than he cared for, that is until some nasty rumors began circulating about the current mayor's Las Vegas gambling junkets. Seems Mayor Whitliff enjoyed a few trips a year to the city where *What Happens Here, Stays Here.* The problem was that what happened in the casinos, and what may have happened afterhours in the private suites above, somehow leaked to Houston news sources.

Granted, the Houston Chronicle refused to run such unsubstantiated rumors. But that didn't stop the Houston Press, an alternative weekly newspaper, from muddying the political waters.

"It's the political equivalent of trying to answer the question, 'Do you still beat your wife?'" Jeremiah Jones explained to his wife.

"Is there anything you *won't* do to win a political race, 3-J?" Grace asked him.

"Not if it's me who's running, Gracie. What, you don't like the idea of being the First Lady of Houston?"

"Not as much as I'd like being the First Lady of East Texas," she replied, patting him on his derriere.

"That's something we don't talk about, Grace, publicly *or* privately. At least not yet!"

"Then what *can* we talk about privately?" she demurred, slipping her blue silk blouse over her head and slowly unzipping her brown leather miniskirt.

"Oh, we'll think of something," Jeremiah assured her.

It was no surprise to anyone in Laredo that Estevan Barrero was elected mayor by a majority of voters, some of whom were deceased.

Governor Swaggart called Mayor Barrero to congratulate him, just as he intended to call all the newly elected mayors of five major Texas cities.

"Why thank you, Governor," Estevan said. "No, thank *you*, Mayor Barrero," Swaggart replied. "Seems to me, the City of Laredo is in fine hands for the time being. But let's not forget that there are bigger plans in the works, Estevan."

"You just tell me when it's time to pull the trigger, Governor."

"I'd prefer you choose a different expression, Mayor."

"Then how about, *El que sabe, sabe,* Governor?"

"What's that mean in English, Estevan?"

"He who knows, knows."

Ponce "El Popo" Ponzio went from Mayor Pro Tem to Mayor of El Paso in a heartbeat, reminiscent of the last heartbeat of the city's murdered mayor. He ran unopposed in a special election the following spring. He quickly began conversations with the brass at Ft. Bliss about a special hardened structure he had in mind on the base.

"Can we count on the city to raise bonds for this little venture?" a Ft. Bliss General asked Mayor Ponzio privately.

"Not only can you count on it, General, you can consider it a done deal," the new mayor promised him.

Five Texas cities, five Texas mayors. Now nothing stood in the way of Bo Swaggart's Project Pentagram.

48

Governor Beauregard Swaggart had run and won as a Republican, not that he considered himself one.

There hadn't been a Democratic governor of Texas since Ann Richards won in 1990. Which was odd, considering the vast majority of the previous 48 governors were Democrats. But not anymore. Bill Clements turned the tide in 1986, thanks in part to the popularity of Ronald Reagan. Once Ann Richards lost to George W. Bush in 1994, every Texas governor since had been a Republican.

Bo Swaggart knew which side of the political bread gets buttered in Texas. Privately, Bo referred to his party of choice as "Republi*cants*," since, to his way of thinking, they were dead set against serving the best interests of all Texans." He referred to Democrats as "Demo*crites*," since he considered them hypocrites who merely kowtowed to the middle class when it served their purposes. Bo considered himself a Populist, in the mold of Andrew Jackson, William Jennings Bryan, George Wallace, and Donald Trump.

Populist Bo Swaggart had big plans. His call for secession was merely a diversion from his real goal. Dividing Texas into five states. Once he accomplished that and placed his four other handpicked governors in place, the next step would be to elect ten

Texas senators, two from each new state. From there, the road to the White House was paved with ill-gotten gold.

"Is it kosher to say, 'Mission Accomplished,' Governor, or does that conjure up memories of one of Dubya's not-so-finest hours?" chief of staff Truman asked her boss.

President George W. Bush had delivered his now infamous "Mission Accomplished" speech aboard an aircraft carrier, declaring the Iraq War over.

PBS commentator Gwen Ifill had said Bush was "part Tom Cruise, part Ronald Reagan."

A New York Times columnist had this to say about President Bush's premature proclamation:

"He flashed that all-American grin as he swaggered around the deck of the aircraft carrier in his olive flight suit, ejection harness between his legs, helmet tucked under his arm, awestruck crew crowding around. Maverick was back, cooler and hotter than ever, throttling to the max with joystick politics…This time Maverick didn't just nail a few bogeys and do a 4G inverted dive with a MiG-28 at a range of two meters. This time Top Gun wasted a couple of nasty regimes, and promised this was just the beginning."

"I won't be making the same mistake of counting my chickens before they hatch, Jules," Bo said. "We've got our mayors in place. If I have my way, they will soon be governors of four of the five new states of Texas."

"Not to sound redundant, Governor, but there's still that little matter of a state-wide referendum to make sure Texans actually *want* the Lone Star State divided into five states."

"Right you are, Jules. And who's to say those same five states won't opt to secede sometime in the future. That will depend largely on who's POTUS at the time."

"No one has ever accused you of being timid, Governor. The next President of the United States will be needing a loyal chief of staff, one would assume," Truman said, testing the waters.

"As my daddy was fond of saying, Jules, 'When you assume, you make an ass out of you and me.'"

"Copy that, Governor. Which one of your new Texas mayors would you like to meet with first?"

"All of 'em, Jules. The sooner, the better!"

Mayor-elect Alexa King thought it was no coincidence that the same Texans who had secretly met with Governor Swaggart a few months ago at the Headliners Club in Austin were the very same Texans who had now been elected mayors of major Texas cities.

Did that mean that those cities, including her beloved Dallas, were likely to be the capitals of the five new states? Dallas and Houston made sense, as did Austin. But Laredo over San Antonio? What was she missing something here? And El Paso, the so-called "Second Safest City in America," was the site of the recent assassination of the city's mayor.

"Let's see," Mayor King said to herself. "I'm the only female mayor. Jeremiah is the only Black mayor. Estevan and Ponce are two Hispanic mayors. And Austin just re-elected their Caucasian mayor.

Alexa jotted down her scorecard. One white, three people of color. Governor Swaggart probably wouldn't face serious opposition for re-election.

"What is that wily sonuvabitch's end game?" Alex wondered. Swaggart's absurd Dome Over the Dome idea was clearly a diversion. But Bo was nobody's fool. He had bigger plans. She just hoped they included her.

"Maybe I should plan another little trip down to Austin, remind Bo what he's missing at home. He's obviously a sucker for kinky videos, and this Texas girl has plenty of those!"

She would call Bo's chief of staff in the morning and set up a private rendezvous soon. That being settled, Alexa picked up her cell phone to call her sexy chauffeur. He was going to have a long night.

49

First Lady Swaggart summoned her staff for an unscheduled meeting.

"I need a fucking cause, y'all! Eleanor Roosevelt had her causes. Human rights, children's rights, and women's rights. Jackie Kennedy had the arts, historic preservation, and culture. Betty Ford had her alcohol abuse centers. I need a cause, goddammit!"

Veronica's staff was accustomed to her frequent tirades. But this one seemed particularly virulent.

"Well, Madam First Lady, there's always the LGBT," one staffer suggested sheepishly.

"Fuck the lesbos and the gay parade they rode in on!" Veronica shouted.

"How about the dreamers, those unauthorized Hispanics brought into this country as children?" another brave staffer offered.

"Dream on! Don't any of you nine-to-fivers have any new ideas? Or are you simply content to suck on the hind tit of the political sow?" Veronica's blood pressure was clearly boiling over.

A young male staffer slowly rose in the back of the conference room. "Opioids."

"Well I'll be damned," Veronica suddenly smiled. "Even a blind hog will occasionally root up an acorn. Talk to me, Jeremy."

Sensing an opportunity, her staffer bravely stood his ground.

"Opioid addiction, or the opioid crisis as the news media prefers to call it, is literally killing America, Madam First Lady. Oxycodone, hydrocodone, fentanyl. Despite their high rate of addiction and overdose, the potency and availability of these substances have made them popular as both formal medical treatments and recreational drugs."

Sensing the angry tide may have turned, Jeremy continued. "Texas recently got a twenty-seven-million-dollar federal grant, provided by the Substance Abuse and Mental Health Services Administration. But it's just a drop in the opioid bucket. Opioid addiction has reached epidemic proportions in Texas, and we need to cure it, Ma'am."

"We need a slogan!" Veronica said. "Not some namby-pamby 'Just Say No' crap. Somebody find Max Sinclair and tell him we need his services, his *pro bono* services, ASAP!"

It was a mirror image of the state of affairs in the nation's capital.

Max Sinclair was a jack-of-all-trades, master of some. Recovering adman. Full-time author. Part-time sleuth. Over the decades, he had written some rather catchy phrases.

Yet Max was cautious when he got a call from the Office of the First Lady of Texas requesting his creative talents.

Max had never met the First Lady. And he wasn't exactly a fan of the Governor of Texas. Max believed secession, while a noble notion, was a terrible idea.

"REMEMBER BREXIT. NIX TEXIT!" would be Max's battle cry, should Texas ever actually consider fleeing from the Union.

Still, he was intrigued by the First Lady's invitation to discuss a top-secret initiative.

Max accepted the invitation and decided to do a little homework on his high-falutin' host. He'd start by asking around at the Cloak Room. If there was dirt on the First Lady, Brenda Prendahl could be counted on to dig it up.

"Mayor Alexa King has requested an audience, Governor," chief of staff Truman told her boss one morning. "What should I tell her?"

"Tell her she's always welcome, Jules. But given my busy schedule these days, we should plan for an after-hours meeting. Somewhere off campus, where we won't be disturbed."

"The Governor's Suite at the Driskill Hotel?"

"Perfecto, Jules. And reserve it overnight. I might just bed down there if my meeting runs late with Alex, er, Mayor King."

"Consider it done, sir."

"And Jules, have security bring Mayor King up on the private elevator. You know how persnickety the rumormongers in this town can be.

"Roger that, Governor. The last thing we need is more fake news."

50

Senator Bethany Jordan couldn't believe she was standing at the podium with her mortal enemy, First Lady of Texas Veronica Swaggart.

The devil herself had given Bethany no options: "Stand with me on the podium when I announce my new initiative, or stand down from the Senate, stigmatized by slander for life."

"Ladies and gentlemen of the Senate, it is my pleasure to introduce the First Lady of Texas as she launches her broad-sweeping anti-opioid initiative today."

Behind Senator Jordan a large banner unfurled.

TEXAS IS NO DOPE!

"Thank you, Senator Jordan. We all know that your distant relative would be proud of all you've been able to accomplish in your short tenure in the Texas Senate. Who knows where you'll go from here?"

Nowhere, the First Lady chuckled to herself.

"One day, I predict that this slogan will not only free Texans from the stranglehold of opioid addiction, it will also replace 'Remember the Alamo!' as our Great State's most memorable battle cry.

Never happen, Senator Jordan chuckled to herself.

The applause in the Senate Chamber was perfunctory at best. President Trump had appointed pundit Kellyanne Conway as his Opioid Czar. That had failed miserably. Most senators assumed the First Lady's ambitious anti-opioid initiative would follow suit.

Opioid addiction in the United States had already killed more U.S. citizens than all the Americans who had died in the Vietnam War. And the numbers were climbing. According to the U.S. Drug Enforcement Administration, overdose deaths, particularly from prescription drugs and heroin, had reached epidemic levels. By 2016, nearly half of all opioid overdose deaths involved prescription opioids.

Curiously, drug lords were cited as the major culprits. The real drug lords, according to some newspaper and magazine reports, were the FDA and Big Pharma, with America's doctors serving as their pushers-for-hire. To make matters worse, the crisis had changed moral, social, and cultural resistance to street drug alternatives like heroin. Opioids, in both urban and rural areas, had been dubbed "hillbilly heroin."

Yet First Lady Swaggart's anti-opioid campaign appeared to be working. Mothers began monitoring their children more closely. Businesses began putting employees suspected of opioid addiction into rehabilitation programs at company expense. Adult O-Zone parties began to be replaced by NO-Zone parties.

Texans were foregoing opioids at an astonishing rate and First Lady Swaggart was getting most of the credit. That did not, unfortunately, affect her own opioid dependency. While she no longer distributed her little pink pills at her Spring Flings, she kept an ample supply for special occasions in her own personal medicine cabinet. Special occasions included happy hours that ranged from dawn until dusk. Sometimes beyond.

☆

Back at the Capitol, the Governor was getting a wee bit jealous of all the attention his wife was garnering.

"Jules, get in here!" he demanded. "I've had it up to here with Veronica's grandstanding. I need something that will wrestle attention from her anti-drug successes.

"You mean something besides your 'Dome Over the Dome' initiative, Governor?"

"You and I know that idea's a dud, Jules.

"That reporter just won the Ellie at the National Magazine Awards for her stories, Governor. I suggest we plow new ground."

"You might be right, Jules. Maybe it's time I plow new ground in my upcoming State of the Union speech.

"Are you suggesting that it might be time to run your Project Pentagram up the flagpole and see who salutes, Governor?"

"That I am, Jules.

Bo Swaggart, 49th Governor of Texas, began writing his State of the State speech that very night in his Capitol office, with a little help from his co-writer, Jack Daniels. He finished his first draft, along with a fifth of bourbon, just before dawn. He left his handwritten yellow tablet draft on his antique oak desk, held in place by his priceless Bowie knife.

Chief of staff Julie Truman would know what to do next.

PART V:
STATE OF DISUNION

51

"MY FELLOW TEXANS," Governor Beauregard Swaggart bellowed from the lectern in the Senate Chamber as he began his annual State of the State Address.

Every news source in Texas was present and accounted for. From the rugged mountains in the west to the sandy beaches in the southeast, from the blustery panhandle in the north to the scraggly high desert in the south, Texans were glued to their television screens. Would this be Governor Swaggart's long-anticipated call for secession?

"As you are all aware, I have run and won the governorship of our great state by claiming our right, as defined in our 1885 Joint Resolution for Annexing Texas to the United States, to secede from the Union at any time of our choosing.""

Millions of Texans leaned in.

"However, I come before you today, not to ask for your permission to secede from the Union. I come to ask your permission to succeed *within* the Union."

Millions of Texans simultaneously shouted, "Huh?"

"As some of you know, when President Sam Houston demanded that certain rights accompany our annexation in 1885, our right to secede was not his only demand. President Houston also demanded that we retain the right to divide our great state into as many as five great states."

Millions of Texans frowned.

"Now I know what some of you may be thinking: Bo Swaggart has lost his ever-lovin' mind! Please, hear me out, my fellow Texans. The Senate currently has 100 members.

Millions of Texans were pretty sure Bo Swaggart had lost his mind.

"Texas, like every other state, has two senators. That's good, but not great. Great is what we Texans aspire to. Am I right?"

Millions of Texans assumed it was a rhetorical question.

"Now imagine, if you will, five states of Texas with ten senators representing them. Now *that*, my fellow Texans, is true power! The power to win debates. The power to determine policy. The power to confirm or deny Justices of the Supreme Court. The power, if you will, to elect Presidents!"

Bo paused for dramatic effect.

"I realize this is a lot to chew on, my fellow Texans. But I suggest that we immediately conduct a statewide referendum, giving every voter in this great state a say in what could be a glorious future for us all."

Millions of Texans blinked.

"There are a lot of other things we could discuss today, my fellow Texans. Unemployment is down. Jobs are up. Texas leads the nation in energy creation. Maybe it's once again time we declare our independence. Secure our sovereignty over our own future. Are you with me?"

It was a bold stroke. Whether of genius or political suicide remained to be seen. Before anyone from the press could ask any questions, Chief of staff Truman stepped forward for an announcement.

"Ladies and gentlemen of the press, I know you have lots of questions for the governor. But we've just been informed that the President of the United States is on the phone. We wouldn't want to keep the President waiting, would we? This meeting is hereby adjourned. Thank you all for attending. And may God bless Texas!"

Of course, the President was *not* on the phone. The President was golfing, with instructions not to be disturbed by insignificant matters. In his mind, Bo Swaggart's bloviating speeches clearly merited that distinction.

Sitting in her apartment, Holly Worthington wondered what had just happened. Unless she was mistaken, the Governor of Texas had just suggested that the Great State of Texas divide itself into five smaller states!

"We don't do small in Texas, Governor Swaggart!" Holly shouted at her television set. "And we don't go back on our promises!"

Holly knew that Bo Swaggart was probably never serious about his promise to secede from Union. But he shook things up. And that got him elected.

But this was clearly a step too far. Holly was pretty sure Texans would squelch Swaggart's divisive plan, assuming a referendum was ever held. But this renewed her commitment to dig further into Swaggart's questionable past.

"I'm comin' for ya, Swaggart!" Holly railed at her television screen.

52

THE RESPONSE FROM Texas news sources to Governor Swaggart's bold State of the State Address was both fast and furious.

The Dallas Morning News blasted the banner THE GREAT DIVIDER.

The Houston Chronicle followed suit with WHAT BO DOESN'T KNOW.

The Austin American-Statesman predicted DIVIDED WE FALL.

The El Paso Times speculated CAPITAL OF WEST TEXAS?

The Laredo Morning Times appeared to break with the other newspapers, showing support for the governor with the front-page headline, ¡EL QUE SABE, SABE! He Who Knows, Knows. Did Laredo know something the rest of Texas failed to grasp?

Laredo Mayor Barrero was quick to sing Governor Swaggart's praises. "Bo Swaggart is a true visionary," the mayor insisted. "Someone who sees a brighter future for Texas, a future that recognizes the value of all Texans, including people of color."

Houston Mayor Jones quickly responded to the local headline. "How about what Texas doesn't know? Texas may no longer be the largest state in the Union. But we can damn sure be the five most powerful states in the Union!"

Dallas Mayor King lauded the governor's bravery. "The time has come for Texas to assume our rightful role. Not just as one state. Five of the most powerful states in the Union. Governor Swaggart reminds us what it means to be a Texan."

El Paso Mayor Ponzio declined to comment. To his way of thinking, the El Paso Times headline said it all. If El Pasoans wanted to ensure their place in the annals of history, they should pay tribute to Governor Swaggart. Soon enough, they would pay tribute to Governor Ponzio.

Austin's mayor was the sole dissenter. "Read the headline and weep, Austin. 'Divided We Fall.' John Dickinson, one of America's founding fathers, wrote those stirring words in *The Liberty Song*. The truth is, Bo Swaggart is bad for business, bad for Texas, and bad for America."

Bo just chuckled when he read those words. He knew that Austin's mayor stood zero chance of re-election once Bo put Project Pentagram in place. But Bo also knew that a little controversy stirs the pot of the people's will. In time, all Texans would know what Bo already knew. Instead of seceding from the Union, Texas would soon divide and conquer the Union.

Max Sinclair was so invested in First Lady Swaggart's new anti-drug campaign that he had failed to anticipate her husband's end game. Dividing Texas into five states. The very thought turned Max's stomach. How could anyone think that dividing Texas into five states would make us stronger? Welcome to the idiocracy!

Max's daughter, Sunny McBee, who was visiting him in Austin, tried in vain to calm him down.

"Now, now, Daddy, don't let that blowhard get under your skin. The last thing I need is for you to blow a gasket. Why don't you head back down to the coast and continue your writing? You know that makes you happy.

There was some truth to that. Max loved writing. He was almost finished with his second novel, and he was already thinking about his third. A devilish tale that would rattle Texas history.

"You're right, Sunny Bunny," Max agreed. "But Bo Swaggart is a burr under my saddle. I can't ride off into the sunset until I get rid of that pain-in-the-ass."

"I brought you one of my famous marble cakes with chocolate ganache, Daddy. You know what they say…"

"The way to a man's heart is through his stomach. I believe I taught you that. How's my grandson?"

"Jackson is growing like a weed, Daddy. He's almost two now."

"Two!? How did that happen so fast?"

"Life is what happens when you're busy making other plans. I believe you taught me that, too. By the way, Jackson was asking about you the other day, GranDude."

"Love his nickname for me. Does he need me to teach him how to spiral a football?"

"You never even taught me!"

"Because you're a gir…never mind. I'll teach you both. Those NFL scouts will be knocking down your door before you know it!"

"So, you'll be heading back down to the coast to write, Daddy?"

"All in good time, Sunny Bunny."

53

Amateur Scientist Max Sinclair had some friends in both low and high places, among them some professors at the Dell Medical School on The University of Texas at Austin campus.

Dell Medical School is UT's graduate medical school. The school opened to an inaugural class of 50 students in the summer of 2016. The school is named after the Michael & Susan Dell Foundation, which pledged $50 million over 10 years to the facility.

Max knew Michael Dell in passing. But he had become good friends with several of the professors at the school since he survived a scare from basal cell carcinoma a couple years prior.

When all the brouhaha surrounding the First Lady's anti-opioid campaign had erupted, Max met with the doctor who had no doubt saved his life.

"Why can't we invent something that will block the effects of opioids, especially in overdose cases, Doc?"

"We can. And we have, Max. We just haven't completed our beta test. And we don't have a name for it yet."

"How long will it take to complete the beta test?" Max asked.

"Probably two more years."

"And if you fast-tracked it, assuming the funds were available?"

"Six months."

"Consider the funds available, Doc. And as for the name, consider that done, too."

"What name would that be, Max?"

Max didn't blink. "NoZone."

NoZone got FDA approval in three months and was on the market in six. It was cheap, readily available, and it worked. Proceeds from brisk sales provided funding for additional UT studies to help remedy Texans' opioid addiction.

Satisfied that he had done his good deed for the moment, Max piled into his vintage French Citroën motorcar and headed toward the coast. He stopped by briefly in San Marcos to say his goodbyes to his daughter Sunny and his grandson Jackson. Sunny convinced him to stay for lunch, knowing that he'd get a much-needed nap before getting back on the road. She served him her famous chicken fried steak with cream gravy, horseradish mashed potatoes, and buttery green beans, followed by a slice of homemade lemon meringue pie.

"Why don't you grab forty winks with your grandson before you hit the road, Daddy?" Sunny suggested.

Forty winks became two hours. Only because Max's grandson Jackson woke him up.

"What? Huh? Oh, it's you, Li'l Big Man. WHOA! Let's get that dirty diaper changed. Then GranDude's gotta light a shuck for the coast."

Sunny held Jackson, who waved as GranDude pulled away in his odd car.

"One day you'll inherit that rust bucket, young man, and it'll be the ruin of you," Sunny warned her toddler.

Jackson just giggled and burbled "wust bucket!"

☆

Seated in the Senate Chamber, Senator Bethany Jordan quietly seethed. She had helped Veronica Swaggart launch one of the most successful anti-drug campaigns in Texas history. To make matters worse, Dell Medical School doctors had invented a successful opiate blocker, and the number of Texans addicted to opioids was decreasing at a record pace. It was hard to get mad at her writer friend Max Sinclair. NoZone, his catchy name for the blocker, had caught on big time. So big that it had become a national success. American doctors had been put on notice by the FDA that overprescribing opioids would cost them their licenses and conceivably land them in jail.

TEXAS IS NO DOPE quickly became AMERICA IS NO DOPE. The First Lady of Texas had become a national celebrity, rivaling her egomaniacal husband, Governor Beauregard Swaggart.

That simply would not do, at least in Bo Swaggart's devious mind.

"My wife needs a vacation, Jules," Bo told his Chief of staff, "preferably someplace far, far away."

"Someplace like the Caribbean, Governor?"

"Too close to home."

"Roger that, Governor. Has the First Lady ever visited the Democratic Republic of Congo?"

"Not to my knowledge. But isn't it very dangerous there?"

"Welll, it can be…"

"Perfect. Book it, Jules. The sooner, the better!"

54

Texas First Lady Veronica Swaggart cordially invited America's First Lady to join her on her whirlwind tour of the Democratic Republic of Congo. That way, she reasoned, she might be able to bum a ride on Air Force One.

America's First Lady politely yet firmly declined Veronica's kind offer. A Travel Advisory had been issued warning U.S. citizens to avoid unnecessary travel to the DRC because of ongoing instability and sporadic violence in many parts of the country. The directive went on to warn that very poor transportation infrastructure throughout the DRC and poor security conditions in the Eastern Congo and Kasai made it difficult for the U.S. Embassy to provide consular services anywhere outside of Kinshasa."

If Governor Swaggart was aware of the current travel warning, he failed to mention it to First Lady Swaggart.

She invited several of her guests from her legendary Spring Flings to accompany her aboard a chartered Gulfstream 650, courtesy of the taxpayers of Texas. It was, Vanessa would assure them, a goodwill mission.

"While we're there, we'll swing by Cape Town to shop, she tempted her friends. And if I have my way, we might even touch down in Paris on the way home."

A handful of Veronica's well-heeled lady friends greedily accepted her invitation.

"Like the song says, girlfrans, 'May the road go on forever and the party never end!'"

At the Driskill Hotel, Dallas Mayor Alexa King was being ushered into a private elevator to the Governor's Suite by a uniformed Texas Ranger.

"My, my, aren't you handsome, Ranger!" Alexa purred to tall security guard.

"I couldn't say, Madam Mayor," the Ranger stammered.

"Then I only have one question for you, Ranger," Alexa said as she brushed his wide shoulder with her pendulous breast. "Is that a gun in your pocket, or are you just happy to see me?"

Before the Ranger could answer, the elevator door slid open and Governor Bo Swaggart met Alexa and her escort wearing a thick Driskill bathrobe and slippers emblazoned with the Governor of Texas Seal. Bo was holding two bubbling flutes of champagne.

"Alex! As I live and breathe. Welcome to the suite life!"

The Texas Ranger quickly pushed the button that would send him and the private elevator quickly descending to the ground floor.

"Is there one of those yummy robes for me, Bo?"

"I don't think you'll need a robe in the hot tub, Alexa."

"No? Then why don't you slip out of yours and into something more comfortable. Me, for instance."

Bo congratulated himself on remembering to reserve his private suite overnight and down a double dose of Viagra.

55

Lone Star magazine printed 100,000 extra copies of the issue with a map of Texas divided into five states on the cover. The lead story, penned by Holly Worthington, was likely to be the most widely read article in the magazine's history.

"BO'S BIG BOO-BOO" the cover shouted. Holly's story made the national news.

Most political pundits assumed Governor Beauregard Swaggart would be incensed. On the contrary, the governor commissioned a giant blow-up of the cover and hung it from the second story columns of the Capitol.

"Seceding is for sissies," Bo scolded reporters from the national and international press. "Sometimes, to get bigger, you have to think smaller. Texas is the second largest state in the Union. But how many senators does Alaska have? Two! How many senators will Texas boast when we're done dividing? Ten! 'Divide and conquer' is my motto, ladies and gentlemen of the press."

The question was, could he sell it to 30 million Texans?

Holly Worthington clearly didn't think so. In her article, Holly suggested that no real Texan would ever agree to divide the Great State of Texas into five smaller states.

"Texas might forgive Bo for his stupid Dome Over the Dome idea," Holly's controversial article began, "but dividing our beloved State of Texas into five statelets is Bo's biggest boo-boo by a long shot."

The map on the cover of the magazine was pure conjecture, of course. Nobody yet knew how the governor planned to divide Texas into five states. But Holly figured that the major cities of Texas would become the capitals of the new states. The cartographer depicted the new capital cities as Austin, Dallas, Houston, San Antonio, and El Paso.

Mayor Estevan Barrero was livid. He paid a bevy of high-priced lawyers to demand LONE STAR magazine recall every single copy of the magazine, to no avail. As his lawyer explained, "That train has left the station, El Jefe."

"Then kill the train's engineer!" Barrero roared.

"And who might that be?" his lawyer asked meekly.

"That reporter, Holly Worthington!" Barrero shouted.

"Surely you're not asking me to order the assassination of a reporter for one of the state's most powerful magazines, Jefe?"

"Of course not. I'm asking the lawyer who will be taking your place today to follow my instructions without question. Now get out of my sight!

It was never Holly's intention to put herself in the spotlight. Truth was, she assumed Bo Swaggart's plan to carve up the state was simply bluster. Another diversion at a time when his popularity appeared to be declining.

"First, he wins by promising secession. Then he concocts a cockamamie plan to build a dome over the Capitol. Then he has the gall to suggest dividing Texas into five states," Holly told the press. "This may prove to be Bo Swaggart's Waterloo moment."

Meanwhile, pundits were digging deeper into Bo's harebrained plan. The prevailing consensus was it might work. Success would depend heavily on convincing five states to vote as a bloc, wrangled by Governor Beauregard Swaggart himself. The Governor of California considered a similar plan. Dividing her state into North and South California. But the plan only produced four senators, whereas the Texas proposal would seat ten senators. California's Senate declared the proposal dead on arrival.

Eastern liberals shuddered to think what would happen if Swaggart pulled off his preposterous plan. "We'd be eating barbecue and two-stepping in the streets of New York City!" they fretted. "We've barely recovered from LBJ and that Bush bunch. Imagine an America with Beauregard Swaggart in the White House!"

The thought that a Texas divided might become America's most powerful swing states was, in a word, inconceivable.

56

ONE DOESN'T TRIFLE with the likes of Rhett McCullum, nephew of the legendary Red McCullum. Rhett was a new owner of the San Antonio Spurs, a not-so-silent partner in the Circuit of the Americas Formula One track in Austin and, rumor had it, the future owner of an NFL team in San Antonio. Rhett liked to think of himself as the King of San Antonio.

A man as powerful as Rhett McCullum just naturally maintained spies in high places. Among those places was the Texas State Capitol. That's how Rhett learned of Governor Swaggart's controversial plan to divide Texas into five states long before the governor announced his intentions to his fellow Texans.

And that's how Rhett learned that Laredo, not San Antonio, was destined to become the capital of what Swaggart was calling the State of South Texas. That would not stand!

"If Swaggart thinks he can sidestep the second-largest city in Texas for a one-horse town on the South Texas border, he's sadly mistaken!" Rhett McCullum ranted to his executive team. "Two can play that game!"

"If you don't mind me saying so, Rhett," his executive vice president said cautiously, "you don't mess with the mayor of Laredo."

That simply infuriated Rhett. "Estevan Barrero? He may have a few billion dollars, but I know his back-story," Rhett had spent a small fortune looking into Estevan Barrero's secretive past. "Rumor has it he's the bastard son of Pablo Escobar, the notorious Colombian drug lord. Once Texans get wind of that, Barrero's political power will evaporate."

"You might have also heard the rumor that Barrero's enemies sometimes disappear, right, boss?"

"You yourself oversaw the installation of the security systems at my home and my ranch. Nobody gets to Rhett McCullum."

Rhett's executive glanced around the room, took note of his team's diverted eyes, and choked back his concerns. "Whatever you say, boss. Meanwhile, we'll alert our shadows on the Dark Net that we may have some wet work for them. Any other bidness?

☆

The Governor of Texas eased into his saddle leather lounge chair, poured himself a stiff double highball of rye whiskey, and settled in to watch the evening news.

Bo typically muted the broadcast until the weatherwoman appeared in a body-hugging dress. "Lemme guess," Bo slurred to the screen, "There's gonna be a big front, with a sudden rise in temperatures right behind."

Tiffany, the bombshell weather forecaster, appeared in a low-cut navy Victoria Beckham knit dress, slit up the side to reveal long, sensuous legs.

"You can eat crackers in my bed anytime, Miss Tiffany," Bo said to the TV screen before refilling his cocktail. Lifting his cell phone from a side table, Bo recorded a reminder. "Jules, invite that weather woman Tiffany to meet me for a cocktail in the Governor's Suite at the Driskill ASAP. Schedule it for right after the late news, so she doesn't have time to change her wardrobe before meeting me."

Bo's wife Veronica suddenly appeared, carrying her ubiquitous vodka martini.

"Did you say something, dear?"

"Just some bidness I need to take care of, sweetheart."

"Oh, really? Who's Tiffany?"

"Now you've ruined the surprise, 'Nessa. I'm getting you a Tiffany lamp for our anniversary."

"How original!" Veronica snorted as she left the room.

"Note to self," Bo whispered into his cell phone. "Jules, find Vee a Tiffany lamp on eBay!"

As usual, Governor Swaggart insisted that his own personal chambermaid, Marina Alvarez, clean up the Governor's Suite at the Driskill Hotel once the Mayor of Dallas was headed back home the morning after.

Marina went about her job with her usual fastidiousness, turning off the still-gurgling hot tub, bagging the rumpled bedsheets that she would wash at home and return, and wiping the lipstick stains from a bedside champagne flute.

Marina had no idea what DNA meant. But she recalled how a semen stain on a blue dress had almost gotten a U.S. President impeached. She slipped a lipstick-stained champagne flute into her utility bag.

Job security, Marina told herself.

57

The Gulfstream G650 touched down on the secluded Congo landing strip just in time for a happy hour celebration.

First Lady Veronica Swaggart and her lady friends were already plenty happy, having indulged in copious quantities of Maine lobster and Louis Roederer Cristal Brut Champagne on the private flight to the Democratic Republic of the Congo. None of them had slept a wink, thanks to the endless supply of pharmaceutical-grade cocaine onboard.

Their gleaming jet was met by a cadre of what appeared to be DRC military in black uniforms and blood-red berets. These were hard men, clearly accustomed to battle. Each of them brandished an AK-47 assault rifle.

As Veronica paraded down the jet's stairway, she was met by the leader of the imposing squadron.

"Greetings, First Lady Swaggart. We've been expecting you. Allow me to introduce myself. I am Commander Duchel Mafinga. I am here to inform you and your esteemed entourage that each of you will be required to pay an entry fee of one hundred thousand U.S. dollars."

"Now wait just a minute, buster!" Veronica interrupted. "Do you know who I am?"

I know precisely who you are, Madam First Lady. Veronica Swaggart of Texas. As I was saying, you and your friends will be required to pay an entry fee of one hundred thousand dollars."

"A hundred grand? That's preposterous. I demand you take me to your leader at once!"

"I *am* the leader, First Lady Swaggart. And I can assure you, you'll not be going anywhere until you and your colleagues pay our entry fee. Fortunately for you, we except credit cards."

By this time, Veronica's friends had deplaned and were anxious to know what the hold-up was.

"It's a hold-up, all right, ladies! This goon thinks he can strong-arm us into paying him a ridiculous sum of money just to enter his puny little third-world country!"

The slap caught Veronica off guard.

"How dare you, you big bully!" Veronica cried, rubbing her reddened cheek.

One of Veronica's millionaire friends decided this was not going to turn out well. She quickly spun around and began walking back toward the Gulfstream jet. A bullet struck her squarely between the shoulder blades and she collapsed to the tarmac in a pool of blood.

The pilot of the Gulfstream had seen enough. He had yet to wind down his twin engines and he immediately began taxiing down the runway. Commander Mafinga barked an order. Three of his squad began raking the jet with gunfire. The pilot suddenly slumped in his seat. But his copilot kept the jet barreling down the runway and the jet began to lift skyward, beyond the withering gunfire.

Another mercenary quickly shouldered a Stinger missile and launched it at the departing aircraft. Instantly the Gulfstream jet erupted in a gigantic fireball.

"As I was saying, Madam First Lady, we will require a $100,000 entry fee from you and each of your guests, including the recently departed. In the meantime, my men will escort you to your quarters. And may I strongly suggest, you do or say nothing more to anger me or my men."

"Do you know who my husband is?" Veronica shouted.

"Indeed I do, Madam First Lady. He is the Governor of Texas, is he not?"

"You don't want to mess with Texas!" Veronica warned.

"Actually, you don't want to mess with me, Madam First Lady!" Commander Mafinga corrected her. "In the meantime, you and your guests look a bit weary. Allow my men to show you to your quarters."

The bold headlines shouted similar messages in every major Texas newspaper:

FIRST LADY HELD HOSTAGE IN CONGO, GOVERNOR REFUSES TO NEGOTIATE

Within hours, the millionaire and billionaire husbands of Veronica's friends had each wired a million dollars to the Congolese terrorists. Everyone, that is, except Texas Governor Beauregard Swaggart.

"Texas does not negotiate with terrorists!" Bo told the assembled news reporters. "I have no control over what other individuals may or may not do. But I can assure you that the Great State of Texas is not going to kowtow to these extortionist demands!"

True to his word, Commander Mafinga released Veronica's friends relatively unharmed, once their husbands paid his exorbitant fees. The bedraggled women stumbled onto a commercial Ethiopian Airlines jet and vowed never to return to the Congo under any circumstances.

A few weeks later, First Lady Veronica Swaggart was secreted across the Rwandan border where she boarded a Rwanda Airlines jet bound for the United States.

Records would later reveal that her million-dollar ransom was paid from the campaign coffers of Texas Lt. Governor Iain McClain.

58

Deep beneath Estevan Barrero's gigantic commercial development in downtown Laredo, Texas, a vast underground railroad was taking shape.

Built over many months by his secluded construction crew, the mayor's massive underground tunnel was an engineering marvel. It had all begun with several hundred tons of railroad track manufactured in South Korea, which Estevan had purchased for pennies on the dollar from bankruptcy court.

Estevan had then leased heavy drilling machinery used in a now defunct tunneling operation in San Marcos. The equipment, which included giant earth-chewing monstrosities, was leased from the U.S. Army after a brigadier general and nefarious Russian spy abandoned an attempt to dig a tunnel for a miniature halide collider.

Now, after months of digging, a huge high-tech tunnel stretched from the bowels of Estevan's project to Nuevo Laredo, Mexico.

The tunnel was lit with low-heat LED lighting, cooled by several hundred tons of industrial air conditioning equipment vented at the surface through artificial Saguaro cacti, and guarded day and night by Barrero's elite security detail.

A driverless mag-lev train, built by the same company that engineered Tokyo's automated transit system, levitated above the rails. The twelve-mile round trip took less than 12 minutes in time trials.

Soon, *El Expreso de Nuevo Laredo* would be transporting marijuana, cocaine, heroin, and the popular opiates known as hillbilly heroine from Barrero's underground drug caches in Mexico, right under the noses of the United States Border Patrol.

Estevan smiled. He was, indeed, the bastard son of the infamous Colombian drug lord and narcoterrorist, Pablo Escobar. His full name, Estevan Colombia Barrero, cleverly concealed his heritage in the first few letters of his given names. Es. Co. Bar.

But where Pablo Escobar had amassed an impressive thirty billion dollars by the early 1990s, Estevan estimated that his operation would generate ten times that much in revenues. Perhaps even more if his stealth operation continued to flourish for 20 years or more.

Three hundred billion dollars would buy a lot of things. Maybe even a United States presidency, Estevan mused. He knew that the Governor of Texas had his eye on the White House. But Swaggart was a moron, in Estevan's opinion, capable of fooling some of the people some of the time. But hopelessly inept at fooling all the people all the time.

Estevan's impressive fortress would be finished in plenty of time to be recommissioned as Estevan's South Texas capitol once he became governor of the new State of South Texas. State capitol by day, U.S.-Mexico drug nexus by night.

Estevan raised a shot glass of his favorite tequila to his namesake, Pablo Escobar. "What say you now, *Papa? ¿Quien es mas macho?*"

Estevan's bravado was suddenly interrupted by the chiming of his cell phone "I told you never to call me at this number!"

"Even if I could make you very, very happy, Estevan?" A woman's voice purred.

Estevan immediately recognized his caller. "Esmerelda, my Emerald. This had better be good!"

"Was it not good for you the last time we met, *mi amor?*"

Estevan smiled at the memory. Esmerelda was also a bastard child of Pablo Escobar, which made her his stepsister. But that didn't seem to matter once the two of them were together. Esmerelda presently lived across the border in Nuevo Laredo. But several times now, she had boarded *El Expreso de Nuevo Laredo* and secretly met Estevan in his private suite in Laredo.

Esmerelda was quite adventurous in bed. "Shall I bring the whips and chains, *El Dominador?*"

Esmerelda, she of the emerald eyes, had taught him sexual deviances he had only imagined before meeting her.

"I'll send *El Expreso* for you at midnight, *mi preciosa.* But you must be back in Nuevo Laredo by dawn."

"Let's see if you hold me to that order in the morning, *El Guapo.*" Esmerelda whispered seductively before the line went dead.

"I'd give my left *pelota* for that woman!" Estevan grinned as he poured himself another shot of tequila. "But I might just need both of them tonight!"

Estevan placed a call to his head of security in the tunnel deep below his private suite, then checked his supply of Viagra in his bedside table.

"Drink up, my friend," he said to his image in an ornate full-length mirror, "for tonight we ride till dawn!"

59

VERONICA THREATENED TO move out of the Governor's Mansion the day she got home from the Democratic Republic of Congo.

She refused to even speak to her husband, who attempted to convince her that he had secretly paid the ransom that freed her from Commander Mafinga and his terrorist Congolese regime.

"Ordinarily, I'd say fuck you, Bo!" Veronica hissed, "but that's something that's never going to happen again. Capiche?"

Bo Swaggart was not one to grovel. Besides, there were plenty of other ports in this latest storm.

"Does that mean you no longer want to be First Lady of Texas, Vee?"

"Why would I want to be First Lady when I can be the Governor?" Veronica replied as she headed for the door of the mansion.

Bo attempted another path to diplomacy. "Did you at least enjoy your Congo adventure?

Veronica stopped abruptly and swiveled menacingly toward her husband. "Adventure? What part of watching one of my best friends gunned down in cold blood, a Gulfstream jet and two pilots getting blown to bits, and me being raped by Commander Mafinga and his gang of goons would you call an adventure, Bo?"

"Mafinga raped you? That wasn't part of the deal!" Bo would gladly have paid a fortune to retract these last few words.

"The deal, Bo? Are you telling me that you had something to do with what happened in the Congo?"

"Of course not, Vee! But I saw what you told the press when you landed, and I find it hard to believe any of your story actually happened.

"Well, believe it Bo! And believe this. If I ever find out you had anything to do with the murder of three people, the destruction of a seventy-million-dollar jet, and me being raped by Congolese soldiers, I won't just see you in court. I'll see you in hell!"

"Vee, listen to me. I had nothing to do with *any* of that. It was your idea to visit the DRC and take your friends along. Who knew that it could be dangerous?"

"I'll tell you what could be dangerous, Bo. Dangerous is when the billionaire husbands of my friends who accompanied me into harm's way decide to quit bankrolling your political ambitions. That, Beauregard, is what even you might call dangerous!"

Bo shuddered. The thought of losing his wife was manageable. The thought of losing funding for his future political campaigns was unthinkable.

"Let's not get ahead of ourselves here, Vee. Why don't you set down your suitcase, pour yourself a martini, and let's figure out how to make this a win-win for both of us."

"What do I stand to win, Bo? Because I'm damn certain what you have to lose."

"How about Vice President of the United States."

"How about you kiss my ass!"

"I'll kiss anything you like, my love, so long as you listen to reason. Why don't you take one of your happy pills and I'll mix you a martini while I swallow some Vitamin V. This time tomorrow, all will be forgiven."

"I will never forget what happened in the Congo, Bo. And I will *never* forgive you for lying to me about it."

Bo just winked. "Now, now, Vee. Here, wash down that happy pill with this martini and join me upstairs for a little beast-with-two-backs."

"You and I will never have sex again, Bo. Not here in the Governor's Mansion and not in the White House, should we get there by hook or crook. Which, in your case, is more likely by crook!"

Bo was pretty sure he could drum up some kinky sex elsewhere. Which reminded him that he had a date soon with that busty weatherwoman Tiffany. Plus, there was always Alexa. And once he got to the White House, it would be open season on sex.

"Alright, you win," Bo acquiesced. "I'll draw you a bubble bath, and we can reschedule the wild thing for another time."

"Read my lips, Bo!" There will be no next time!"

60

Cowgirl of Liberty Christmas ornaments were selling like hotcakes at the Bob Bullock Texas State History Museum in Austin.

When Governor Swaggart asked for a statewide referendum on dividing Texas into five states, Lt. Governor McClain had countered with a request for a referendum replacing the Goddess of Liberty atop the Capitol dome with his Cowgirl of Liberty.

While Governor Swaggart's divisive idea was drawing fire from several quarters, it appeared Texans were ready to embrace a neon-lit Cowgirl of Liberty statue atop their beloved State Capitol.

"Our gay Lt. Governor has outrun his coverage on this one!" Governor Swaggart ranted to the press. "It's one thing to remove statues of our proud Confederate heroes from the Capitol grounds. But it's quite another to defile our blessed Capitol with a vulgar cowgirl!"

Yet Texans appeared to be warming to idea of a Lone Star-lassoing cowgirl to replace the Goddess of Liberty. A straw poll indicated that Texans believed the Lt. Governor's spirited cowgirl proposal topped the Governor's harebrained dome proposal by a margin of five-to-one.

☆

Elsewhere in the news, the First Lady of Texas had doubled her staff at taxpayers' expense, apparently with the tacit approval of her husband, the governor. Talk of her moving out of the Governor's Mansion had quickly subsided. In addition, it was quietly announced that the First Lady would be redecorating the upstairs rooms at the Governor's Mansion. This prompted a brief bit of chatter in the Twittersphere. But there were larger issues looming on the horizon.

Governor Swaggart had started a rumor that what the Lt. Governor really had in mind was topping the State Capitol with two cowgirls.

"Texans won't tolerate another Brokeback Mountain!" the Governor railed.

But Texans were onto the governor's swaggering. His plan to divide Texas into five states was largely falling on deaf ears. And his popularity numbers were plummeting precipitously.

Bo needed to do something fast. Who could he turn to? Why, Jeremiah Jones, of course!

"Governor, how nice to hear from you!" Mayor Jones said, recognizing Bo on his Caller ID.

"Let's cut the bullshit, shall we, 3-J? I'm in a world of hurt over here in Austin. Which means we could all be in a world of hurt if things don't change. Pronto!"

"Hold on a minute, Bo. Who's this 'we' you're talking about?"

"You and the mayors of every other major Texas city, thanks to me!"

"We all got what we bargained for, Bo. So what is it that you want in return?"

"I need for thirty million Texans, or at least the forty percent who actually go to the polls, to vote for dividing the Lone Star State into five states."

"Bo, I can assure you that you won't get eleven thousand Texans to vote for dividing Texas in a referendum."

"What I need you to assure me is that roughly forty percent of Texas voters will feel the need to vote in this referendum, Jeremiah. Think you can do that, Mr. Mayor?"

"That's a big hunk of meat, Bo. Let me chew on it for a couple of days."

"Fine. Call me on Monday once you've put that diabolical mind of yours to work over the weekend, 3-J. Remember what's at stake here. The future governorship of the State of East Texas."

Before Jeremiah could protest, Swaggart was gone.

"Damn!" Jeremiah shouted, throwing his glass of cognac across the room, where it shattered spectacularly against his office wall.

"Is something wrong, Mayor?" his chief of staff stuck her head in his office and asked sheepishly.

"Looks like it's time to pay the piper, Cookie. Before the rats start coming out of the woodwork."

"Would you like me to assemble the Council, Mayor?"

"Hell no! This one is strictly off the books."

With that, Jeremiah Jones began flipping through his private address book. This was going to be tricky. Heads might have to roll…

61

Holly Worthington jogged every day before dawn on the Butler Hike & Bike Trail around Austin's Lady Bird Lake, come rain or come shine.

This morning was chilly. So she donned her sweats, grabbed her cell phone and ear buds, and headed for her morning run. It was dark and would remain dark this time of year until around 7 a.m. By 8 o'clock, she'd be showered, dressed, and sipping a latte at the offices of LONE STAR magazine. Publisher Lev Gingrich insisted that there was always plenty of caffeine handy to keep his writers focused.

Holly crossed the footbridge just off Lamar Boulevard, headed south, then turned east along the south banks of the Colorado River. This section of the river, originally called Town Lake, had been renamed in honor of President Lyndon Baines Johnson's widow, Lady Bird.

As usual, there were almost no other joggers up this early. Holly punched classic rock on her cell phone and began to jog. Slowly at first, then faster as her muscles began to loosen up. She passed by the north end of Zilker Park, crossed the tracks for the Zilker Zephyr miniature train, and started down the slope that ran along the riverbank.

Over the driving beat of Led Zeppelin's classic 'Whole Lotta Love,' Holly sensed another presence. Glancing behind her, she spied another jogger. A male, in dark sweats and a black knit cap trailed closely behind her. But what struck Holly as particularly odd was that the dude was wearing sunglasses. Sunrise wasn't for another couple of hours.

Holly turned off her tunes and picked up her pace. The Man In Black picked up his pace, as well. There had been a spate of sexual assaults on the hike and bike trail in recent months, which had prompted Holly to purchase a self-defense pepper spray canister. But lately the city responded by increasing patrols along the trail. Assaults had all but ended. This morning, she had left her pepper spray at home.

A waning moon barely lit the winding trail. Holly accelerated to a dead run, trying desperately now to retrieve her cell phone from her sweatpants and dial 911. She hazarded a quick glance behind her, shocked to see that the Man In Black was almost upon her. But what shocked her more was the appearance of a shiny object in his left hand and a feral grin on his face. That's when she tripped on an exposed tree root and tumbled to the ground.

Running at full speed, the Man In Black went sailing over her prone body and landed hard on the crushed granite trail beyond her. Struggling to get up and reverse her direction, Holly heard a blood-curdling groan. The Man In Black had fallen on a large knife, which was now protruding from his midsection.

For a moment, Holly regained hope of escaping. But as she stood to run, her right ankle exploded in pain. *Damn! Great time to twist your ankle, Holly Girl!*

She stole a quick glance behind her. The Man In Black was standing now, and Holly watched in horror as he grimaced and slowly removed the fearsome knife from his bloody belly.

"Now I kill you, *coño!*" he hissed through gritted teeth.

Ignoring the searing pain in her ankle, Holly began backtracking on the trail, praying that someone would come to her aid. Gripping his bleeding torso, the Man In Black somehow matched her pace. Suddenly, he began to gain on her.

I am not going to die on this trail today, Holly promised herself.

But the Man In Black was slowly catching her. She could hear his labored breathing and imagined she could feel his fetid breath on the back of her neck.

Suddenly a bright spotlight blinded Holly and, with any luck, her assailant.

"Hold it right there, sir! Drop the knife or I'll shoot!" shouted a uniformed park ranger.

The Man In Black staggered to a halt, grinned a wolfish grin, then did what every Estevan Barrero lieutenant had sworn to do in this circumstance. He slowly slit his own throat.

Holly screamed as great gouts of the killer's blood splattered across her back and into her hair and eyes.

This can't be happening to me! Holly told herself as she collapsed into the park ranger's arms.

"You're late!" Lev Gingrich admonished his favorite reporter as she slunk into the office.

"Yeah, the trail almost killed me this morning," Holly replied sarcastically.

"Writing, not running, is what earns raises around here," Gingrich reminded her.

"Yeah, well I might have stumbled upon a cover story for the next issue this morning, Chief. What if I told you that my meddling almost got me killed today?"

"I'd say you need to go easy on the caffeine, Worthington. Last time I checked, jogging wasn't a blood sport."

"Oh yeah? Remember my cover story on Governor Swaggart's stupid Dome Over the Dome idea, Chief? That was, as I predicted, merely a diversion for Swaggart's real agenda. Dividing Texas into five states.

"Then go do that voodoo that you do so well, Worthington," Gingrich ordered.

62

"I NEED YOU!" Lt. Governor McClain called his Chief of staff, Rory Minton.

"You got me, Governor!" Minton replied as he hurried into McClain's office.

"Rory, I think we're on the verge of breaking Swaggart's stranglehold on Texas politics.

"If you're talking about the Cowgirl of Liberty, I agree," Minton said. "The Cowgirl's numbers are off the charts in the referendum!"

"I'm not talking about the Cowgirl, Rory. Although she has clearly captured the hearts of Texans. I'm talking about bringing down Swaggart and his band of billionaire bullies. We both know that he had a hand in getting the mayors of the major Texas cities elected. I don't think he plans to stop there."

"You think he's serious about dividing Texas into five states, Boss? Believe me, that's never going to happen!"

"Never say never, Rory. Swaggart's smarter than you think. But he's also got some dirty laundry. I intend to air it in public."

"What do you need *me* to do, Iain?"

"I need you to take one for the team."

☆

Tiffany Taylor finished the 10 o'clock weather and headed toward her dressing room.

"I hung your street clothes in the closet, Tiff," her assistant told her.

"Nothing casual about tonight, Angie. I've got a meeting with the governor."

"Kinda late for a meeting, isn't it?"

"He insisted we meet tonight in the Governor's Suite at the Driskill."

"Sweet!"

"Don't get any ideas, Angie. The governor's a married man. But there may come a time when I need a political favor. So I might as well start at the top!"

"As long as you don't start on your bottom, Sister!" Angela giggled.

"Not to worry," Tiffany assured her.

She should have worried.

When Tiffany Taylor stepped off the private elevator to the Governor's Suite, Bo was standing there in a silk smoking jacket, holding two flutes of champagne.

"Wellll, if it isn't my favorite weathergirl!"

"Meteorologist, Governor. Weather forecaster if you prefer."

"I'd prefer to offer you a glass of bubbly. Please, come inside," he said with a wink.

"If this is about the story the station did on your Dome Over the Dome idea, I had nothing to do with that, Sir."

"I'm sure you didn't, Tiffany. I don't think you would have called my idea 'Dumb Over the Dumb,' would you?"

"Again, not my story. I'm responsible for the weather."

"Do tell! I always figured that was God's domain. But then, who's to say God isn't a She, right?"

"May I ask why you've called me here tonight, Governor?"

"You certainly may, Tiffany. You know, I recently bought my wife an antique Tiffany lamp. Perhaps you'd like one as well?"

"No thank you, Governor. Now, about this important meeting?"

"Right. The truth is, I just wanted to see if you were as beautiful off screen as you are on screen. And it's clear to me that you are," he said, ogling her from head to toe. "Have a bit of bubbly, my dear. It's Dome Pear-ig-nome," Swaggart butchered the name of the fine French champagne.

Tiffany reluctantly took a sip. "

"You realize, Governor, that this champagne is named after Dom Pérignon, a monk and cellar master at the Benedictine abbey in Hautvillers, France.

Bo refilled her glass. "Tell me more," he encouraged her.

"Whoa, Governor! I need to slow down if we're going to have a conversation."

"Funny you should say 'conversation,' Tiffany. Are you aware it comes from the French word for intimacy?'"

"It's getting late, Governor, and I've got to do the weather early tomorrow morning. Why don't we reschedule this meeting for another time?"

"You're already dressed to do the weather tomorrow, Tiffany. Why don't you just stay the night. You can shower here in the morning and be on your way. The station is just down the road."

"And what would your wife have to say about that, Governor?" Tiffany asked, her eyes flashing daggers.

"Fifty Mile Rule."

"Fifty Mile Rule?"

"When you or your spouse is more than fifty miles from home, anything goes. And Vee's in Houston tonight."

"Thanks, but no thanks, Governor. I'll be leaving now."

"As you wish. But how about a little goodnight kiss for your Governor?"

Bo suddenly grabbed Tiffany, pulled her into a sickeningly tight embrace and kissed her, all the while pawing her with his hands.

Tiffany's reaction was swift and crushing. She kneed the Governor violently in his crotch and dumped a full flute of Don Pérignon over his head before spinning around and heading toward the private elevator. But not before predicting the weather:

"Tonight, there should be late swells, clearing slowly tomorrow. Ice is suspected until mid-morning, followed by intermittent patches of blue."

Writhing in agony on the floor, the Governor was not amused.

"Let me get this straight," his clearly perplexed chief of staff asked the Lt. Governor of Texas. "You want me to meet with the First Lady of Texas?"

"That's precisely what I'm suggesting, Rory," McClain said. "It's time she knew the truth about her visit to the Congo."

"And you actually think the First Lady of Texas is going to invite me to the Governor's Mansion?"

"Leave that to me, Rory. I'll come up with some reason you need her expert opinion. She'll probably think we want her to endorse the Cowgirl of Liberty."

McClain's Chief of staff chuckled. "If she's anything like I've heard, she'll probably want to model for the statue."

"Let her think what she wants, Rory. But wait until she hears the real reason you're meeting with her."

"And that would be?"

"To draw a line in the sand between the First Lady and her husband that the governor would be a damned fool to cross."

63

SOMEONE SET FIRE to the Governor's Mansion with a Molotov cocktail on June 8, 2008, while then-Governor Rick Perry and his wife Anita were in Europe.

They had relocated to a temporary mansion off-site in October 2007 while a ten-million- dollar major maintenance project on the mansion began in January 2008. Ironically, the project was to include a fire suppression system. The State Fire Marshall told the press that investigators had evidence that an arsonist had targeted the 152-year-old mansion.

In February of that year, the assistant director of the Texas Rangers announced that a person of interest had been identified who was connected to an Austin-based anarchist group. That same perpetrator had also been linked to an attack involving a Molotov cocktail planned for the Republican National Convention in St. Paul.

No one had ever been charged with the crime, and there had never been any evidence linking the incident to an anarchist movement.

In May 2009, twenty-two million dollars was allocated to the restoration of the Governor's Mansion, eleven million of which came from the American Recovery and Reinvestment Act of

2009. An additional three-and-a-half million was raised through private funding.

Security had been significantly increased throughout the mansion grounds. Texas State Troopers guarded every conceivable entry point 24 hours a day.

The Lt. Governor's Chief of staff was met at the main entrance to the Governor's Mansion by an armed state trooper. While the Ranger knew full-well who Rory was, he was required to ask for official identification.

Rory was tempted but wisely declined to make any jokes about cocktails, Molotov or otherwise. After presenting his credentials, the trooper stepped politely aside as the front door of the mansion opened.

"Good morning, Mr. Minton!" said a cheery, matronly-looking woman. "My name is Bonnie Caldwell and I'll be your docent today."

"Actually, I'm here to see First Lady Swaggart," Rory said.

"And see her you will, Mr. Minton. But first, the First Lady has asked me to show you around our beautifully renovated public spaces."

"That won't be necessary, Ms. Caldwell. I…"

"Not only is it necessary, Mr. Minton, it will be my pleasure. First, let's step into the Blue Room, followed by the Green Room, the State Dining Room, the Family Dining Room…"

"I'll take it from here, Bonnie," the First Lady of Texas said as she slowly descended the impressive master staircase from the second floor in a striking Armani Collezioni featherweight wool suit and Jimmy Choo pumps.

"But Madam First Lady, we were just getting started," the docent protested.

"As I said, Bonnie, that will be all. A pleasure to meet you, Mr. Minton. How have I rated a visit from the Lt. Governor's handsome Chief of staff?"

"Lt. Governor McClain sends his warmest regards, Madam First Lady. He heard through the grapevine that you may have taken an interest in his Cowgirl of Liberty project."

"That I have, Mr. Minton. Shall we continue this conversation upstairs, in the First Family Quarters? Besides, I'd love to show you my recent renovations."

"How can I say no to a private tour, Madam First Lady?"

"You can't, Rory. I insist!" Veronica said, taking Rory's arm and guiding him up the richly carpeted grand staircase.

"This is the Governor's Master Bedroom," Veronica sneered. "As you can see, Rory. May I call you Rory? It's dreadfully boring, wouldn't you agree?" Rory fidgeted nervously.

"And this is my masterpiece. My very own Governess's Suite Bedroom. This is how lots of money and lots of class can transform a useless guest bedroom into a showstopper. Now, if you'll excuse me, I think I'll slip out of this fancy dress and into something a bit more comfortable. Feel free to look around."

Rory silently cursed his boss for putting him in this uncomfortable predicament.

When Veronica returned from her dressing area, she was wearing a scarlet silk kimono. Apparently not much else. Rory averted his eyes.

"What's the matter, Rory? Don't like what you see?"

"I've just come to deliver a private message from the Lt. Governor, Madam First Lady, nothing more."

"Nothing more, Rory? Perhaps this will change your mind." With that, Veronica let the slinky kimono slide to the floor, revealing that she was very tan. Very fit. And very naked.

"Lt. Governor McClain simply wanted you to know that it was he who paid your ransom to the Congolese terrorists, Madam First Lady," Rory blurted as he headed for the door.

"If that's true, Rory, I owe him my life. Should I repay him. Or his messenger?"

Rory brushed by docent Caldwell on his rush out of the Mansion.

"Did the First Lady let you in on any state secrets, Mr. Minton?" she asked coyly.

"Indeed she did, Ms. Caldwell. She bared her soul."

Part VI:

E Unum Pluribus

64

E Pluribus Unum. Latin for Out of Many, One. It is the traditional motto of the United States, appearing on the Great Seal.

If Texas Governor Beauregard Swaggart got his way, the gold and silver commemorative coins of Texas, which currently bear the Great Seal of Texas on one side and 'Don't mess with Texas' on the reverse, would have the following motto added: E Unum Pluribus. Out of One, Many. Confirmation of Swaggart's controversial mission to divide Texas into five states.

Privately, Bo had already commissioned a coin maker to cast such a coin. He would secretly receive a generous commission for his idea.

The Five State Referendum, which the press now referred to as TX5, was unexpectedly gathering steam. Apparently, Dallas was warming to the idea of being the capital of North Texas. Houston responded by supporting their "inalienable" right to become the capital of East Texas.

Mayor Alexa King was busy measuring the drapes for her planned major renovation of the sprawling Dallas Infomart into her very own capitol. "When I'm done, the North Texas Capitol will be the crown jewel of World Heritage Sites," she mused.

Houston Mayor Jeremiah Jones was sipping a wee dram of The Macallan 18 single malt whisky and puffing on a Montecristo

No. 2 Cuban cigar when his chief of staff interrupted his reverie. "Mayor, that famous architect is here to see you, sir."

Mayor Estevan Barrero had all but paid for the votes to ensure that Laredo would become the capital of South Texas, a new state that would faithfully elect him governor.

One hundred fifty miles to the northwest, Rhett McCullum was blowing a gasket. "It'll be a cold day in hell when Laredo becomes the capital of South Texas! Laredo is nothing but a suburb of the magnificent city of San Antonio. Texans remember the Alamo, not some one-horse border town!"

Out in the West Texas town of El Paso, Mayor Ponce Ponzio was inspecting the masterplan for his underground capitol building on the Ft. Bliss Army Base grounds.

Recovering from a recent injury to his nether regions, Governor Beauregard Swaggart was nonetheless ebullient about the recent polls showing statewide interest in his Project Pentagram.

"If I can pull this off, I can own the world!" he told himself. "The Western world, at least."

"What the fuck?!" Lt. Governor McClain shouted.

"Are you referring to the new numbers on TX5, Boss?" chief of staff Minton asked.

"Swaggart's idiotic plan to divide Texas is polling even better than my plan to replace the Goddess of Liberty with the Cowgirl of Liberty.

"Welcome to the Tea Party, Iain.

"I'm in no mood for levity, Rory. Yesterday, Texas was prepared to dance with my Cowgirl of Liberty. Today they're letting the biggest phony in politics cut in. How does that happen?"

"In a word? Greed. Bo Swaggart might as well be Gordon Gekko.

"But don't Texans understand that dividing Texas into five states will help Swaggart and only hurt them?"

"Maybe it's time we trump Swaggart, boss. Maybe it's time we brought in the big guns."

"Just who do you have in mind, Chief?"

"A gang of Texas cowgirls. You know what they say, 'Hell hath no fury like a woman scorned.' And believe me, Swaggart has scorned his fair share of Texas women!"

"Sounds like it may be time to wrangle us some cowgirls, Rory. Just remember, mum's the word!"

"Ma'am's the word, boss. And I think I know just where to begin wrangling."

65

A PRIVATE GATHERING of strong-willed Texas women was scheduled at the Cloak Room on a Sunday afternoon when the dive bar was officially closed.

Among the invitees were the Cloak Room's own Brenda Prendahl. Holly Worthington, who invited Max Sinclair. Texas Senator Bethany Jordan. The First Lady's private caterer Becky Walford. And three late additions. Local weather forecaster Tiffany Taylor. Sister Mary Celine. And the Governor's chambermaid, Marina Alvarez.

Author Max Sinclair was assigned double duty. Gatekeeper and scribe. Max met each attendee at the door. Once they were all gathered, he stepped inside and slid the deadbolt.

Max surveyed the gathering. "Ladies, there haven't been this many strong women in a room together since the MeToo Movement. You all know why we're here. Texas has a governor intent on dividing our great state into five states."

Holly blushed. She was, she realized, one of the reasons this meeting had been called. Her recent articles in LONE STAR had clearly unmasked Governor Swaggart as a braggart and laid bare his devious intentions. Holly suddenly had a quick flashback to her attempted assault on the Hike & Bike Trail. She shuddered uncontrollably. LONE STAR publisher Lev Gingrich had offered to provide her with around-the-clock security. Holly had politely yet resolutely declined.

The women shuffled nervously, waiting for someone to take charge.

Senator Jordan rose to the occasion. "Ladies, may I suggest we take our seats at the table Ms. Prendahl has so graciously reserved for us."

Everyone waited for the Senator to choose her seat, then quickly took their places around the table.

"Ladies, may I offer you a cocktail or a glass of wine?" Brenda Prendahl asked. "After all, it's five o'clock somewhere. Drinks are on me."

Senator Jordan ordered a double bourbon, neat. Holly requested a shot of tequila to calm her nerves. Becky Walford opted for the Green Fairy, absinthe. Tiffany Taylor, who had to go on camera in a few hours, settled for iced coffee. Sister Mary Celine surprised everyone by ordering red wine. At first, Marina Alvarez politely declined, then reconsidered. "Mezcal, *por favor!* And don't forget the *gusano,* the worm!" she giggled.

Max Sinclair ordered the usual. A Templeton Rye Double Old Fashioned.

Brenda set to work mixing drinks behind the bar, occasionally stopping to take a healthy slug of her own special poison. A Vesper made with top shelf gin, a mildly bitter aperitif, and a lemon twist. According to legend, it was James Bond's favorite martini.

When everyone had been served, Senator Jordan tapped her glass. "Let's get this party started. I successfully infiltrated one of First Lady Swaggart's infamous Spring Flings, where she treated her millionaire and billionaire friends to quite an evening. At the taxpayers' expense, mind you. Unfortunately, she saw through my flimsy disguise as one of Becky's catering staff and had the nerve to threaten me. Said she could end my career with a snap of her finger. Well, pardon my French, ladies, but I have a message for the First Lady. Bring it, bitch!"

"Maybe I should chime in here," Becky Walford interrupted. "I have video on my laptop of the shenanigans after you were dismissed, Senator. Believe me when I say that the First Lady can ill-afford for this video to see the light of day. At the very least, her billionaire BFFs would run like scalded dogs. And imagine what Texas taxpayers would do if they found out the First Lady was hosting wild parties, with male escorts, in their beloved Capitol!"

Tiffany Taylor just smiled and sipped her coffee. "Let me just say, ladies, that if the Governor plans to sing in the church choir anytime soon, he'll be singing soprano."

Sister Mary Celine blushed. "Well, this certainly isn't what we were taught in the convent. To be perfectly honest, it was Governor Swaggart himself who went to bat for me when his predecessor tried to throw me under the bus for aiding and abetting a peaceful protest for Planned Parenthood. But frankly, I don't like him and I don't trust him," she said, emboldened by her glass of wine.

"Are there any other revelations we should know about?" Senator Jordan asked.

Maria cleared her throat sheepishly. "My job is to clean up after Governor Swaggart's messes. I may know something about his after-hour meetings with a woman who isn't his wife.".

"Got anything to top that, Max?" Holly asked.

"As a matter of fact, I just might," Max grinned.

66

"A LITTLE BIRDIE told me that our good Governor might have been involved in collusion with some of our recently elected Texas mayors," Max said, winking at Brenda Prendahl. "And there's a rumor that he might have higher offices in mind for his hand-picked mayors."

"Are you suggesting that Swaggart is conspiring to get certain individuals elected governors of his five new states of Texas?" Holly Worthington chimed in. "That would be…"

"…grounds for impeachment, Holly?" Max concluded. "It would, indeed. But it wouldn't stop there. I'm no lawyer, but my guess is some pretty high-falutin' Texas politicians might be spending some quality time behind bars right along with him."

"Let's not get ahead of ourselves here, ladies and gentlemen," Senator Jordan interrupted. "Collusion is a mighty strong word. I trust we have some equally strong evidence?"

"Without naming names, Senator, a friend of mine overheard Governor Swaggart offer to make one of our new Texas mayors the Governor of the State of West Texas, right here in the Cloak Room."

All eyes turned to Brenda, who continued to sip her Vesper.

"Not that there's anything illegal about the governor discussing future political elections," Max said. "But if those future political elections were for positions that don't exist, it might raise some eyebrows in the State Senate and House. Not to mention a few Texas courts-of-law."

"Are you suggesting that Swaggart is trying to stuff the ballot box with his own favorite sons, Max?" Senator Jordan asked.

"Certainly sounds like it, Senator. "I have it on good authority that Swaggart is grooming both three men and one woman for his five-state boondoggle. As Governor of Central Texas, he'll round out the quintet."

"As I understand the law," Senator Jordan said, "collusion includes any secret or illegal cooperation or conspiracy whose aim is to cheat or deceive others."

Max nodded. "I see you know your law, Senator. If, in fact, Swaggart instigates a coup, with his handpicked mayors becoming his handpicked governors, I'd say that constitutes collusion."

"Claiming collusion and proving it are two very different things," Senator Jordan reminded him.

"That's where the women in this room have an opportunity to repay the State of Texas for its many blessings," Max replied.

"Count me in!" Holly Worthington said, raising her shot glass.

"In for a penny, in for a pound!" Senator Jordan chimed in.

"Guess I just lost my plum catering job with the First Lady!" Becky Walford said, indicating to bartender Prendahl that her glass of absinthe had mysteriously evaporated.

Tiffany raised her empty mug. "Another iced coffee, please, Brenda. And this time, splash a little Bailey's in it. I've got a feeling that tonight's weather is about to get a little inclement. Or perhaps I should say, indictment!"

"Oh Lord!" Sister Mary Celine shrugged. "I usually ask what Jesus would do. But this one time, I believe I'll side with my sisters."

"*¡Madre de Dios!*" Marina whispered, tears in her eyes. "I am too old to find a new job. But I'm tired of letting that gringo determine my fate."

"That just leaves you, Brenda," Max said. "I know we'd hate to see you lose your job, or worse yet, see the Cloak Room shut down."

"Don't worry about me, Max. I've got enough dirt on enough Texas politicians to send 'em all straight to hell in a handbasket. Like the slogan says, 'Don't mess with Texas. Or Texas women, for that matter!'"

"Then it's decided," Max said, making eye contact with the women in the room one-by-one, eliciting a hesitant nod from each. "God Bless Texas!" Max raised his glass and proclaimed.

"And God Bless Texas Women!" the attendees toasted in unison.

Less than a block away, Governor Beauregard Swaggart strode restlessly around his office, his precious Bowie knife in his fist.

"If no one gets in my way, I might actually be able to pull this off!" The governor stabbed the huge dagger into his desk for emphasis.

67

"Admiral Vanessa Ingram, to what do I owe the honor of this call?" Max asked, cradling his cell phone to his ear as he drove along a Texas backroad in his vintage French automobile. Max knew Admiral Ingram, director of Defense Clandestine Service, an arm of the U.S. Defense Intelligence Agency, from previous experience.

"Please, just call me 'Six,' Max. Everybody else does. And after our little adventure in San Marcos a couple of years ago, I believe we can dispense with any formalities. How the hell are you?"

"Never better, Admir…Six. Although I have to say, things seem to be heating up again here in the Lone Star State."

"So I hear. Which is why I'm calling."

Max pulled off the side of the road. "So this isn't a social call, I take it?"

"Anything but, I'm afraid, Max. Tell me what you know about this kerfuffle I hear about dividing Texas into five states."

"Kerfuffle is too kind a word, Six. Our governor has taken it upon himself to hold a referendum to see if he can convince Texans that his cockamamie plan is in their best interest."

"Cockamamie. Another great word, Max. You should consider writing," Six teased. "I'll give Texans the benefit of the doubt on how they'll vote. But what I can't abide is what seems to be happening right under Uncle Sam's nose down in Laredo."

"Are we talking about Mayor Estevan Barrero's construction project?"

"Precisely. And I'm much more concerned about what's going on below ground than what's rising above."

"You want me to go snoop around down there, Six?"

"Actually, I'd prefer you look into what's going on in El Paso."

"Are we talking about the homicide that put Ponce Ponzio in the mayor's office?"

"Whether it was a homicide or simply an unfortunate accident has never been proven. That's where you come in, Max."

"You want me to drive out to El Paso and see what's what?"

"I want you to drive to Ciudad Juarez, across the border from El Paso, and nose around."

"I'm afraid my Spanish *no es muy bueno,* Six. About all I can manage is *¡Otra cerveza, por favor!* and *¿Donde es el baño?*'"

"You'll do fine, Max. Money talks in Mexico. Especially greenbacks from gringo*s.*"

"Do I have a choice, Madam Director?"

"Ask not what your country can do for you, Max. Ask..."

"...what I can do for my country. I get it. Okay, count me in."

"That's the answer I was looking for. How's your daughter Sunny and that new grandson of yours?"

"Sunny's doing great in her new job. And Jackson is a firecracker!"

Six chuckled. "Gee, I wonder where he gets *that*, Max? Your daughter was very brave during that incident at Texas State University, Max. And I know where she gets that."

"And I'm guessing that the first female member of SEAL Team Six knows a little something about bravery."

"It's a job, just like...whatever it is you do, Max."

"Recovering adman. Full-time author. Part-time sleuth. Need I go on?"

"In the interest of time, let's stick to the plan, shall we? I'll email you my directive via secure server within the hour. How soon can you head to El Paso?"

"As soon as I receive your directive, along with an ample supply of walkin' around money, Madam Director."

"Roger that. And I'll make you a deal, Max. You don't ever call me Madam Director and I won't ever call you Maximilian."

"You know my given name?"

"Max, rest assured, there is nothing I don't know about you."

"Now *there's* a scary thought!"

"Max let's not have any secrets between the two of us. Do you have a handgun handy? And a concealed-carry permit?"

"Texas is pretty much open carry these days, Six."

"Yeah, well I don't think it's wise to saunter into a bar in Juarez with a weapon visible."

"Point taken, Six. What do you suggest?"

"Tomorrow you will receive a FedEx package that you'll need to sign for. Inside you'll find a rather unusual weapon. One of only a half-dozen 3-D printed revolvers we seized from a Japanese yakuza. It's designed to fire six .38-caliber bullets. It's called a Zig-Zag, modeled after the German Mauser Zig-Zag."

"Hold on, Six. This sounds like I'm getting in way over my head!"

"Not to worry, Max. We'll have eyes on you. Just remember, when the shooting starts, you might want to zigzag a bit yourself."

68

A slow night in Austin meant you could usually find the First Lady of Texas, seated on her private swivel stool at the Driskill Hotel Bar.

The Driskill Hotel is well-known political hangout. On August 31, 1934, Lyndon Baines Johnson and Claudia Alta Taylor went on their first date, meeting for breakfast in the Driskill Dining Room.

On November 3, 1964, President Lyndon Baines Johnson watched the returns of the 1964 Presidential Election in the Jim Hogg Suite. The hotel later served as the White House Press Center when the President and First Lady were in Texas.

In March 1991, the rock band Concrete Blonde penned their hit, *Ghost of a Texas Ladies' Man,* about the ghosts that supposedly haunt the hotel. Some believe LBJ himself may be among those spirits.

President William Jefferson Clinton stayed in the four-room Cattle Barron's Suite when he visited Austin in 1999.

On this particular night, the First Lady of Texas was sullen. Her husband, the governor, was out of town yet again, this time in Dallas, and probably screwing Alexa King. Veronica nibbled half-heartedly on some homemade beef jerky and fiddled with a tray of wild boar mini corn dogs.

"Bring me another Double B, Johnny!" she slurred to the bartender. Her cocktail of choice was the Brazos Batini.

"Coming right up, Vee!" the bartender replied. Given how often Veronica haunted this downtown bar, she allowed the bartender to call her Vee. Besides, he was kind of cute, in a boyish way. Nothing like the dark, handsome gentleman seated across from her who had been eyeing her all evening.

"The gentleman in the navy suit would like to buy this round," Johnny told Veronica when he placed her third martini in front of her.

"Well, well, well!" Veronica brightened. "Tell the gentleman there's an empty stool right here next to mine if he'd care to join me. Be sure you tell him I don't bite. At least not this early in the evening."

"Name's Daniel," the tall stranger said as he eased onto the stool beside her. "And if I'm not mistaken, you're the First Lady of Texas."

"I have a name, too, Daniel. It's Veronica. This might be the most handsome man she'd ever met. Or at least the most handsome man she'd met this evening.

"Would you like to come up to my place for a nightcap, Daniel? My bar never closes.

"Someplace where we can talk privately would be nice, Veronica."

Upstairs in the Governor's Mansion, in the newly remodeled Governess Suite, Veronica slipped out of her stilettos and pointed toward her private wet bar.

"Why don't you mix us up a couple of vodka tonics while I slip into something more comfortable, Daniel."

"My pleasure, Mrs. Swaggart. But don't get too comfortable. We really need to talk."

Veronica winked. "Talk is cheap, Daniel. I'm not."

The stranger mixed a light vodka tonic for her and a straight tonic for himself.

When Veronica reappeared, it was in a luxurious Giacomo dressing gown. In her carefully manicured right hand, she held a small white packet with a red triangle in the corner. In her left hand she held a small pair of scissors. As the stranger watched, she slit open the packet and removed a celluloid square. Daniel immediately recognized the fentanyl transdermal patch. Veronica expertly snipped off a quarter of the celluloid square and popped it in her mouth.

"While I chew on this patch, Daniel, why don't you chew on my patch," Veronica purred, untying her gown to reveal her Brazilian-waxed nether regions.

"This might be a good time to formerly introduce myself, Mrs. Swaggart. I'm Agent Daniel Mueller with the Austin office of the Federal Bureau of Investigation. An autopsy on your friend who was murdered in cold blood in the Democratic Republic of Congo revealed traces of alcohol, cocaine, and fentanyl in her bloodstream. I'm here to inform you that you are under investigation for possession and distribution of unlawful controlled substances. It also appears that you just placed a quarter patch of fentanyl in your mouth. Do you happen to have a prescription for that?

"Wh…WHAT??? Do you know who I *am*, Agent Mueller?" Veronica shouted, gathering her gown around her. "Get out! Get out of my house! NOW! Don't make me call security!"

"That won't be necessary, First Lady Swaggart. I alerted your security of my presence when I entered the Mansion. And for your information, this is not your house. The Governor's Mansion belongs to all Texans. You are merely a visitor. And, if I may be permitted to speculate, not for much longer."

69

Sleuth Max Sinclair sat patiently in his vintage Citroën, mired in a long line of cars waiting to cross the Bridge of the Americas spanning the Rio Grande between El Paso, Texas and Juárez, Mexico.

He wore faded blue jeans, a jaunty silk shirt, mirrored sunglasses, a gaudy pinkie ring, and a Panama hat. Max found the name Panama mildly humorous, since he knew the classic straw fedoras were handmade in Ecuador.

Max turned off his engine to save gas, which tripped the hydropneumatic self-leveling suspension, lowering his odd-looking French automobile several inches.

After a long wait, Max was next in line. He muted legendary jazz saxophonist John Coltrane's *Giant Steps,* rolled down his window, and handed the Mexico border guard his driver's license.

"*Buenos días, Señor Sinclair.* What brings you to Juárez? Business or pleasure?"

"A bit of both. I'm writing a book about the borderlands, and I have a meeting with someone to learn more about life south of the border."

The border guard glanced suspiciously at Max's car. "Just what kind of car is this, if you don't mind me asking, Señor."

"Not at all, Officer. This is a French-made 1975 Citroën DS 23 Pallas. Perhaps the finest motorcar ever built."

"Looks like an *escarabajo*. A beetle."

"I get that," Max said. "Some say it looks like a horseshoe crab. To me, it's Brigitte Bardot on wheels."

"Mind if I ask what is in the box in the backseat, Señor Sinclair?"

Max turned around and stared at the object in the back seat as if he wasn't aware it was there.

"That? Looks like LEGOs, those plastic construction bricks kids love to play with. Guess my grandson Jackson must've left 'em the last time he was in my car."

"May I have a look, Señor Sinclair?"

"Be my guest. My grandson never seems to finish any of his creations. So there may be a few unfinished masterpieces among the bricks."

Max handed the box to the border guard. It did, indeed, contain hundreds of multicolored plastic bricks, along with a few odd-shaped plastic pieces the border guard assumed were some of the grandson's creations.

"Looks like your grandson is *un arquitecto*, an architect, Señor Sinclair. Enjoy your visit in Juárez."

"This is one of those in-and-out, nobody-gets-hurt kind of trips, Officer. I'll be back in the good old U.S. of A. by nightfall."

"*¡Buena suerte*, good luck. Some say Ciudad Juárez is *muy mal*, very bad. *¡Vaya con Dios!*"

When Max was safely across the bridge, he pulled over to the side of the road and reached for the LEGO box in the backseat. Inside, he rummaged around until he found the plastic parts he'd hidden among the partially completed constructions.

Slowly, Max reassembled the random plastic pieces into the Zig-Zag 3-D printed revolver that Admiral Ingram had sent him.

Then he opened a concealed chamber in the French car's elaborate console and inserted six .38-caliber bullets into the plastic gun. Shoving the weapon into the rear waistband of his blue jeans, Max started the fuel-injected four-cylinder engine. The hydropneumatic suspension automatically raised the car several inches.

Max glanced at the map he retrieved from the door pocket, where he had circled Juárez City. A quick Google search had told him more than he wanted to know about Juárez City. "Welcome to Mexico's Murder Valley, a ghost town so dangerous even police don't dare enter."

Unfortunately, that's where Admiral Ingram had told him to meet his target, a shady informant named Pedro Gutierrez.

Juárez City lived up to its reputation: Burnt bodies in the streets. Blood splatters against the walls. Home to dangerous drug cartels locked in a never-ending war. Only 5,000 of the original 60,000 inhabitants had dared to remain. The rest had fled in fear of their lives.

Max drove slowly down the dusty streets, searching for the rendezvous point, a ramshackle bar named *El Diablo*. He drove past it twice before realizing that there was no sign, save for a crudely drawn horned figure, engulfed in hand-painted flames.

What's that old Irish prayer? Max asked himself. *May you be in heaven three days before the devil knows you're dead.*

The inside of *El Diablo* was worse than the outside. Dirt floor. A bar constructed of rusted corrugated metal and splintered driftwood. Kerosene lanterns hanging from the cobwebbed ceiling. Crippled folding chairs surrounding a few ancient cable spools that doubled as tables.

A lone mustachioed bartender smoking a vile-smelling cheroot glared at him when he pushed through swinging doors. The joint was empty, except for one skinny, disheveled soul with his back to the wall in a dark corner.

"*Dos cervezas, por favor,*" Max said to the bartender, using four of the few Spanish words he knew.

The bartender reached under the bar, causing Max to flinch, and produced two dusty bottles of Modelo Negra. "*¿Limón?*" the bartender grunted. "*Por favor,*" Max answered.

Easing slowly over to the pitiful figure in the corner, Max placed the two beers on the table. "Might you be Pedro Gutierrez?"

"*¡Si, Señor!*" the wizened man answered, glancing around furtively, clearly nervous.

"My name's Max. I only have one question for you, Señor Gutierrez. Who ordered the murder of the former mayor of El Paso?"

"*No lo sé*. I don't know, Señor Max," the Mexican whispered.

"Perhaps this will jog your memory, Pedro," Max said, slipping the pinky ring off his finger. "This is a pink diamond from Australia. I'm told it's worth five grand. That's what? Half a million Mexican pesos?"

The old man stared at the ring, then back at Max. "*Dámelo.* Give it to me."

Max complied, and the old man lurched over to the mirror behind the makeshift bar and scratched it roughly across the blotchy surface. The pink diamond etched a deep scar in the mirror. Satisfied, the old man stumbled back to the table and drank his beer dry. Then he muttered an unintelligible name.

"Pepe?" Max said. "That's all you've got, Old Timer? Give me back that ring!"

"Not *Pepe*, Señor, *Popo.* Perhaps you've heard of him? Ponce Ponzio?"

Max couldn't believe his ears. According to this informant, vetted by Admiral Ingram herself, the man who ordered the murder of the former mayor of El Paso was the current mayor of El Paso.

When Max turned back to the table, the old man was gone. So was the bartender. And outside the bar, Max heard a strange hissing sound.

70

THE HISSING STOPPED. As Max approached the dilapidated swinging doors of *El Diablo* bar, everything got unnervingly quiet.

Outside, three thugs surrounded his vintage car. Two of them were shorter, dark-skinned Mexicans. The third was taller and fairer. Perhaps Colombian.

The first thing Max noticed was that his right rear tire was flat. Not low, flat. As if someone had recently punctured it with a sharp object.

"*¡Mala suerte, Señor!* Bad luck! It appears you won't be going anywhere," the Colombian grinned, exposing crooked yellow teeth.

"I'm just minding my own business here, gentlemen. Perhaps you three amigo*s* should do the same."

The sound of a switchblade snicking open cut short the conversation.

"*De lo contrario, Señor,*" the knife-bearing Colombian sneered. "Your business here *es terminado.* Finished, just like you!"

The Colombian with the switchblade lunged toward Max, who had just enough time to retrieve the pistol from his waistband and fire a .38-caliber round into the attacker's kneecap.

"*¡Hijo de puta!*" the Colombian shouted as he dropped to the ground. His compadres wasted no time running from the scene of the crime.

Leaning over the wounded man, Max grabbed the switchblade from his clenched palm.

"I've always wanted one of these, amigo," Max whispered menacingly in the groaning man's ear. "But switchblades are illegal in the United States. Oh well, what the hell!"

Max closed the blade and slipped the illicit weapon into his jeans pocket. "Better have someone look at that knee, amigo."

"*¡Chinga tu madre!*" the Colombian hissed through clenched teeth.

"Let's leave my mother out of this, if you don't mind," Max growled, then kicked his assailant fiercely in the jaw, knocking him out cold.

"Okay, Brigitte, let's show these hooligans what you can do, mi amour," Max said, stroking the fender of his beloved French motorcar.

Max slid into the driver's seat, withdrew the car keys from his jeans pocket, slid them into the ignition and started the engine. Almost immediately, the Citroën's hydropneumatic suspension lifted the car from the mud-caked road. The flat right rear tire was now suspended several inches off the ground.

"We gringos have a few tricks up our sleeves as well!" Max leaned out the driver's window and spat at the unconscious assailant.

Max shifted into Drive and headed toward the Bridge of the Americas on three operable tires. He drove with his knees as he disassembled the plastic revolver and placed what he hoped were unrecognizable pieces back into the LEGO box.

"Welcome back to El Paso, Sir," the U.S. guard said, while eyeing the interior of the odd-looking car. "Do you have anything to declare?"

"I declare I'm glad to be back in the good old U.S. of A.!"

"Would you mind stepping out of the car, Sir?"

"What I meant to say, Officer, is that I have nothing to declare."

"Just a formality, Sir. May I see your driver's license, your passport, and your proof of insurance? And would you open your trunk, please.

Miffed, but not foolish, Max complied.

The U.S. border guard probed the capacious Citroën trunk, tossing fishing gear aside and lifting the floor mat, exposing the spare tire. He shone a flashlight in the nooks and crannies before roughly slamming the trunk shut.

"Easy does it!" Max said.

The border guard paid him no mind. "What's in the box in the backseat, Mr. Sinclair?"

"Oh that?" Max answered. "Are you familiar with the plastic building blocks called LEGOs? Do you have grandchildren?"

"Children. Three boys."

"Tell you what, Officer. My grandson has thousands of the damned things. Why don't I just give these to you for your kids," Max said handing him the box.

But instead of thanking him, the border guard opened the box and began rummaging through the plastic pieces inside.

Suddenly two people appeared. A high-ranking American border officer and a tall woman in a grey business suit.

"This man is with us," Admiral Vanessa Ingram said to the U.S. border guard, flashing her Defense Department credentials.

The U.S. border guard simply saluted and handed the box of LEGOs back to Max.

"Keep 'em," Max said. "Maybe your boys can make something that will come in handy in El Paso. I'm told it's the second safest city in America."

"Follow me, Max," the Admiral barked, pointing to a convoy of armored black Suburbans.

71

The good news, of which there seemed to be precious little these days, was that First Lady Swaggart's anti-drug program was a surprising success.

Thanks in part to tremendous strides made by the School of Social Work at The University of Texas at Austin, opioid abuse was trending downward.

The cannabis supply from Mexico had decreased, with increases instead coming from the use of home-grown and hydroponic methods and the availability of high-quality cannabis from Colorado.

Cocaine was still readily available. But the supply had been unstable given the cartel wars, with amounts seized at the Texas-Mexico border down by double digits.

At the same time, methamphetamine use was increasing.

Heroin was trending downward. A result of abusive over-prescription of hydrocodone.

PCP remained a problem. While the number of PCP items identified by forensic labs was dropping, patients who required hospital care had often taken "K2" or "Spice," which exhibits the classic PCP signs.

Yet, despite the First Lady's personal predilection for fentanyl, more and more Texans were ditching, or at least limiting, their opioid use.

The University of Texas at Austin School of Social Work had recently received a twenty-five million dollars donation from one of its regents.

The regent, a serial entrepreneur, didn't have a background in social work. But he had always been focused on supporting institutions and causes that directly helped people with addictions.

He should know. He was a recovering alcoholic himself.

"I think we have a great society, but in every social system, parts of it break from time to time and the social workers are there to pick up the pieces, whether in the hospitals or recovery centers, assisted living facilities and the prisons," the regent said in an interview.

Texans have had a legendary love affair with alcohol. Many Texans were descendants of hard-drinking Anglo-Saxon ancestors. They faced a life of rural hardship and tedium and a diet consisting largely of meats preserved by heavy salting. Salt makes one mighty thirsty.

When Texans decided to give up or at least cut back on opioids, they decided to dial-up their consumption of alcohol. Austin had recently been listed as the 16th drunkest city in America.

First Lady Swaggart chalked that up as a victory. True, Texans might be hitting the bottle a bit more often. But at least fewer Texans were dying of opioid poisoning.

"I'll drink to that!" Veronica said over breakfast the next morning. And drink she did.

72

GOLD FOR DIAMONDS. That was an offer that Duchel Mafinga, commander of an elite cadre of DRC troops, simply could not refuse.

The offer to purchase blood diamonds in exchange for gold bullion came from a reputable figure within the United States military. Commander Mafinga had done business with shady sources within the U.S. military before.

While the Democratic Republic of Congo's newly elected President accepted economic assistance from the U.S. government, Commander Mafinga found it easier and more profitable to conduct business with soldiers of fortune like himself.

The offer was tempting, indeed. Ten million dollars of untraceable gold bullion in exchange for a bagful of diamonds mined in a war zone and sold to finance an insurgency. The new President's days were numbered, by Mafinga's estimate.

Mafinga's instructions were crystal clear: Just before sunrise, a U.S. Air Force Lockheed AC-130 aircraft was to land at Kitona Air Base, a Democratic Republic of Congo military airport. The plane was to be met only by Commander Mafinga and his elite squad. The exchange, gold for diamonds, would take place in less than two minutes, and the American airplane would be airborne again.

If things went according to plan, Commander Mafinga would be named the new Major General of the DR Congolese Air Force. From there, the DRC presidency was but a coup d'état away.

The date agreed upon was 17 May, DRC Liberation Day. The military airport was a ghost town, save for Commander Mafinga's elite force and one of his hand-picked air traffic controllers.

Just as the sun rose, a ghost-grey Lockheed AC-130 appeared on the horizon. Commander Mafinga mustered his troops to attention near where the plane would land and instructed them to be on the alert for anything suspicious.

Unbeknown to Commander Mafinga, this AC-130 was the latest black-ops version of the aircraft, code-named the AC-130J Ghostrider. Ghostrider is military parlance for a gunship armed with a 105mm cannon and Standoff Precision Guided Munitions comprised of wing-mounted GBU-39 small diameter bombs, AMG-176 Griffin laser-guided missiles, and a 30mm GAU-23 Bushmaster Automatic Cannon side-firing chain gun.

Commander Mafinga squinted as the large aircraft floated in for a landing, massive tires smoking as the pilot braked hard on the pitted macadam. Mafinga thought he could just barely make out the name on the nose of the ominous military plane. ANGEL OF DEATH.

The AC-130J taxied to a stop, then slowly began to taxi toward Mafinga's men, standing at attention, AK-47s resting on their shoulders. Slowly, the plane presented its port side. To seasoned battle commanders, this might have set off alarms. But Mafinga had never laid eyes on such an imposing aircraft and he simply grinned broadly, awaiting delivery of his precious gold bullion.

What he and his cadre received, instead, was heavy metal.

The gas-operated AK-47 assault rifles that Mafinga's men shouldered were chambered with 7.62x39mm rounds, rimless bottlenecked intermediate cartridges of Soviet origin. No match for a GAU-23. While the AK-47 was designed to kill, the chain gun was designed to vaporize.

A moment too late, Mafinga realized what was about to happen. His plan was always to attack first. But like any good military man knows, no plan survives first contact with the enemy.

The first contact with the Ghostrider's chain gun was utterly devastating. Commander Mafinga and his entire squad were instantly reduced to a fine red mist. Moments later, one of the Ghostrider's laser-guided missiles slammed into the airfield's control tower, killing the sole air traffic controller before he could alert the rest of the Congolese Air Force, who were slowly sobering up from the Liberation Day festivities.

"Don't mess with Texas!" the soldier manning the chain gun shouted.

"Wheels up!" the co-pilot ordered the Ghostrider pilot.

"Aye-Aye, Six," the pilot replied to Admiral Ingram before taxiing down the runway and lifting off as the sun rose over the DRC.

DRC President Tshisekedi would later order a full-scale investigation of what happened at the Kitona Air Force Base that day. But the grim truth would never see the light of day.

Back in the United States, the family of the slain friend of First Lady Veronica Swaggart and the families of the two dead pilots were solemnly handed handsome presentation cases containing Lone Star flags, along with deepest sympathies for the families' unfortunate losses.

73

THE DARK WEB is a very scary place. A secret space for drug dealers, arms traffickers, hackers, and political dissidents. Some believe it is funded by the U.S. government.

Jeremiah Jones was no stranger to the Darknet, where retail sites function like Amazon, except that you can purchase psychedelics and AK-47s instead of woks and lawn ornaments. This evening, Jeremiah was searching for a toxicologist. Not just any toxicologist. One who specialized in poisoning people for profit.

The name Salvatore Minelli had been mentioned to the mayor by one of his sketchier acquaintances, Mikey the Mole.

"Get it?" the Mole had chuckled. "Salvatore Minelli. Sal Minelli. Salmonella?" Mikey clearly thought the guy's Darknet handle was a serious knee-slapper.

After threatening the Mole with his life if he mentioned this conversation to a soul, Jeremiah began searching the Darknet for the mysterious Salvatore Minelli. It was easier than he thought. On a site called ToDieFor, he was redirected to a site called DeathWish, which redirected him to ToxinSurance.

Jeremiah requested a face-to-face meeting with Salvatore Minelli. The response was short and not particularly sweet.

☆

Deposit $10K earnest money in non-refundable Bitcoin, along with the requested data on you and your target. Someone will get back to you shortly. If you are legit, welcome. If you are a Fed, have someone else start your car in the morning. ~S. Minelli

Jeremiah hesitated, but only for a moment. Bo Swaggart had asked him only one question: "How bad do you want to be governor?" Jeremiah reasoned that poisoning the Lt. Governor of Texas was about as bad as you can get.

The meeting took place in Washington, D.C., in a little out-of-the-way bar called Off the Record in the Hay-Adams Hotel. When Jeremiah googled the joint, one reviewer noted "You'll barely register the hushed conversations between the movers and shakers who haunt this quintessential Washington lounge, hidden in the basement of the historic hotel."

The meeting was set for 3 p.m. Jeremiah arrived 30 minutes early to case the joint. The Off the Record bar was described as a good place to have a private conversation. And this conversation was very private. What LONE STAR magazine publisher Lev Gingrich referred to as "death talk."

"Good afternoon, Mayor Jones," said a furtive man with a pencil-thin mustache as he approached Jeremiah's table in the corner.

"Do we know each other?" Jeremiah asked.

"We've done business online recently," the man answered, glancing around the mostly empty bar. "Allow me to introduce myself. Salvatore Minelli."

Jeremiah was somewhat taken aback. The fellow didn't look particularly Italian, except perhaps for the mustache and the gold chains around his neck.

"Let's cut to the chase, shall we, Mayor? You've deposited ten grand, non-refundable, to have this meeting. You made some vague mention of a high-ranking political figure as your target. I'll need you to be more specific. What kind of poison did you have in mind?"

Jeremiah glanced nervously around the bar before answering. "What if I told you that the target was, hypothetically, the Lt. Governor of Texas?"

"Then I'd say the price just doubled. Make that tripled."

"Are you kidding me?" Jeremiah blurted. "Thirty grand to off a gay dude?"

Salvatore Minelli stood up to leave.

Jeremiah stopped him. "Wait! I didn't say I wouldn't pay! What kind of poison are we talking here."

"I'm guessing you don't want him to die in your presence, am I correct?"

"Oh, hell no!"

"Then I recommend Polonium 210."

"Polonium? Isn't that the radioactive stuff the Russians used to kill that Russian spy?"

"Alexander Litvinenko? Yes. Properly dosed, your target should succumb in roughly three weeks."

"And there is absolutely no way this can be traced back to me, right?"

"The truth is, they'll probably suspect the Russians are trying to tamper with another election.

"One question?"

"Fire away."

"I'm guessing Salvatore Minelli isn't your real name."

Salvatore Minelli paused for a moment, staring intently at Jeremiah before answering.

"Good guess, Mayor Jones. Let's just say my friends call me Joey G."

74

Mayor Ponce Ponzio's phone jingled in his El Paso Mayor's office.

"Mayor Ponzio, this is Brigadier General Audrey Murphy over at the Army Base calling, Sir." General Murphy was the great-granddaughter of one of the most decorated American combat soldiers of World War II. Her grandfather had received every military combat award for valor available from the U.S. Army. His great-granddaughter Audrey was the first woman Commander of Ft. Bliss Army Base.

"Sir, I'm calling to inform you that we have completed the preliminary excavation on that top-secret project you and I discussed privately a few months ago. I thought you might like to come over and inspect the progress."

Ponce winced. "I trust you haven't mentioned my little project to anyone else, General Murphy?"

"Sir, no sir! Only a handful of corps engineers know about it. I've threatened them with courts-martial if they so much as breathe a word about it."

"Good! The answer is yes. I'd love to inspect the progress. When did you have in mind?"

"Well, sir, I know you're a busy man. Why don't you pick a time when you've got an hour or so on your schedule? I suggest you wear comfortable clothes and hiking boots. We're going to do a little caving."

"Roger comfortable clothes and hiking boots, General. And may I add that I'm very excited about reviewing your progress. Just remember, no one is to know about this. Are we clear?"

"Crystal, sir."

Mayor Ponzio's limo pulled up to the guard station at Fort Bliss a week later.

"Mayor Ponzio to see Base Commander Murphy," his limo driver told the guard.

"We've been expecting you, Mayor Ponzio. Protocol demands that you exit your limo, Mayor, and join me in my Humvee for transportation to the excavation site."

"No problem, Lieutenant," the mayor replied. "I'm very interested in the improvements General Murphy has been making on these hallowed grounds."

"Sir, I wouldn't know anything about improvements." Ponce noted the guard's confusion over his secret project. Ignorance is bliss, he chuckled to himself.

The Humvee stopped by the Commander's quarters, where General Murphy and two strapping young MPs stepped into the armored vehicle.

"Good morning, Mayor Ponzio!" General Murphy saluted. "I've asked these two corpsmen to join us, to make sure your inspection isn't interrupted.

Now this was how Ponce Ponzio liked to be treated! Like a visiting dignitary from an important state. Soon to be *his* State of East Texas.

As the Humvee slowed at an imposing chain-link fence topped with concertina wire, General Murphy offered a brief explanation:

"Mayor Ponzio, this is merely the preliminary excavation for what will obviously be a much larger excavation for your top-secret project."

Ponce immediately glanced at the two MPs, who appeared to be staring straight ahead, oblivious to the conversation. "I understand fully, General. I see that you were kind enough to install makeshift stairs to the cavity below. And I'm pleased that you've added temporary lighting, as I imagine things can be downright scary underground."

"See for yourself, Mayor Ponzio."

Ponce observed that the two MPs followed them down the stairs. For his own safety, he presumed. Standing at the bottom of the stairs was a man with a familiar face, although he couldn't quite place it. And standing beside him, a man in a dark suit holding a black leather satchel. Behind them, Ponce thought he could just make out a barred metal door. Like you might see in a prison.

"Good morning, Mayor Ponzio, said the familiar face. My name is Max Sinclair. I'm a writer by trade, but from time-to-time my government calls on me to assist them in solving cold cases. Allow me to introduce you to the gentleman beside me. This is Special Agent Daniel Mueller with the FBI.

"Good morning, Mayor Ponzio. It is my pleasure to welcome you to your new home, courtesy of the FBI."

Ponzio teetered momentarily, not sure if he was hearing what was being said. There was a sudden ringing in his ears.

"Excuse me, Mr…Agent Mueller. Did I just hear you say, 'Welcome to my new home?'"

"Indeed you did, Citizen Ponzio. As of this moment, you are being charged with the murder of the former mayor of El Paso. You will await trial in this underground jail cell, constructed especially for you by the brave men and women of Ft. Bliss Army Base. I regret to inform you that, given the status of dockets in our judicial system, it could take several months before your trial. Correction, it could take several years before you face trial."

Former Mayor Ponce Ponzio sank to his knees. The two MPs helped him to his feet and roughly shoved him into the dank, dimly lit underground prison.

"You haven't heard the last from me!" Ponce shouted. "I'm personal friends with the Governor of Texas!"

Agent Mueller simply smiled at Max and turned his attention back to the ex-mayor. "Perhaps the governor would like to visit you here in your new home, Prisoner Ponzio.

The sound of a hardened lock clicking closed sealed former Mayor Ponzio's fate.

75

SCULPTOR DAVID DEMING smiled. After almost a year, his latest masterpiece, the Cowgirl of Liberty, was almost finished. All that remained was for a legendary Texas neon artist to craft a swirling neon lasso encircling a glowing Lone Star.

The truth was, Deming would have crafted the Cowgirl for free, given her proposed perch atop the Capitol of Texas. But Lt. Governor McClain had dipped into his campaign coffers and paid Deming handsomely for the 16-foot cast aluminum statue that now graced his studio.

And true to his word, Deming had given the Cowgirl a strikingly beautiful face. It was far more pleasant than the garish countenance on the current Goddess of Liberty.

Lately, Deming had had an epiphany: Why not paint the Cowgirl's billowing fringe skirt, along with her cowgirl boots, her cowgirl shirt, and her cowgirl hat? Deming consulted with some permanent paint experts and settled on turquoise boots, a denim skirt, a red-and-white plaid shirt, and a white Stetson Open Road hat.

Of course, Texas voters had to approve the Cowgirl of Liberty. She had won hands-down in the referendum. But she would never see the light of day unless she won the hearts of a majority of Texas voters.

There was one small problem: Governor Swaggart had sworn an oath to prevent the Cowgirl of Liberty from ever topping his beloved capitol building. But it wasn't really his capitol building. It was every Texan's second home.

When Lt. Governor Ian McClain, accompanied by his Chief of staff Rory Minton, first encountered the finished Cowgirl of Liberty, they both shouted in unison. "Yee-HAW!"

The Cowgirl of Liberty was quite fetching. McClain pulled a photo of the Goddess of Liberty out of his suit pocket and held it up to Deming's masterpiece.

"Gee, tough decision!" McClain joked. "What do you think, gentlemen? Does Texas salute a golem? Or do we tip our ten-gallon hats to this gorgeous cowgirl?"

Not surprisingly, the Cowgirl of Liberty got their three votes. Question was, could they muster several million more?

"I'd bet my boots they'll vote our way," Lt. Governor McClain wagered.

"Wonder how Governor Swaggart will vote?" McClain's chief of staff chuckled.

"Word on the street is, he's got his hands full with a few other issues, Rory."

Swaggart had his hands full. One of his hand-picked mayors had just gone missing. He'd tasked another mayor with a deadly assignment. And rumor had it, the future governor of South Texas was spending more time with a certain lady friend than on his construction project. At least he could depend on the Mayor of Dallas to toe the line. And speaking of lines, Bo had recently discovered his wife's cache of cocaine in her new Governess's Suite in the mansion. Maybe he should invite the Mayor of Dallas to join him in the Governor's Suite over at the Driskill Hotel for a little R&R while his wife was gallivanting around Texas.

"Alex? Bo, here."

"Bo? Would that be Bo Diddley? Or Beau Bridges? Or maybe Bo Dallas, the professional wrestler?" the Mayor of Dallas joked.

"None of the above, Madam Mayor. Luckily, it's the best-looking Bo you know!"

"Oh, of course, Bo Derek!"

"It's me! Bo Swaggart! I thought we might spend a little quality time in the Governor's Suite at the Driskill."

"Are you tryin' to sweet-talk me, Mr. Governor? Because if you are, it's working!"

"How about this Saturday night? Besides, we need to chat about some of your fellow mayors. I get the feelin' a few of them might've slipped off the reservation lately."

"Well, you know where I stand…and lay down, Bo."

"So it's a date?"

"It's a date."

"And Alex, I may be able to procure a taste of the First Lady's Peruvian marching powder if you play your cards right."

"My cards are always on the table. Just make sure your flouncy wife doesn't get wind of our little rendezvous."

"Never happen."

"By the way," Alexa probed, "how's your little plan to divide Texas into five states shaping up?"

"Leave that to me, Alex."

76

THE STEALTH HELICOPTER hovered over the commercial edifice in Laredo. The soon-to-be-renamed *Casa Blanca del Sud*. The time was zero-dark-thirty in military speak. An unspecified time in the early morning before dawn in civilian speak.

A small cadre of SEAL Team Six operatives fast-roped swiftly and silently to the dome-shaped bell tower atop the construction. They were fully armed and armored, including Alpha High-Cut ballistic helmets and Gen 3 Night Vision goggles. Dressed entirely in black, the SEAL Team was virtually invisible in the moonless night.

One of the operatives extracted a small C-4 charge from his vest and placed it atop the locked trap door inside the bell tower. The teamed quickly scrambled away before an operative pressed a button that lifted the door off its hinges.

Not a word was spoken as the team entered the building. Communication was executed with hand signals. Their target was ten floors below, in the subbasements of Estevan Barrero's private world.

In the second subbasement of the breached building, Estevan Barrero was entertaining his girlfriend, Esmerelda. They were both quite nude, frolicking in satin sheets on the California King bed in Estevan's lavish private apartment two floors above the underground tunnel to Ciudad Nuevo Laredo. A bottle of Roederer Cristal Brut champagne chilled in an ice bucket nearby. Several lines of uncut cocaine trailed across a solid gold hand mirror.

"Soon this building will be the Capitol of South Texas," Estevan whispered in his lover's ear. "I will be Governor and you will be my Governess."

Esmerelda responded by licking his earlobe licentiously, then leaning over him, her breasts tickling his chest hair as she snorted two lines of cocaine before playfully coating her nipples with the pure white powder.

"But what will people say about me?" Esmerelda pouted. "Will they call me 'First Lady,' or Primera Puta?'"

Estevan ignored her question, easing atop her and deftly tonguing the cocaine from her breasts before sliding down toward the cocaine in her navel.

As if on cue, members of SEAL Team Six burst into Estevan's private quarters.

Estevan instinctively reached for the Beretta 9mm pistol he kept by his bedside. But hesitated when he spied a red laser dot on his outstretched hand.

"I wouldn't advise that, Estevan," the team leader said quietly as she lifted off her ballistic helmet. "My name is Vanessa Ingram, Director of the U.S. Defense Clandestine Service. You, sir, are under arrest for willingly possessing, cultivating, manufacturing, and selling controlled substances across international borders."

Far below, several massive explosions rocked the entire structure.

"What the hell was that?" Estevan shouted.

"That, Mayor Barrero, was the sound of three bunker buster bombs obliterating the elaborate tunnel system you and your minions have built over the past year beneath the Texas-Mexico border. We've been monitoring your excavation using infrared satellite technology for the entire time. I must admit, we've marveled at both your ingenuity and your seemingly boundless access to enormous sums of money."

"I will kill you and your entire family!"

"Well, good luck with that, Mayor Barrero, because you'll have to do it from the confines of your cell in Gitmo."

When Estevan failed to grasp the full meaning of what she had said, Six continued. "You may know it by another name, Estevan. The U.S. Naval Station Detention Camp on the coast of Guantanamo Bay in Cuba."

Esmerelda reacted indignantly. "I don't even know this man! I was kidnapped and brought here against my wishes and raped! *Por favor, Señora Director,* may I please be permitted to leave now?"

"You'll both be leaving, Esmerelda. You'll have adjoining cells at Gitmo before the sun sets today."

And with that, the of Clandestine Service turned over the spoils of the war on drugs to her trusted team. Before exfiltrating aboard the hovering stealth chopper, she reminded her teammates:

"This. Never. Happened."

Within a month, developer and self-ascribed King of San Antonio Rhett McCullum had secured the property rights to what was now never to become *Casa Blanca del Sud.* Rhett had begun transforming it into a major tourist destination that would include a swanky hotel, a Borderlands Museum, and a Six Flags Over Texas theme park.

"Fuck you and the horse you rode in on, Estevan Barrero!" Rhett bellowed." As for Laredo becoming the Capital of South Texas, *bésa mi culo, amigo!*"

Unfortunately, Rhett's message never reached Estevan's ears. He was preoccupied with his own troubles down in sunny Guantánamo Bay.

Part VII:
The Eyes of Texas

77

Houston Mayor Jones arranged a meeting with Texas Lt. Governor McClain under the auspices of making a sizeable contribution to McClain's campaign.

The meeting was scheduled for the Press Box Bar in the Headliner's Club.

Jeremiah Jones arrived early, to surveil the bar. He was pleased to see that, for the most part, the bar was empty.

The Lt. Governor arrived promptly at 5 p.m., accompanied by his chief of staff, Rory Minton.

"Always good to see anotha brotha in these hallowed halls!" Jones fist-bumped Minton, who seemed unamused by Jones' fake camaraderie.

McClain intervened, reaching out to shake Jones' hand. "Congratulations on your recent election as Mayor of Houston, Mr. Jones."

"Who'd have guessed a black man would be elected mayor of the largest city in Texas, Governor?"

"Some folks say a mayorship is simply a steppingstone to greater things, Mayor Jones. Don't you agree?" McClain asked, staring directly into the mayor's eyes.

"I wouldn't know anything about that, Governor. I'm just lucky to be where I am."

"And I'm lucky to meet someone who has promised a sizeable contribution to my campaign, Mayor. How have I earned such a gracious gesture?"

"We elected officials gotta stick together. You never know when somebody's gonna try to rain on our parade. May I buy you a cocktail? I highly recommend the Headliner Stinger. It's a classic here, I'm told."

"If that's what you're having, make it two, Mayor. Club soda and lime for Rory."

Mayor Jones pointed the Lt. Governor and his Chief of staff to a table in the far corner, then sidled up to the bar and addressed the bartender.

"Double Stingers for me and the Governor, my good man. And a club soda and lime for the sissy with him. I'll carry them to the table, no trouble."

For some reason, the bartender sensed there *was* trouble brewing. But he shrugged it off and crafted two signature cocktails, along with a club soda and lime. When he placed them on the bar, Mayor Jones caught his attention.

"I don't suppose you have any cigars. Preferably Monte Cristo No. 2s."

"I've got some in the back, sir. I'll just be a moment."

Jones took the moment to reach into his coat pocket and pull out a small lead capsule. Glancing around to make sure no one was watching, he carefully unscrewed the capsule and poured the contents into one of the Stingers.

"I'll take those," he heard someone say. The bartender, he assumed.

"No worries. I can handle the Stingers. You bring the sissy drink."

"I said I'll take those," the voice repeated. "And don't make me say it again, Mayor Jones."

Jones turned to see a familiar face, albeit without the familiar pencil-thin mustache.

"Sal Minelli? What are you doing here?"

"What I'm doing here is arresting you for the attempted murder of a state official, Mayor Jones. It might not surprise you that we don't look too kindly on attempted murder in the Lone Star State. And for the record, the name's Joseph Greenfield. Agent Joseph Greenfield, with the Austin office of the FBI."

Jeremiah suddenly felt faint. Luckily, someone grabbed his shoulders, arresting his fall, then abruptly jerked his hands behind his back and snapped them tightly in handcuffs.

"Hold on, now! Do you realize who I am?" Jeremiah demanded.

"I realize who you *were,* Mayor Jones. But now that you've attempted to poison the Lt. Governor of Texas, I believe your new title will be Inmate Jones."

Agent Joseph Greenfield winked at the Lt. Governor as he perp-walked the former Houston Mayor out of the Press Box bar.

Good news travels fast. Bad news, even faster.

Word of his self-appointed Mayor of Houston's incarceration reached Governor Swaggart like a landslide, crushing any hope he had of putting his chosen candidate into the governors' office of one of his proposed five states of Texas.

"Goddammit, Jules!" he railed at his chief of staff. "What the hell is happening? "El Popo has gone missing in El Paso. Word has it Estevan Barrero has been kidnapped by some rogue Colombian drug lords. And now you're telling me that Jeremiah Jones has been arrested for attempted murder?"

"That's about the size of it, Governor. And to make matters worse, the polls show voters are beginning to sour on TX5."

"That's impossible!" Bo ranted. "What about my plans to be President?"

"You know what they say, Governor. 'The best laid plans of mice and men…"

"Are you saying I'm a mouse, Jules?"

"Not at all, Sir. But I'm afraid I have some more bad news."

"What could possibly be worse than all this?"

"I quit."

78

"We've got problems, Alex," Bo grumbled into his private cell phone.

"You're damn right we've got problems, Bo," Alexa King shouted back at him. "I trust this is a secure line?"

Bo grimaced before replying. "Certainly more secure than the future of the five states of Texas!"

"Is it true what I've heard, Bo? Ponzio's gone missing. Barrero's been kidnapped? And Jones is in jail on a murder rap?"

"I know it doesn't look good…"

"Doesn't look good?" Alexa interrupted. "It looks like we're up shit creek without a paddle. How could you let this happen?"

"How could *I* let this happen? Let me tell you something, darlin'. I made all you sons-of-bitches mayors of some of the biggest cities in Texas. And what do I get in return? A goddamn shit show, that's what!"

"Don't cry to me, Beauregard Swaggart! You and I are all that's left of your big plan to divvy up Texas. Guess that's what I should expect from a college drop-out."

"Now wait just a minute, Alex. I got my college diploma from Sul Ross, just like you."

"Yeah, well my diploma was legit. You bought yours."

"Calm down, Alex. I may have pulled a few strings to graduate. But the world doesn't know a thing about that. That is, unless you've told someone?"

"Your secret's safe with me, Bo. Besides, you and I have lots of little secrets that will never see the light of day. Capische?"

"I get it, Alex. The point is, where do we go from here?"

"Well, do you still plan to run for President, Beauregard?"

"I've asked you not to call me that, Alex. But to answer your question, yes. There's only one thing standing in my way."

"Would that one thing be that bitch you call a wife?"

"You always could read my mind, Alex. Question is, what do we do about it?"

"I thought you'd never ask, Bo. Leave that to me."

Becky Walford's catering business was going down the tubes. She had lost the First Lady's Spring Fling contract. Now Veronica had blackballed Becky with all her rich girlfriends.

Apparently, Veronica blamed Becky for Senator Bethany Jordan masquerading as one of Becky's catering staff. That evening had gotten a little out-of-hand, what with the male strippers and all.

The truth was, Becky didn't hire the Senator. But she recognized her the minute she took the place of an ailing staff member. Becky thought it was kind of funny. The First Lady obviously had a different opinion.

Becky Walford was down to seeds and stems. She was late on her house payments, and the bank was threatening to foreclose if she didn't get current. The dealership where she leased her BMW sent notice that they'd be coming to repo her car at the end of the month. She'd run through her savings and had even borrowed some money from her parents, who could ill-afford to loan their grown daughter money.

The only thing Becky had of any value was the videotape she'd shot on her cell phone the night of the First Lady's Spring Fling. Some nights, after a bottle of cheap wine, she'd break it out and look at it again.

It was downright damning. There was the First Lady, stripped down to her Victoria Secret undies, snorting coke and strutting around on stage with some male strippers.

And right beside her, in a conga line of rich, nearly naked women, were the wives of some of Texas' most successful businessmen.

"That's gotta be worth something to somebody," Becky mused. True, she had pledged allegiance to the band of women who'd gathered at the Cloak Room a few months before. But none of them were facing her financial straits.

I wonder what Veronica Swaggart and her fancy-schmancy friends would pay to see this video go away, Becky wondered. *Ten grand? A hundred grand? A million? What the hell, think big! After all, what have I got to lose?*

What Becky Walford had to lose was more than she might have imagined. Veronica and her friends were not people you messed with. But there was one person Becky might never have guessed would have an interest in her racy videotape. That is, until she got a phone message one evening.

"Becky Walford? This is Alexa King. We've never met. But you may have something for which I might be willing to pay a considerable sum of money. Can we meet sometime very soon? I guarantee I'll make it worth your time."

79

ONE MILLION DOLLARS. That's how much Becky planned to tell Alexa she wanted for her video.

Alexa, of course, had no intention of paying that kind of money. But once she'd seen the video, she knew who would pay a bucket of money. Veronica Swaggart's rich girlfriends. They had everything to lose. Their reputations. Their marriages. Maybe even their lives.

"Has anyone else seen this video?" Alexa asked Becky over martinis at Clark's Oyster Bar on West 6th Street.

"Not a soul, Ms. King," Becky assured her. Becky, of course, had done her homework. She had googled Alexa King and discovered she was the mayor of Dallas and an heir to the King Ranch fortune. She apparently also had plenty of political pull at the state capitol.

"How much are we talking about here, Ms. King?"

"Please, call me Alexa. I was thinking a hundred grand."

"And I was thinking, add a few more zeroes," Becky said, followed by a deep swallow of her second Vesper martini.

"And I'm thinking this conversation is over," Alexa said, tossing some bills on the table and standing to leave."

"Wait. Hold your horses, Alexa! I'm a reasonable woman. I also know this video is worth a lot of money. Let's say...a million dollars."

"Let's say a hundred grand."

Becky smiled. "I have a feeling somebody would pay dearly for a copy of this video."

"Okay, okay! One million dollars. But I want the original. If I ever learn you've made a copy, life as you know it will be over. Do I make myself clear?"

"Very," Becky assured her. She waited for Mayor King to leave before she got up and skittered to the restroom. At some point in the conversation, she had wet her pants.

Alexa's newly acquired video included the Who's Who of Texas high society. Wives, trophy wives, and mistresses of some of the richest men in Texas.

Alexa had to admit, she was a pleasantly distracted by some of the virile young men on the video. Sipping her third martini, Alexa realized she was touching herself in places ordinarily reserved for her male companions.

She had paid her caterer a cool million dollars for this video. But she figured that was chump change compared to what some of Veronica's friends would pay for this video to go away.

Meanwhile, she began making a list of Veronica's Spring Fling attendees. Some she recognized, or at least thought she did. She could nail the rest using facial recognition software she'd recently purchased for her soon-to-be-christened Crystal Capitol.

There was just one big problem. Bo Swaggart's plan to divide Texas into five states appeared to be disintegrating right before her eyes. Well, there was more than one way to skin that cat. Perhaps she could convince Bo that all he really needed was a North and South Texas, with him as Governor of South Texas and her as Governor of North Texas. It had worked for North and South Carolina. North and South Dakota, too. And it was probably just a matter of time before those screaming liberals on the West Coast divided their state into North and South California.

"I don't know if that will get Bo elected president one day," Alexa admitted. "But I know what *could* get him elected. Only one thing stands in the way. And I plan to remove her from the equation."

Alexa replayed the video. It just got better the more she drank.

"Randall, I know it's kinda late, but could you come over to my condo?" Alexa cooed into her cell phone.

"Of course, Mayor King," her chauffeur replied. Will you be needing a ride somewhere this evening?"

"I'll definitely need a ride, Randall. And you're just the stud to give it to me."

80

Prisoner Ponzio blinked, but the bars that confined him to his underground cell beneath the Fort Bliss Army Base were still there.

How could this happen to me? Ponce asked himself for the hundredth time. *I haven't done anything wrong. Sure, I gave the order for one of the Los Zetas snipers to wing the mayor of El Paso. But that was just to put the fear of God in him, so he'd vacate his office. I never dreamed those bastards would kill him!"*

When he got out of this godforsaken prison, some heads would roll. The question was, how the hell was he going to get out? Then it hit him. Los Zetas were experts at tunneling. That's how they got drugs across the border right under the U.S. Border Patrol's noses.

What Ponce didn't realize was that his little home-away-from-home was not only 30 feet below ground, it was also 30 miles from the Mexican border. El Popo wasn't going anywhere.

☆

Estevan Barrero looked down at the orange jumpsuit he was wearing and cursed under his breath. On the rare occasions when the US. Marines let him out of his cell, they placed a black hood over his head.

"How am I supposed to work out with this fucking hood on my head?" Estevan asked his captors.

"You'll just have to work that out, scumbag," a Marine answered while his fellow guards snickered.

"You gentlemen know that money is no object with me, right? I can make every one of you a millionaire if you'll just get me out of this hellhole."

"Who needs money when we've got that pretty little girlfriend of yours to keep us company?" another guard said.

"Touch Esmerelda and I will cut off your balls and feed them to you, you worthless cocksuckers!" Estevan roared.

"Wow! How did you guess what's for dinner tonight, Prisoner 11816?" the Marine goaded him. Jokes were the currency at Gitmo, right down to Barrero's prison number. It was the day the 45th President of the United States was elected.

"The good news is, the ex-president may one day be your cellmate."

Jeremiah Jones was looking forward to his one phone call a month. He wouldn't be calling his wife, Grace. No, Jeremiah would be calling the governor of Texas. If Bo couldn't spring him from this deathtrap, nobody could.

In the meantime, Jeremiah had been thinking a lot about how he'd been set up. Bo himself had suggested that Lt. Governor McClain needed to disappear. No way to misinterpret what the governor had meant by that.

Okay, maybe slipping over to the dark side and trusting some unknown toxicologist from the Darknet had been a bad idea. There was almost no way to vet such sources. But the name Salvatore Minelli should have been his first clue.

When he got out of here, 3-J's first stop would be to strangle that snitch, Mickey the Mole.

But first things first. He'd call the governor and the governor would spring him. Plead entrapment, or whatever it took. And then Jeremiah would go looking for one Joey G, aka Joseph Greenfield, FBI agent. He'd never know what hit him.

"Hey, Screw, when do I get my phone call?" Jeremiah shouted to the guard with the key to his cell.

"Oh, didn't I tell you?" the guard taunted. "Your phone privileges have been rescinded. Something about the laws governing possession of stolen radioactive material."

"Hey, I didn't steal any radioactive material. It was given to me!"

"By the Russians, from what I hear. You're just lucky they even feed you, Big Man. You might want to turn out your cell light and make sure your meals don't glow in the dark! And call me Screw again and I'll see that's just what you get. Screwed, blued and tattooed!"

Things were not going well for three out of four Texas mayors that Governor Swaggart had helped get elected. And things were about to get even worse for the fourth mayor. The ever-popular Alexa King.

81

"WATCH THIS VIDEO, Vee, and let me know when you're done," Bo ordered his wife before retiring to the Governor's Master Bedroom next door to her separate Governess Suite.

"I'm not watching your porn anymore, Beauregard," the First Lady informed him before tossing the flash drive into the hallway outside her private domain.

"It's not porn, Vee. Well, I take that back. It's pornographic. But I think you may recognize some of the actors, including yourself." Chuckling maliciously, the Governor of Texas shut the door to his private quarters.

"What the hell?" Veronica Swaggart said aloud. Picking up the flash drive from the hallway, she reentered her private quarters, slammed the door, and locked it.

It took her a moment to figure out how to plug the flash drive into the high-end AV system she'd had installed in her suite. Grabbing the remote control and her half-empty vodka martini, she settled into her queen bed, adjusted the satin sheets, and hit play.

"Oh My God!" she shrieked as the video began. Hitting pause, she poured herself another generous martini. She crawled back into bed, kicking off the sheets and wiping a few nagging drops of perspiration from her forehead.

There she was, in her favorite Victoria Secret thong panties and peek-a-boo bra. At the same time, a crew of jockstrap-clad policemen paraded around her. The sex-laden lyrics of *The Big Bamboo,* blasted over the speaker system:

Veronica was soon joined onscreen by some of the richest women in Texas. They, too, were nearly nude, and frolicking with the male dancers in ways that made most online porn look relatively tame.

Veronica gasped as, on screen, she ripped off her bra and tossed it to one of the faux policemen. Hitting pause and clumsily setting down her martini, Veronica raced to her private bathroom and vomited into her gold-plated toilet.

"You'll pay for this, you sonuvabitch!" Veronica screamed through the walls of the Governor's Quarters.

"I already have!" she heard her husband reply. "But it was worth every penny. Besides, I'm guessing your girlfriends will be more than happy to pay me a tidy profit for that video to go away."

"And what about me, you bastard!"

"Let's talk in the morning, once you've had a chance to sober up."

"You know I hate runny eggs, you idiot!" Veronica shouted at the breakfast server the next morning.

"Pay no attention to the First Lady's rantings, Clint," Bo told the server. "She's not herself this morning. More like a diva, if you ask me."

"Out! Out, all of you!" Veronica screamed. "And see that we're not disturbed, or I'll have your heads!"

"Now, now, Vee. It's not the helps' fault that you've decided to change careers, my dear. As a matter of fact, I honestly believe you could be the next big porn star!"

"Do you know all the crap I have on you, you miserable sonuvabitch? Don't you think I don't know about you and your conquests, not the least of which is that horse-humping whore in Dallas?"

"Settle down, Vee. Let's settle this like adults."

"Adults?" Veronica shouted. "That's something no one would ever accuse you of!"

"Enough of this Mr. Nice Guy bullshit. Let me lay it out for you, Vee. First, you're going to get your girlfriends to cough up a hundred thou each, assuming they want to go on living the lifestyle to which they've grown accustomed. Second, you're going to admit to having extra-marital affairs with several unnamed male friends. Third, and this is the juicy part, you're going to ask me for a divorce."

"Ask you for a divorce? You've gotta be kidding me, Beauregard!"

"You know I don't like it when you call me that, Vee. Now, any questions?"

"Just one. When might you have some time to watch a video that may interest *you?*"

82

Marina Alvarez shuddered, something she did every time she replayed the video on her cell phone.

At first, she thought of showing it to her new friends from the secret Cloak Room meeting a few months ago. After all, it seemed to her that they all shared her feelings about Governor Swaggart.

Marina had even considered showing it to the governor. But that thought faded quickly when she remembered that frightful knife he kept hidden in his desk.

Why not simply send it to the First Lady's cell phone and let her deal with her adulterous husband? The First Lady would never know where it came from, would she?

Veronica Swaggart loved her monthly Lake Austin Spa treatments. A facial, followed by a mani-pedi, followed by some quality time with her favorite masseuse, Rommel. Today she planned to fully surrender to Rommel's fickle fingers.

A phone message jarred her from her reverie. Veronica glanced down at her cell and, not recognizing the sender, ignored it.

"Is that the best you can do for my crow's feet?" she nagged the facial specialist. "I looked younger when I walked in here!"

"According to your chart, Mrs. Swaggart, you're overdue for your Botox treatment."

"Well, unlike the rest of the world, I'm a very busy woman, Sally. You have no idea the pressure I'm under helping my husband run this great state of ours. My friends think I'd make a better governor than Beauregard!"

"Most women would," Sally agreed. "You've got pluck!"

"Speaking of pluck, thread my eyebrows while you're at it. And that stuff you gave me to make my eyelashes longer hasn't helped at all if you ask me!"

Sally hadn't asked her. But she quietly let the First Lady's tantrum pass.

"Do you know if Rommel's here today, Sally?"

"Rommel was dismissed, Ms. Swaggart. There were, um, some complaints about his massage technique. I think he might have been getting a little handsy, if you know what I mean."

Veronica knew exactly what she meant. Which was why Rommel was her favorite masseuse.

"Damn! That really ruins my day!"

"There is that new guy. He was the assistant sports doctor for the gymnast camp over near Huntsville for a while."

"I like his credentials. See if he's available for a deep-tissue massage when we're done here, Sally."

☆

Once she hit SEND on her cell phone, it was as if the weight of the world had been lifted from Marina's shoulders. Now that her video of the Governor of Texas and the Mayor of Dallas cavorting in his private chambers was somebody else's problem. That somebody else being the First Lady of Texas.

She worried for a moment about whether the First Lady would know who sent it to her. But she was quickly distracted by the workday ahead. The governor was hosting a gathering of visiting dignitaries in his office later that day, demanding that everything be up to his usual standards.

Marina considered deleting the video from her cell phone, then changed her mind. She still might show it to her new lady friends if they ever met at the Cloak Room again. Deep down inside, she wanted to see the looks on their faces when they saw their governor and his lady friend committing adultery.

Marina turned her attention back to cleaning the governor's office, carefully avoiding his desk, as she had been warned when she first took the job.

83

SLEUTH MAX SINCLAIR sometimes had a funny feeling. Usually his funny feelings pointed to trouble.

Max was aware of the recent events that had left three major Texas cities without their mayors. Mayor Ponce Ponzio of El Paso had simply disappeared from the face of the earth. Mayor Estevan Barrero of Laredo was reportedly serving time at the Guantanamo Bay U.S. military prison for treacherous acts. Mayor Jeremiah Jones was incarcerated at Allan B. Polunsky supermax prison near Livingston.

The only remaining mayors of major Texas cities were the recently re-elected mayors of Austin and San Antonio, along with the newly elected Mayor of Dallas.

Max plotted to himself one morning over breakfast tacos at Torchy's Taco trailer on South Congress. "Maybe it's time I meet with Holly Worthington and get her take on this." After draining his second cup of java, Max pinged Holly's cell phone.

"Max Sinclair! How the hell are ya, old friend?"

"Better than I deserve, Holly."

"I bet you're wondering what the hell is goin' on in this Great State of Texas of ours, am I right?"

"Bingo! How'd you know?"

"Because you only call me when you can't figure something out on your own, Maximilian."

"Please, that's not my name."

Holly chuckled. "Oh, but it *is*, Maximilian. Your momma done told me so!"

"Enough about me. What's happening to all our bigshot Texas mayors?"

"You mean like…"

"I mean like Ponzio, Barrera and Jones. One has disappeared and the other two are in prison. That's weird, even by Texas standards!"

"I couldn't agree more, Max. In fact, I'm writing a story about these strange goings-on for the next issue of LONE STAR."

"I figured you'd just be sitting around waiting for them to award you the Pulitzer Prize for your exposé on Governor Swaggart, Holly."

"Oh, that old thing? Naw. I'm onto something even bigger. Something about Bo Swaggart's college degree doesn't add up. And call me crazy, but I think there may be some hanky-panky going on with Alexa King."

"I knew it! When can we meet to discuss these ideas of mine?"

"For starters, they're my ideas, not yours. How about we meet at Clark's Oyster Bar for happy hour oysters and martinis this afternoon at, say, 4 o'clock? And you're buyin'."

"Don't I always?"

Clark's Oyster Bar on West 6th Street is a popular Austin hangout. During the week, oysters and martinis are happy hour specials. They also serve what some believe is the best burger in town, which comes with a mountain of shoestring potatoes they call French fries.

Max arrived early and grabbed a table outside, where things were quieter. He took the table at the far end, closest to the street.

"I'll just have water until my writer friend arrives," Max told his waiter. "But make it a double!" he joked. The waiter brought him a large glass of ice water and a tray of homemade bread, fresh cut radishes, whipped butter, and a tiny mound of sea salt. Like most regulars, Max knew to dip his radishes in butter, then salt.

"Buy a girl a drink, stranger?" Holly said as she as she eased into the chair across from Max.

"My pleasure, young lady. Are you sure you're old enough to drink?"

"Are you sure you're young enough to handle me when I do?"

Max motioned to the waiter. "Two Hendrick's Gin martinis up, with a splash of orange bitters and a slice of cucumber, please."

"Coming right up, sir. Some oysters with that, Mr. Sinclair?"

"A dozen of your finest, Josh. Six from the East Coast, six from the West Coast. And some Worcestershire Sauce and Tabasco on the side."

When the waiter was gone, Max got down to business.

"I don't know what's going on, but I think it all leads back to the Governor's office, Holly."

"I agree. If you ask me, this is all about the Governor's plan to divide Texas into five states."

"But what's in it for him? He'll wind up just being Governor of Central Texas if he gets his way,

"Mind if I share a little of that yummy bread?" Holly said, reaching.

"Be my guest. But if you reach for my radishes, you might draw back a nub," Max joked.

"Truth is, I don't think Swaggart's plan ends at the governorship of a smaller state of Texas," Holly said, playfully nabbing one of Max's precious radishes and expertly slathering it with butter before dabbing it into the diminishing salt mound.

"Surely we're not talking about the presidency, are we?"

"Indeed we are," Holly said. "And don't call me Shirley."

"But Swaggart has zero chance of ever becoming President of the United States."

"People said the same thing about the 45th president. Look where that got us!"

"Another round!" Max instructed the waiter. "And this time, we'll switch to Rye Manhattans, with two Luxardo cherries each." He then made a production of concocting his secret cocktail sauce, suggesting Holly test it on her half dozen oysters.

"Damn! That's righteous, Max. And what, pray tell, is a Luxardo cherry?"

"The second-best thing you'll ever put in your mouth."

"You're incorrigible, Max," Holly said, shaking her head.

"Were you considering encouraging me?"

Holly wisely changed the subject. "Let's get back to Swaggart and what's going on right in front of our noses, shall we? I believe that Bo Swaggart lied his way into the Governor's office. I also believe that he has designs on that Dallas hottie mayor, Alexa King, although I can't prove it just yet."

"If what you're saying is true, we're talking…"

"Treason, Max? It wouldn't be the first time in recent history when a good-for-nothing politician was accused of that, now would it?"

Max had to agree. "No, it would not."

Two Rye Manhattans arrived, each with the requested two Luxardo cherries.

"So," Max said conspiratorially, "Shall we collaborate on bringing down the Texas Chainsaw Governor?"

"Only if you let me use that as the headline for my next article. You know, sometimes you can be quite creative, Max."

"Creative is my middle name," he said, polishing off his Manhattan and signing the check.

84

First Lady Veronica Swaggart was very relaxed from her massage session with the handsome former gymnast trainer. What was his name, again? Lech? Oh well, no matter.

One thing was still nagging at her. She had received a phone message from an unfamiliar sender and had summarily sent it to her junk file. It appeared to be a video of some sort. What the hell?

Flustered, Veronica retrieved the message and swore to herself she'd look at the video later. The sender was simply listed as marina. com. A marina? Why would a marina be sending her a video?

The original Grove Wine Bar & Kitchen is an indoor-outdoor restaurant in West Lake Hills. The lunch menu consists of tasty bruschetta, crisp house salads, savory soups, thin-crust pizzas, and yummy New American eats. And wine. Lots of it.

Veronica arrived early and ordered the first of what would be several bottles of wine. A 2009 Morlet Family Vineyard Cabernet Sauvignon called Passionnément. It was $350 a bottle. But that was chump change compared to what she was about to suggest her friends pay her husband to destroy the video she was about to share with them.

"How's my bestie this fine afternoon?" the first girlfriend to arrive asked.

"Ask me after we've had a few more bottles of this stuff," Veronica answered, pouring her friend a tall glass of Cab.

They were soon joined by a handful of likewise gleeful besties. Gleeful, that is, until Veronica lowered the boom.

"I suggest we just skip lunch today and concentrate on drinking as much of this wine as my entertainment budget will allow, ladies," Veronica suggested, pouring her third glass of red.

"What is this, like, all about, Vee?" one of her girlfriends asked nervously.

"It's, like, the end of life as we know it if we don't pony-up to my asshole of a husband," Veronica slurred. And with that, she turned her cell phone toward them.

"Oh my fucking God!" one of her besties almost shouted, spitting a mouthful of wine on the tablecloth.

"My thoughts exactly," said Veronica. "Somehow, my husband got his hands on this video someone took at our little Spring Fling."

"We're dead! We're all dead!" another friend moaned.

"Either that or we pay our way out of that bastard's blackmail and never look back," Veronica said.

"What are we, like, talking about here?" one of the billionaire wives asked. "Ten grand?"

"Try ten times that amount. For each of us."

"A hundred grand apiece? Fuck that! No offense, Vee."

"No offense taken. But we need to consider what the lifestyles we lead are worth to us. Y'all have lots more money than me."

"Some lunch, ladies?" a waiter approached cautiously and asked.

"Two more bottles of Passionnément," Veronica answered. "And make sure you don't run out. We might be here for a while."

"Excuse me, Madam First Lady, but you do know how much that wine is per bottle, right?"

Veronica shot the waiter the side-eye. "You do know how much I give a shit, right?"

While the waiter scurried off to procure more wine, Veronica leaned toward her friends conspiratorially. She had everyone's complete attention now.

"Like my daddy always told me, 'It ain't over 'til it's over.' Let's pay the piper, then set a trap that will cost him his job."

"What do you have in mind, Vee?"

"I don't know yet. But believe me, I'm working on it. Can I depend on a hundred grand from each of you by, say, the end of the week?"

Each of her friends nodded tentatively, then helped themselves to more wine.

Veronica had almost forgotten the suspicious phone message by the time her driver deposited her back at the Governor's Mansion.

Stumbling up the grand staircase, she reached into her purse for her cell phone.

"Where did I put that damn phone message," she asked herself. "Oh, of course, right where it belongs. In my junk file!"

Veronica slipped off her designer heels and plopped down on her silk duvet before accessing the file. Her mind was sufficiently wine addled, but she was eventually able to open the mysterious file.

She recognized the room immediately. It was the Governor's anteroom, where he entertained guests on special occasions. On the wall, a movie was playing on the large flat screen. A movie about horses? Wait! It was a movie about horses fucking!

As Veronica stared in amazement, the camera panned to the opposite end of the conference table, where one Beauregard Swaggart, Governor of Texas, was pile-driving the blonde-haired, blue-eyed Mayor of Dallas, who screamed:

"That's it! That's it, you stud, you! Show that stallion how we do the wild thing!"

Veronica couldn't believe her eyes. "Alrighty, now! Two can play this game!"

Checking first to make sure the governor wasn't in his quarters, Veronica quietly closed and locked the door to her bedroom, poured herself a dry martini, and began plotting.

It never occurred to Veronica to figure out where the video had come from. All she cared about was finding the perfect moment to spring it on her unsuspecting husband.

After dinner in the Mansion a week later, she invited Bo up to her bedroom for a nightcap.

"Well, well! And here I thought those days were over, Vee," Bo grinned. "I guess you just can't get keep a good man down!"

"That's right, stud. But there's something I think you need to see first." With that she hit play on her remote. A most unwelcome scene appeared on her flat screen TV.

"Oh my fucking god!" Bo gasped.

Veronica grinned. "My sentiments exactly!"

85

THE LARGE CHECKS began arriving at First Lady Swaggart's office on Friday morning, some delivered by private courier, others by registered mail. All the checks had two things in common. Each was made out in the amount of $100,000. None listed the intended recipient. None of Veronica's girlfriends were brave enough to list Governor Beauregard Swaggart on the "Pay to the Order of" line.

The First Lady, of course, knew something none of her besties knew. She had countered Bo's threat with one of her own. "Post the video of me and my girlfriends at my Spring Fling, and I'll post the video of you and Alexa King's doing the wild thing."

Stalemate, with one exception. Here sat Veronica with upwards of $1 million dollars in checks. Neither her girlfriends nor her soon-to-be ex-husband would ever be the wiser if she simply pocketed the money herself. All she had to do was write in "Gov. Swaggart" and assure her bank that these checks were for *Governess* Swaggart. They were, after all, all signed by her closest, richest female friends.

That revelation called for a stiff drink. Maybe even two.

To say that Bo Swaggart was caught off-guard by this lurid video was an understatement. Hornswoggled might be closer to the truth.

Where had Veronica gotten her hands on this video? It had to be one of the after-hours Capitol staffers. A roving State Trooper, maybe. Or one of the cleaning staff. He'd have Capitol security retrieve videos of his office corridors. Whoever was responsible would rue the day they thought they could get away with blackmailing the Governor of Texas. Heads would roll! And not just figuratively speaking.

Veronica had offered to erase all copies of her video, assuming he would do the same with his. If she was foolish enough to believe him, that was her problem.

On the other hand, Alexa had told Bo that she paid a cool million for the video in her possession. Taking that kind of money out of his campaign coffers would be tricky. Tricky, but not impossible.

"My wife somehow got hold of a tape of you and me doing the wild thing in my office, Alex," Bo told Alexa on his private cell line.

There was a long silence, then Alexa stated the obvious. "Well, then erase our tape of her if she erases her tape of us, and nobody's the wiser, Bo. There is one problem, though."

"What's that, darlin'?"

"A matter of one million dollars, lover boy."

"I've thought about that, Alex. Let me work on it. But I think I can squeeze a mil out of my campaign coffers without raising too many eyebrows."

"You do that, Bo. Oh, and Bo, I think it's time we dispensed with the extra-marital hanky-panky until you divorce your precious Veronica.

"No need to go *that* far, Alex. Besides, My wife and I are sleeping in separate bedrooms now!"

"So are we, Bo, unless and until you get me that million bucks."

☆

Veronica waltzed into her bank like she owned the place. Her personal banker saw her and immediately rushed over to welcome her.

"Madam First Lady! How may I assist you today?"

"Just making a few deposits in my personal account, Oliver. And I'm late for an appointment. So let's take care of this little matter without any undue delay, shall we?"

"Of course, Mrs. Swaggart!"

"Here are ten checks made out to me from some of my closest friends, for a whirlwind tour of Europe we have planned. The total, if I recall, is one million dollars."

"One million dollars?" her banker stammered. "Sounds like quite a trip!"

"We're traveling by private jet, Oliver. You can just imagine what that will cost, I'm sure."

"Not really. But no matter, ma'am. Do you have the checks with you?"

Handing him the checks, she made it clear she was in no mood for dilly-dallying. "Of course, I do. Why would I waste my time coming here?"

Eyeing the checks, the private banker said nervously, "But Mrs. Swaggart, these checks are made out to Governor Swaggart."

"Actually, they're abbreviated, Oliver. Pay to the Order of *Governess* Swaggart."

"Right! I'll have a receipt for you in a jiffy."

"Thank you, Oliver," Veronica purred, "and here's a little something for your trouble." With that she handed her personal banker a crisp one-hundred-dollar bill.

Her banker blushed. "I-I…can't accept this."

"Oh hush, Oliver. After all, it's hush money."

86

THE SECOND MEETING of strong-willed Texas women was again held at the legendary Cloak Room on a Sunday.

Present and accounted for were Brenda Prendahl, the Cloak Room bartender. LONE STAR magazine reporter Holly Worthington. Senator Bethany Jordan. The First Lady's ex-caterer, Becky Walford. Local meteorologist Tiffany Taylor. Sister Mary Celine. And the governor's chambermaid, Marina Alvarez. Max Sinclair had once again been included.

Senator Jordan quickly took charge of the meeting, announcing, "No alcohol today, folks. Welcome Max. Given what we need to discuss today, we could use a little testosterone in the room. Brenda, if you'd be so kind as to take coffee and tea orders, we'll start this meeting. Hard stop in one hour. Do we all agree?"

Once the coffee and tea were served, the meeting began in earnest.

Everyone nodded, including Max, who wasn't sure why he'd been invited.

Once the coffee and tea orders delivered, the meeting began in earnest.

"Folks, I've been doing a little digging behind the scenes over at the Capitol," Senator Jordan said, "and I believe I have uncovered enough evidence of inappropriate spending on the First Lady's part to warrant an investigation.

"What about the governor?" Tiffany Taylor interrupted. "I can almost guarantee he's been dipping his grubby fingers where he shouldn't be."

"Let's stick to the First Lady for a moment, shall we? Does anyone else have anything they'd like to share with us regarding First Lady Swaggart?"

"I have that video from Veronica's Spring Fling that I told you about," Becky Walford said nervously. "But I'm not sure I should be sharing it."

"If we intend to make the First Lady and the Governor pay for their sins, we need to put all of our cards on the table," Senator Jordan reminded them. "Let's see what you've got, Becky."

The First Lady's caterer produced her cell phone from her purse, turned it toward the Cloak Room gathering and hit PLAY.

"Am I seeing what I *think* I'm seeing," Sister Mary Celine asked, clearly aghast.

"I'm afraid so, Sister," Becky answered. "And I apologize to all of you for the sexual content of this video."

"Well, hell, that trumps anything I've got!" Senator Jordan had to admit. "And I'm guessing the good taxpayers of Texas got the tab for this little, what should we call it?"

"The First Lady's Last Spring Fling," Becky suggested.

"Go Directly to Jail. Do Not Pass Go, Do Not Collect One Million Dollars," Max added, paraphrasing the popular board game Monopoly.

"I think I might have something just as devastating on the governor," Holly Worthington said quietly. All eyes turned toward the reporter.

"I have uncovered proof that Beauregard Swaggart never graduated from Sul Ross University. Not only did he lie about it, certain regents at Sul Ross are clearly complicit."

"That will definitely embarrass him," Senator Jordan said, "but I doubt if it'll get him kicked out of office. After all, lying has become standard behavior in politics these days. Besides, if I know Bo Swaggart, he'll just spin it as fake news. Doesn't anyone have something on the governor that will stick?"

Marina Alvarez shuffled her feet and glanced furtively around the room before answering.

"*Perdóname*," Marina apologized for the little white lie she was about to tell, "but I found this cell phone in one of the governor's trash cans a few months ago. I think there's something on it I think you should see."

Hands shaking, Marina grasped the phone in both hands and hit PLAY.

Sister Celine fainted. Fortunately, Tiffany Taylor caught her before she smacked her head against the table.

"Bingo!" Max shouted.

"Bingo!" Holly repeated.

Raising her head, Sister Celine whispered, "Mother of God!"

"*Madre de Dios!*" Marina chimed in.

"Celebratory cocktails, ladies and gentlemen?" Brenda offered. Everyone accepted.

Unaware of what was transpiring just a block away, Governor Bo Swaggart paced his office in the Capitol like a caged tiger.

Alright, alright, alright! Bo told himself. himself. *Vee erased her tape. I erased my tape, except for one copy. I submitted a bill to my communications consultants for a million dollars. I'll argue that it's time I get on TV and remind my fellow Texans how important it is that we stay the course to divide Texas into five states. No one has connected the dots between those three missing mayors and me. I can always find new governors. What else? Oh, note to self. I need to hire a new chief of staff.*"

When you're up to your neck in alligators, it's hard to remember why you drained the swamp in the first place.

87

"TEXAS CHAINSAW GOVERNOR" read the cover story of the latest edition of LONE STAR magazine. Governor Bo Swaggart wore a leather mask, brandishing a menacing-looking chainsaw. Behind him hung a wooden map of Texas, which had already suffered several swipes of the vicious saw blade.

The parallels to the classic horror movie, *Texas Chainsaw Massacre,* were all too obvious. Swaggart was, for all intents and purposes, the movie character Leatherface, whose frightful mask was sewn from the skin of his victims.

But the real horror story was inside the magazine on page 87, as told by LONE STAR magazine's rising star, Holly Worthington.

Holly had wasted no time exposing Governor Swaggart for the pathological liar he was. For openers, the governor had lied about his degree in Political Science from Sul Ross University. Despite a sustained cover-up by a former regent, Holly had uncovered that Bo had apparently never finished his course work for a degree in Animal Husbandry. His degree from Sul Ross University was entirely bogus. Offense Number One: Lying about a college degree when submitting his curriculum vitae to run for governor.

While Holly had been digging up dirt on the governor, she discovered that Governor Swaggart had been deeply involved in strong-arm fundraising tactics for the new mayors of four Texas cities. Holly speculated Swaggart's end game was to make those four mayors the governors of four of the new states of Texas. Provided he could sell his insidious plan to unsuspecting Texas voters.

Holy attributed the *coup de grace* to an anonymous source who was dead certain Swaggart's personal end game was the U.S. Presidency, with the support of ten newly minted U.S. senators. Holly's anonymous source was none other than Max Sinclair.

LONE STAR magazines flew off the shelves. For the second time in the magazine's storied history, publisher Leviticus Gingrich was ecstatic to print tens of thousands of additional copies. Much to the governor's chagrin, Gingrich projected the magazine cover on a tall building on Congress Avenue, in clear view of the Capitol.

"Zoë, bring me the résumés for the chief of staff candidates," the Governor of Texas bellowed from his massive oak desk.

"Uh, Sir, there aren't any," a clearly nervous temp answered.

"What do you mean, there aren't any?"

"Just what I said, Governor. The mail arrived a few hours ago. So far this week, there have been exactly zero résumés submitted for the chief of staff position. Sorry, sir."

"Sorry? I'll tell you what's sorry, young lady! The worthless Capitol mail service, that's what! Get me the Lt. Governor on the phone. Wait! Tell the Lt. Governor I want to see him in my office. Pronto!"

Ten minutes later, Iain McClain, Lt. Governor of Texas, drifted into the Governor's office.

"What's up, boss? Having a little trouble filling that vacant chief of staff post?"

"No trouble at all," Bo lied. "But I need someone for the next couple of weeks while my new hire honors her two-week severance agreement. How's about I borrow your chief of staff. What's his name again?"

"Rory Minton? You've must be kidding!"

"I don't kid, Iain. Think of it as an executive order."

"Just one problem, Governor."

"Yeah? And what might that be?"

"Rory would quit before he would come to work for you."

"Then tell him he's fired!" Bo roared.

"I think not. You can't hire and fire my staff, any more than I can yours. Although in your case, people seem to be more apt to quit."

"Get out of my sight!" Bo yelled, droplets of spittle escaping from his mouth.

"No problem. But may I ask you one small favor?" McClain asked innocently.

"What???"

"Can I count on your vote for the Cowgirl of Liberty on the next ballot, Governor?"

"Get OUT, you turncoat! Fuck you and your cowgirl! It'll be a cold day in hell before that monstrosity ever sits atop this Capitol!"

"Sooo, I shouldn't count on your vote then?" the Lt. Governor said sarcastically, politely shutting the governor's office door.

Moments later, there was a loud THUNK as Swaggart's Bowie knife slammed point-first into the other side of the door.

88

Governor Beauregard Swaggart stared at the computer screen on his desk late the following evening. On screen, the halls outside his office and his antechamber were cloaked in darkness. Only a dim light flickered beneath the door.

Swaggart glanced again at the video datemark. If memory served, this security video was from the evening Alexa King had visited him with her stud ranch video. Hence the flickering light beneath the door, which was slightly ajar.

For the longest time, no one approached in the hallway outside.

Wait a minute! Did a small shadow just appear on the door outside the anteroom? Much too small for a State Trooper wearing a Stetson hat. This was more like a medium-sized child's shadow. Or perhaps a small adult female.

"Oh hell no!" Bo shouted. He couldn't make out who it was in the shadowy corridor, but the Puebla dress was a dead giveaway. "That's Marina! What's she doing there at that time of night?"

The following frames answered Bo's question. At first, there was merely the shadow of a feather duster. Apparently, she was dusting the wainscoting, something he had seen her do countless times before. Then suddenly, a small blueish-white light appeared.

"Now what?" Bo wondered. Then he recognized the screen of a cell phone. The light only shone for a few seconds, maybe twenty or so at best. Then it flickered off. Twenty seconds. Just long enough to doom his career as governor and destroy any chance of him ever becoming President of the United States.

The governor's temporary assistant Zoë handed Marina Alvarez a handwritten note in the hallway the next day.

"Governor Swaggart is so pleased with your work here, he'd like to thank you personally. Would you be available at the end of the day tomorrow?"

Alarm bells began clanging inside Marina's head. She had rarely spoken to the governor and never more than a few words. Why did he want to see her now? In his office. After-hours.

Could it have anything to do with the video of the Governor and the Mayor of Dallas? Impossible. She had shown it to that nice gentleman Max Sinclair at the Cloak Room, who transferred it to his phone, then immediately deleted it from hers. No one would ever be the wiser.

Maybe the Governor was simply pleased with her service these past few years. Perhaps he had noticed how thoroughly she cleaned and dusted his office, always skirting his desk.

Maybe she was finally getting the raise she so richly deserved!

"*¡Si, si, Señorita!* Please tell the *gobernador* I would be most honored to meet with him in his office," Marina replied nervously.

Governor Swaggart had much larger problems. The latest issue of LONE STAR magazine was a textbook case of character assassination.

"How dare that lamestream reporter Holly Worthington accuse me of lying about my college education? Or try me in the court of public opinion about three Texas mayors that I hardly even know?" Bo asked his temp.

"Sir, I'm afraid I have no idea," Zoë answered.

"That's the problem!" Bo bellowed. "Nobody around here has any ideas these days! Bring me today's résumés for my chief of staff position."

"Sir, there are no resumés. Not today. Not this week. And sir, my two weeks run out on Friday."

"What? You're going to desert me, too, Chloë?" Bo said.

"It's Zoë, sir. I have another job that starts next Monday."

"Then get a jump on it. You're FIRED!"

"As you wish, Governor Swaggart. And may I say, it has been an enlightening experience working for you, sir."

"Now I know how Colonel Travis felt at the Alamo when no one would come to his aid!" Bo groused. "Well, I've got the same message for all those sonsabitches who want to attack the Governor or Texas. Victory or Death!"

"Will that be all, then, sir?" Zoë asked.

"No, that won't be all, little lady! Show me your tits!"

"Pardon me? Did you just say what I think you said, Governor?"

"Just a little joke. Something we Sul Ross Lobos used to yell when we got drunk during Mardi Gras in Nawlins back in the day."

"Then for your sake, I'll pretend I never heard you say it, sir."

"You do that, little lady. And while you're at it, pretend I give a damn about you or your feelings. Now, get OUT!"

89

"Seems to me we've got Swaggart dead-to-rights, Holly," Max Sinclair said between bites of the chicken parmesan lunch special at La Traviata Italian Bistro on Congress Avenue.

"Dead to rights, maybe," Holly said. "He might be better off dead. Off the record, of course."

"Wishful thinking, Holly. But I have to say, you pretty much killed Swaggart, figuratively speaking, in that LONE STAR article of yours. Wow! Lying about graduating. And what's all this about him handpicking the mayors of four major Texas cities? Do you really think he was planning to nominate them for governors of his ridiculous five states of Texas?"

"Yes, to the lying. Maybe, to whether he was colluding to put Alexa King, Estevan Barrero, Jeremiah Jones, and Ponce Ponzio in the capitols of North, South, East, and West Texas. Saving Central Texas for himself, of course."

"What's his end game?"

"I honestly believe the governor has designs on the presidency."

"Of the United States?" Max sputtered.

"Yep. Think about it. Bo divides Texas into five states, which is perfectly legal, according to our 1845 Annexation Agreement with the Union. Then the five new states of Texas get to elect two

U.S. Senators each. Ten total. Do you know how much power ten United States Senators would yield?"

"Enough to elect a con artist like Swaggart president?"

"We elected a shady talk show host, didn't we?"

"Not *we*, Kemo Sabe," Max replied. "And I blame the forty-plus percent of Americans who didn't vote as much as I blame the ones who voted for that subliterate sociopath."

"Easy, Tiger. You've gonna give yourself indigestion."

"Too late. Waiter, a double espresso, please. Anything for you, Holly?"

"I kinda had my eye on those profiteroles they just served the table next to us."

"Those *what*-a-rolls?" Max asked.

"Profiteroles," the waiter chimed in. "Puff pastries with vanilla and chocolate ice cream, drizzled with warm chocolate sauce."

"Then make that *two* orders," Max said. "And bring her the check."

"Bring me the check?

"I guess you're right. Separate checks," Max winked to the waiter. "Just kidding. Great job, Lady Worthington. You may have just saved the Great State of Texas from itself."

"That's more like it, Max. I don't care what they say about you. You're not all bad!"

"Ouch!"

"Just kidding. We make a great team, if you ask me, Sir Sinclair."

"Indeed we do, m'lady!"

Two orders of profiteroles and a double espresso interrupted their mutual admiration society. While Max tucked into his dessert and sipped his high-octane java, Holly appeared distracted.

"What now, Holly?"

"I get the feeling we're missing something, Max. No idea what it is, but my spidey-sense tells me that this Texas Two Step isn't over just yet."

"I know what you mean. Seems like the other shoe hasn't dropped just yet. What else could go wrong?"

"Well, Swaggart's still in office, although without a proper staff. But Bo's the vengeful type. Last week I installed two more deadbolts on my door at home and signed up for a security service. I only jog with two or more friends. And I've got one of those date rape gadgets to test for GHB."

"GHB?"

"Gamma-Hydroxybutyric acid. It's a psychoactive drug some sickos slip into unsuspecting dates' drinks."

"Are you sure you're not overreacting a bit?"

"Has anyone tried to stab you to death on the hike-and-bike trail lately?"

"Okay, okay. I get your point. Better safe than sorry."

"Better safe than dead."

"Which is exactly what you wished on Governor Swaggart when this conversation began, I must remind you."

"Strictly off the record, I must remind you, Max. Suffice it to say, I think we're treading on thin ice here. Would you mind walking me to my car?"

Max stared at her. "In broad daylight?"

"Oh, so nobody gets killed in broad daylight anymore?"

"Point taken. After you, m'lady."

"And knock it off with that m'lady malarkey, okay?" Holly said, punching him playfully before lacing her arm securely through his.

90

BECKY WALFORD WAS in no mood to bargain. She was finally back in the black, thanks to Dallas Mayor Alexa King. A million dollars in the black.

Sitting in the First Lady's plush private office in the Capitol Annex, Becky wondered why the First Lady had summoned her. Certainly not to rehire her as Veronica's private caterer.

Twenty minutes later, the First Lady of Texas sauntered into her office and quietly shut the door.

"So nice of you to join me, Becky," Veronica said coolly.

"Didn't know I had a choice, Veronica."

"You may address me as Madam First Lady."

"Of course, Madam First Lady."

"It is my understanding that you sold a certain video from my recent Spring Fling to Alexa King, the Mayor of Dallas and my worthless husband's paramour.

Becky smiled ruefully. "Correct on the first part. I couldn't speak to the second part."

"Well, here's what's going to happen now, Becky. You and I will erase your copy of that video from your cell phone, and you're going to give me half of what Mayor King paid you so she could blackmail me. I believe that would be, what, half a million dollars?"

"You must be out of your mind, Veron…Madam First Lady. I don't have that kind of money!"

"Oh, but you do," said Veronica. "You'd be surprised how powerful the Office of First Lady can be in persuading certain bankers to divulge the contents of their clients' bank accounts when faced with charges of aiding and abetting treason against the State of Texas."

"Treason for what?" Becky asked, clearly shaken.

"Invasion of the privacy of a state official on State of Texas property," Veronica answered, "which carries a substantial fine and up to ten years in a Texas prison."

"That's preposterous!" Becky gasped.

"Actually, that's the law," Veronica lied. "So, for your own sake, I suggest you hand me your cell phone so we can erase your felonious video. And you need to bring a cashier's check for five hundred thousand dollars to my office by close of business tomorrow."

Becky did the math. She'd still walk away with half a mil, and the First Lady would summarily drop any charges against her.

"Sweeten the pot." Becky said.

"You've got some nerve!" Veronica said.

"You've got your philandering husband over a barrel," Becky reminded her. "Why not get the half mil from him?".

"Oh, I plan to get much more than that, Becky dear. Look at it this way. You still get to keep half a mil, you stay out of prison, and I'll give you your old job back."

"When you put it that way, I guess it's not all that bad," Becky calculated.

"On the contrary, Becky, it's all good! Do we have a deal?"

Becky hesitated, but only for a moment. "Deal."

"Now, break out that cell phone of yours and let me see you erase that video. It's the only copy besides the one you sold to Alexa King, right?"

"Right," Becky lied. It was, in fact, *her* only copy. But she had allowed Max Sinclair to download a copy.

Becky opened her cell phone, found the video, and allowed Veronica to watch as she hit the delete button. Becky winced as the screen went blank.

Veronica let out a little cheer. "Shall we celebrate?

"Sure. Why not?"

Veronica hit a button on her desk phone and spoke to her chief of staff.

"Leslie, a bottle of chilled Roederer Cristal Brut, please. And two champagne flutes."

In less than a minute, Veronica's chief of staff appeared with a chilled bottle of bubbly and two crystal flutes.

"Here's to a new day in Texas!" Veronica toasted.

"Beats a cold day in hell, I suppose," Becky replied, and clinked glasses with one of the most devious women she'd ever met.

"Guess we better get started on next year's Spring Fling!" Veronica said.

"Am I just responsible for the dinner, or would you like me to arrange for the entertainment, as well?" Becky half-joked.

"Do you have someone in mind?" Veronica asked, clearly intrigued.

"Well, RuPaul is a personal friend."

"Oooh, drag queens! My besties would love that!"

"I'll get right on it, Madam First Lady."

"You do that, Becky. In the meantime, I've got a very busy day ahead of me. Stay in touch."

Veronica's eyes narrowed as Becky Walford left her office. As soon as the door closed, she picked up the phone on her faux Louis XV desk.

"Attorney General Haggard? First Lady Swaggart here. You may begin the proceedings on the State of Texas vs. Becky Walford tomorrow. The charge? Theft of State Secrets."

Part VIII:

Cut to the Chase

91

Marina Alvarez completed her cleaning chores and made her way to the staff dressing room in the Capitol building. There she changed out of her workday clothes and put on her Sunday best for her meeting with Governor Swaggart.

Marina studied her reflection in the full-length mirror. She was pushing fifty, but she'd been blessed with her mother's genetics. Her skin was smooth and virtually unwrinkled. Her long, straight hair was still dark brown, with only a few traces of gray that she plucked religiously. She was not a tall woman, but she was delicately proportioned. She had birthed three children, yet she still carried herself with a certain grace befitting a woman half her age.

Still, she had to admit she was nervous about meeting with the governor after hours. She removed her rosary from her hand-embroidered purse and quietly recited her *Padre Nuestros* and *Ave Marias*.

The clock on the dressing room wall read 6 o'clock. Time to meet with the most powerful man in Texas. To calm her jitters, Marina took one small sip of tequila from a flask in a zippered compartment of her handbag. *¡Por valor!* she told herself. For courage!

☆

"Señora Alvarez! Do come in! Make yourself at home!" Bo greeted Marina after she knocked gingerly on his massive office door. "May I offer you a small token of my appreciation, Ms. Alvarez? A little taste of Don Julio 1942 Tequila? I'll join you if you don't mind."

"*Muchas gracias, Gobernador,*" Marina replied unsteadily. "But only *poquita, por favor.*"

Bo made an elaborate show of filling two crystal shot glasses to the brim, then handing one to Marina before downing his in a single gulp.

"*Mas tequila?*" Bo asked, before refilling her glass and holding the bottle out to Marina. "C'mon, pretty lady, drink up! How do you Mexicans say it? *Tragos!*"

Marina held forth her shot glass, her hand trembling. "*Solo uno más, por favor.* Just one more, please."

"Come now, Marina. May I call you Marina? We have a lot to celebrate. Please, have a seat. I have a little story to tell you." Taking a seat in his leather desk chair, Governor Beauregard Swaggart began his tale:

Back in 1836, long before either of us was born, a ragtag regiment of what was then called Texians drove all Mexican troops out of what was then called Mexican Texas. About 100 Texians were then garrisoned at the Alamo near the present-day city of San Antonio.

The Texian force grew slightly with the arrival of reinforcements led by Alamo co-commanders James Bowie and William B. Travis.

On February 23rd, approximately 1,500 Mexican soldiers marched into San Antonio de Béxar with the mission of retaking Texas. For the next several days, the two armies engaged in several skirmishes, with minimal casualties to either side. Knowing his army could never withstand a full-on attack by such a large force, Colonel

Travis sent multiple letters pleading for more men and armaments. Fewer than 100 men answered his call.

Marina Alvarez shifted nervously in her chair, the hair at the nape of her neck standing on end.

I suspect you know the rest, Señora Alvarez. In the early morning hours of March 6th, the Mexican army, led by General Antonio López de Santa Anna, advanced on the Alamo. After repelling two attacks, the brave Texians were unable to fend off the third attack. As Mexican soldiers scaled the walls, most of the Texians withdrew to interior buildings. Defenders unable to reach those buildings were slain by the Mexican cavalry as they attempted to escape.

By most accounts, some 257 Texians died that day. None were spared, including James Bowie, whose fabled knife I now hold.

Sometime during his storytelling, Bo had retrieved his beloved Bowie knife from the secret compartment in his desk. As he finished his story, Bo stabbed the blade fiercely into his desktop for emphasis.

Marina leapt from her chair, stifling a gasp.

"Please be seated, Señora Alvarez!" Bo demanded. "I'm not quite finished with my story," Bo said, lightning flashing behind his dark eyes. "You see, I never thought the Battle of the Alamo was a fair fight. I mean, c'mon! A couple hundred Texians against a couple thousand Mescan regulars?

A tear trickled down Marina's left cheek.

"I've always said that, one-on-one, a Texan can whup a Mescan six ways from Sunday. Care to test my theory, señora?"

92

Governor Beauregard Swaggart pushed a hidden button on his desk and Marina flinched involuntarily as a deadbolt on his massive office door engaged.

"There! Now nobody can bother us, Señora. Texan versus Mescan, one-on-one, fair-and-square, just like the Good Lord willed it. Only I have one small advantage," Bo said, holding up his menacing knife so that it caught the light and glinted in Marina's face.

Marina furtively reached into her purse, desperately searching for the small canister of pepper spray her daughters insisted she always carry. Where was it?

"What? You gonna pull a switchblade on me? Did you really think the Governor of Texas wouldn't find out who took videos of the Mayor of Dallas and me simply doing what God intended for a man and a woman to do?"

"Please, Señor Gobernador, you don't have to do this!" Marina pleaded.

"Oh, but I *do*, Señora Alvarez. If not for me, for the 257 Texians who were murdered by Santa Anna and his banditos back in 1846. I just call it deferred judgment."

With that, Bo rose slowly from his desk, Bowie knife in hand, and began narrowing the gap between himself and Marina.

Still searching for her pepper spray, Marina rose from her chair and began backing toward the office door, knowing all-too-well that it barred any hope of escape.

Bo advanced on Marina like a coyote on its prey. He circled, then feinted, cutting the distance between them in half.

"Please, Gobernador, I beg you! I have no quarrel with you!" Marina whimpered.

"Ah, that's where we differ, Señora. Because I have a very big quarrel with you. That little video of yours has cost me my one dream in life, and likely my governorship. Thanks to you and that nosey reporter from LONE STAR magazine, my time is just about up here. But not before I set things right with you. I'll take care of that good-for-nothing reporter later."

Bo was now no more than ten paces from Marina. As he lunged forward for the kill, her hand found purchase on the pepper spray canister in her purse. Dodging his first parry, Marina sprayed him with a potent blast of pepper spray.

"You've blinded me, bitch!" Bo screamed. "But there's no escape. Remember the Alamo!"

Marina, the smaller, more agile combatant, deftly dodged and circled toward the Governor's desk. Meanwhile, Bo's eyes welled with tears and slowly began to clear, although the pain was excruciating. While he could only make out her shadowy form, Bo knew he was backing her into a corner.

Marina slowly slumped to her knees and began praying aloud.

"God won't save you now, you miserable wretch!" Bo bellowed triumphantly. One lone chair remained between him and his hapless victim. Bo shoved it aside viciously. One of the chair legs caught the corner of the rug that bordered his desk.

Lunging blindly, Bo's Lucchese boot tip snagged on the rug, sending him sprawling toward his desk. Bo reached out frantically with his left hand, his right hand still grasping his prize Bowie knife.

On the bright side, his left hand cushioned his fall. On the dark side, the enormous Bowie knife buried itself to the hilt just below his sternum, penetrating his wildly beating heart.

"Governor Swaggart, sir! Open this door or we will be forced to kick it down!" a State Trooper shouted outside the governor's office.

Crawling at first, then slowly rising from the horrific scene before her, Marina Alvarez stumbled toward the governor's desk and found the button that released the lock.

"My God! What have you done to the governor?" one of the troopers gasped as he forcibly grabbed Marina's arms, spinning her around before clicking handcuffs on her tiny wrists.

The lead trooper began shouting into the mic on his epaulet. "Bowie is down! I repeat, Bowie is down! We need a medical team STAT! The suspect is in custody! Repeat. The suspect is in custody!"

Within moments, a full medical team surrounded the fallen form. They glanced at one another, then at the State Troopers, and slowly shook their heads. The figure beneath them, once the mighty Governor of the Great State of Texas, looked somehow smaller now, as if he had been deflated by the fatal wound to his chest.

"Be careful not to disturb anything!" the lead trooper ordered. "Don't step in the governor's blood! A CSI team will be here in minutes. This is a crime scene. And don't anyone breathe a word about what you see here!

"Yes, sir!" the assembled team dutifully replied.

As she was being escorted from the governor's office, Marina glanced at the blood pooling beneath the governor's prone body. So much blood. Then something caught her eye in the corner of the ceiling. A small red light. The governor's departing spirit? *Rojo*, red, made perfect sense, Marina thought to herself. The *gobernador* would be welcome *en infierno*. In hell.

93

Beauregard Swaggart's Funeral was one for the history books. Revisionist history.

Officially, Governor Swaggart perished in a freak accident involving the knife rumored to have been wielded by James Bowie at the Battle of the Alamo. He lay in state in the Capitol Rotunda for three hours, after which his casket was escorted by an honor guard to the Texas State Cemetery. He was be laid to rest in a private ceremony for his family.

Unofficially, the full details of Bo Swaggart's death were never shared with the public. An unidentified State Trooper reported that Swaggart tripped over a loose rug in his office. He had been admiring his relic Bowie knife and fell in such a manner as to drive the enormous twelve-inch blade straight through his heart.

The mortally wounded governor was reportedly found by his personal chambermaid, Marina Alvarez, who had immediately summoned help. Although his state trooper detail arrived within moments, the governor had sadly succumbed to his mortal wound. The Criminal Investigation Department investigated the accident thoroughly and found no one at fault except Fate herself.

Although she was temporarily detained for questioning, Ms. Alvarez was soon released on her own recognizance.

There was never any mention of a bottle of expensive tequila or two shot glasses found at the scene. Nor was there any mention of a lingering mist of pungent pepper spray. Marina Alvarez explained that various cleaning fluids often smelled vile.

Veronica Swaggart, the First Lady of Texas, attended the funeral. Also attending was Alexa King, the Mayor of Dallas. There were reports of strident words exchanged between the two powerful women. But those reports were written off as mere expressions of grief.

Acting Governor Iain McClain attended the services, accompanied by his Chief of staff, Rory Minton. After the services, Governor McClain reportedly regaled the press with stories about his proposed Cowgirl of Liberty statue.

Also in attendance was former State Senator and newly appointed Lt. Governor Bethany Jordan.

Included on the list of dignitaries and guests was author Max Sinclair, who consulted with First Lady Swaggart from time to time. Mr. Sinclair appeared to take copious notes during the funeral proceedings. When asked if he was planning to write a book about the governor, Sinclair reportedly simply smiled and said, "Wouldn't that be a twisted Texas tale!"

Not on the list of dignitaries and guests was LONE STAR magazine's investigative reporter Holly Worthington, who had previously penned several damaging articles regarding the Governor's college education at Sul Ross University and his subsequent interference in mayoral races in several major Texas cities. Also conspicuously absent was Leviticus Gingrich, publisher of LONE STAR magazine.

Due to his untimely death, a proper memorial is currently being designed for Governor Swaggart. Several local artists submitted designs for the governor's tombstone. Some were more respectful than others.

It has been reported that Governor Swaggart's prized Bowie knife was laid to rest with its owner. In truth, it had been preserved for the State Archives, to be displayed at the Bob Bullock Texas State History Museum.

In the aftermath of the Governor's demise, Sul Ross University invited credentialed historians to visit its campus and inspect its records regarding Beauregard Swaggart's attendance and subsequent graduation. Thus far, no historian had accepted their invitation.

The cities of Houston, Laredo, and El Paso had recently held elections and replaced their missing and presumed ineligible mayors. The upcoming election for Mayor of Dallas would pit King Ranch heiress and incumbent mayor Alexa King against an SMU graduate with a PhD in Texas history.

Talks of dividing Texas into five states ground to an abrupt halt. Talks of Texas seceding from the Union continued to bubble to the surface every few years, with little or no chance of ever reaching a call for a vote.

Texas, while still a largely Republican-leaning state, was beginning to see a return to its former Democratic dominance with the election of several high-profile Democratic State and U.S. Senators.

Epilogue

The bold headline in the Austin American-Statesman was an interesting choice of words:

EMBATTLED GOVERNOR FALLS ON HIS SWORD

While the full details of the governor's death might never reach the mainstream, Texans were acutely aware of the shenanigans Governor Beauregard Swaggart was trying to foist on them.

Between Holly Worthington's recent scathing article, the release of pirated YouTube videos depicting the Governor and the Mayor of Dallas *in flagrante delicto*, and the video of First Lady Swaggart's tawdry Spring Fling, Texas politics was poised to add yet another sordid chapter to its storied past.

Newly dethroned Veronica Swaggart resigned in disgrace, ending her short reign as First Lady of Texas. Veronica retreated to France, where she married a famous couture designer.

Sister Mary Cecile was named Director of Planned Parenthood of Texas at a salary of $1 per year.

Found not guilty of Theft of State Secrets, Becky Walford retired to Belize with her newfound wealth and quickly found the Knight in Shining Armor she'd always wished for. Together they franchised and opened a Jimmy Buffett Margaritaville Bar and were making a killing on fishbowl-sized Parrot Head Margaritas and Cheeseburgers in Paradise.

Within days of the untimely death of Governor Swaggart, Lt. Governor Iain McClain was sworn in as temporary Governor of Texas. There would be a statewide election in the Fall, and McClain was expected to win easily, most likely with no opponent.

In his temporary status as acting Governor, McClain elevated State Senator Bethany Jordan to the temporary post of Lt. Governor, over fierce objections from the opposing party. Most Texans assumed that Lt. Governor Jordan would be elected governor if Governor McClain ever moved on to bigger and better things.

Governor McClain's celebrated "Cowgirl of Liberty" statue was a big hit with Texas voters and was scheduled to replace the garish Goddess of Liberty statue sometime the following year.

The whereabouts of former El Paso Mayor Ponce Ponzio remained a mystery. Some said he may have joined the military. But the brass at Ft. Bliss Army Base has no record of his enlistment.

Likewise, there was no record of a prisoner by the name of Estevan Barrero among the inmates listed at the U.S. Naval Detention Camp on the coast of Guantanamo Bay in Cuba.

Jeremiah Jones, alias 3-J, lost his bid for a retrial and remains imprisoned at the Allan B. Polunsky supermax prison five miles southwest of Livingston, Texas, on FM 350 in Polk County.

Alexa King lost an embarrassing run for re-election. A pariah in Texas, she quietly retired to a small hacienda on the sprawling King Ranch, never to be seen or heard from in public again.

Holly Worthington finally won her coveted Pulitzer Prize in Journalism for her investigative article on the "Texas Chainsaw Governor," her exposé on the colorfully corrupt Governor of Texas. She eventually wrote a novel of the same name, which remained on the New York Times Best Seller List for over a year.

Rhett McCullum's multibillion-dollar real estate development in Laredo went bust when it failed to attract enough visitors from the rest of Texas. Rhett blamed it all on the newly constructed border wall and used the verb "trumped" to excuse his bankruptcy to his investors, who were not at all amused.

Marina Alvarez was exonerated once the videotape from Governor Swaggart's office was reviewed. She kept her job at the Capitol, where today she holds the title of Docent.

Max Sinclair returned to writing. Rumor had it his next novel would take a devilish twist.

Acknowledgements

The conversation between 10th U.S. President John Tyler and 1st and 3rd President of the Republic of Texas in the Prologue is pure fiction. I can only imagine such a repartee between these two powerful men.

There is, indeed, a provision in the Texas Annexation Agreement of 1845 allowing Texas to be divided into as many as five states. There is also a provision allowing the state flag to fly at the same height as the United States Stars & Stripes, although it rarely does.

Beauregard Swaggart is likewise a figment of my imagination. He is not actually related to any Pentecostal evangelist who may or may not have fallen on hard times. Likewise, there is no First Lady Veronica Swaggart. No Chief of staff Julie Truman. None of the mayors depicted exist.

There is no Alexa King, a fictionalized descendant from the legendary King Ranch.

There really is a Sul Ross University in West Texas. It is a fine institution of higher learning.

There is no LONE STAR magazine, although there is a TEXAS LONE STAR magazine published by the Texas Association of School Boards. There is no LONE STAR publisher Leviticus Gingrich and no investigative reporter named Holly Worthington.

You may recognize the fictional Max Sinclair from my previous novel, TRASH TALK, and fictional Admiral Vanessa "Six" Ingram makes another appearance, as well.

Legendary American lawyer, educator and politician Barbara Jordan was, and will always be, one of my all-time heroes. Alas, there is no actual Senator Bethany Jordan to follow in her footsteps.

The same goes for imaginary Iain McClain, the handsome, Harvard-educated, trust-funded, gay Lt. Governor of Texas. I still hold out hope that his Cowgirl of Liberty statue may one day replace the Goddess of Liberty atop our beloved Texas Capitol.

The topic of Texas seceding from the Union rears its head from time to time, but is, for the most part, hastily dismissed. The same cannot be said for Great Britain "brexiting" from the European Union, a controversy that has raged nonstop since the United Kingdom European Union membership referendum took place in 2016.

Last yet noteworthy, the Lone Star State has many more secrets. Some, no doubt, worthy of additional storytelling. Yet I feel drawn to the notion of "organized religion," which permeates Texas life and politics in the most peculiar ways. As the old saying goes, "The devil is in the details."

SPECIAL THANKS

FIRST AND FOREMOST, I want to thank my rowdy readers. Without you, my scribblings might go unnoticed.

STATE SECRET is a treasonous treatise. While every state has its secrets, Texas has the biggest secret of all. The right, by law, to divide itself into up to five independent states. In the wrong hands, fictional Governor Beauregard Swaggart for instance, the results could be disastrous. The only thing worse, in my opinion, would be for Texas to secede from the Union, which is also our right.

I would also like to thank my small cadre of writers and readers, those souls who share my passion for both. Texas fiction author Ben Rehder has proven to be both a mentor and true-blue friend. Likewise, Texan expat author Michael Stout, who advised me, "Write for yourself. If someone else chooses to read what you've written, all the better!" I have also benefitted mightily from the wise counsel of formidable Texas authors Stephen Harrigan and Lawrence Wright.

I owe my greatest debt of gratitude to the late, great Texas author C.J. Klinger. Chuck not only edited STATE SECRET, he made me a better writer.

Thanks, too, to my weekend warriors, Jim Wimberly and David Mattka, who offered their valuable feedback at our Saturday morning musings over coffee.

Special thanks to my older daughter, Alison McClure Blair, who spent hundreds of hours reading and ultimately giving a thumbs up to my scurrilous screed.

Through it all, my wife and our two grown children have offered their opinions when I occasionally slipped off into the deep end of the Texas gene pool.

Finally, I am thankful for the time I've been allotted to write this, the second novel in what I trust will be a trilogy. The first, TRASH TALK, teams an unscrupulous Texas landfill operator with an American traitor and a Russian spy. This second thriller, STATE SECRET, pillories Texas politics. With any luck, the third novel, tentatively titled DEVIL'S CLAW, will reckon with organized religion.

Texas isn't just a state. It's a state of mind.

About the Author

Tim McClure is a native Texan. He coined the phrase *Don't Mess With Texas*, the most successful anti-litter campaign in history. Also a screen writer, Tim wrote and executive-produced *Texas: The Big Picture*, the first IMAX movie about the Lone Star State. STATE SECRET is part of his trilogy of twisted Texas thrillers. He is married to Samantha Arzonetti McClure, lives in Austin, and travels the world with his family. Tim is a global member of The Explorers Club.

For a glimpse of Tim McClure's next twisted thriller, DEVIL'S CLAW, please turn the page to discover how a flood of Texas-sized proportions can turn hellish.

Prologue to Perdition

Great deluges punctuate our planet's prehistory.

Noah's Flood is part of the deluge myth, a narrative in which a great flood sent by a deity destroys civilizations, often as an act of divine retribution. Stories of great ancient floods pervade the mythology of many cultures. While most Westerners are familiar with the story of Noah as told in the Old Testament book of Genesis, great floods are recorded in folklore from cultures around the world, from the Middle East to the Americas, India, China, and Southern Asia.

Texans are no strangers to great floods, the latest being the spawn of Hurricane Harvey, tied with Hurricane Katrina as the costliest hurricane on record, inflicting $125 billion in damage, primarily from rainfall-triggered flooding in the Houston metropolitan area.

In a four-day period, many areas were inundated with more than 40 inches of rain as the system slowly meandered over eastern Texas, causing unprecedented flooding. With peak accumulations exceeding 60 inches, Harvey was the wettest hurricane on record in the United States, inundating hundreds of thousands of homes, displacing more than 30,000 people, and prompting more than 17,000 rescues.

But nothing prepared Texas for the deluge that inundated Austin, Texas in the second quarter of the 21st Century. It began, innocuously enough, with a broken backbone, which led to an ominous flood surge that breached a critical dam and leveled sections of downtown Austin.

When the massive flood waters finally receded, a remarkable discovery was made. Beneath the streets of Austin lay a hidden underworld, one that had existed since the late 20th Century.

Not discovered until sometime later was a secret society that simply calls itself, The Brights.